Book 7

Test # 146338

Level 2.6

Points 1

THE MEANING OF LIFE... AND OTHER STUFF

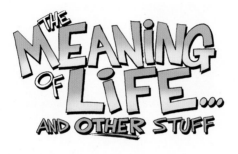

"Side-splittingly hilarious. . . . Highly recommended for all ages
and all libraries."
—*Library Journal*

"Full of wise-cracking jokes and quips, ingenious gags, screamingly funny
dialogue, and the best of classic comic book antics."
—Megan McDonald, author of the Judy Moody series

"Amelia Rules! is . . . absolutely essential. Not only is it one of the
finest comics of all time, it is one of the best examples of children's
literature I have ever read."
—Kidz Corner Comic Reviews

"Smart and genuine."
—David Fury, writer/producer for *Lost* and *Buffy the Vampire Slayer*

"Inspiring and uplifting in ways that will make you want to stand up and
cheer. . . . Here's hoping the series continues for a good long time."
—the-trades.com

"Amelia's family and friends will take up permanent
residence in your heart."
—Bob Schooley and Mark McCorkle, creators of *The Penguins of Madagascar*

"Wonderful all-ages comic."
—*New York* magazine

"Gownley excels at putting a powerful message inside of
a kid-friendly story."
—BSCKids.com

"Amelia Rules! . . . is a delightful entry for lovers of comics and
realistic fiction. . . . She is a character to rival Ramona and Judy Moody."
—*School Library Journal*

"These kids are real . . . Gownley is a genius at capturing
their perspective."
—ComicsWorthReading.com

MEET THE GANG!

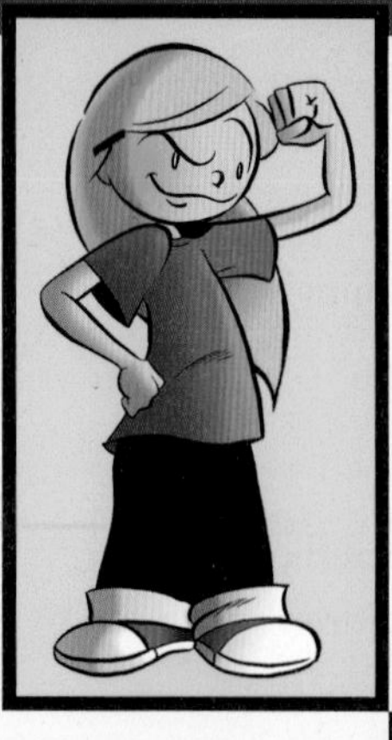

Amelia Louise McBride:
Our heroine. Wise cracking, yet sweet. She spends her time hanging out with friends and her aunt Tanner.

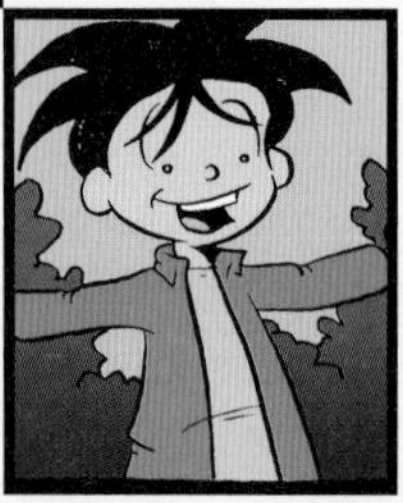

Reggie Grabinsky:
A.k.a. Captain Amazing. Founder of G.A.S.P., which he forces . . . er, encourages, his friends to join.

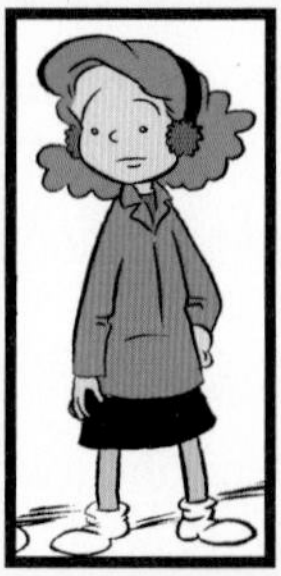

Rhonda Bleenie:
Smart, stubborn, and loud. She wears her heart on her sleeve and it's filled with love for Reggie.

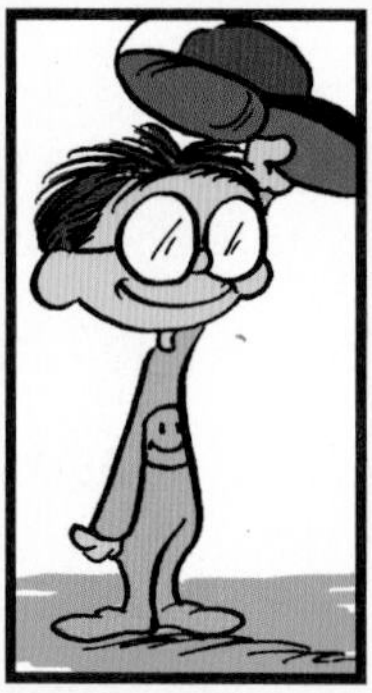

Pajamaman:
Never speaks. Always cool. His feetie jammies tell you what's on his mind.

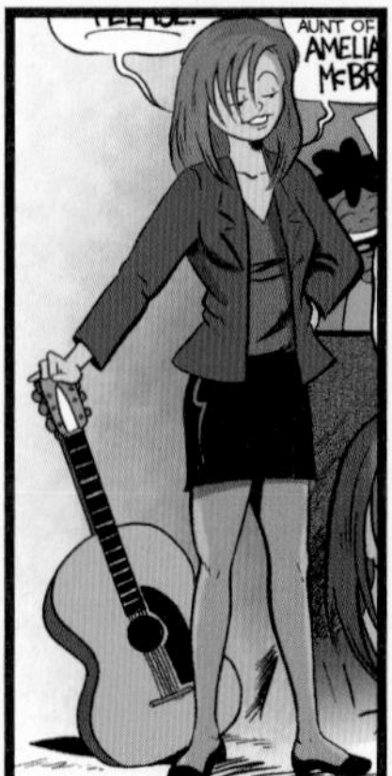
AUNT OF
AMELIA

Tanner:
Amelia's aunt and a former rock 'n' roll superstar.

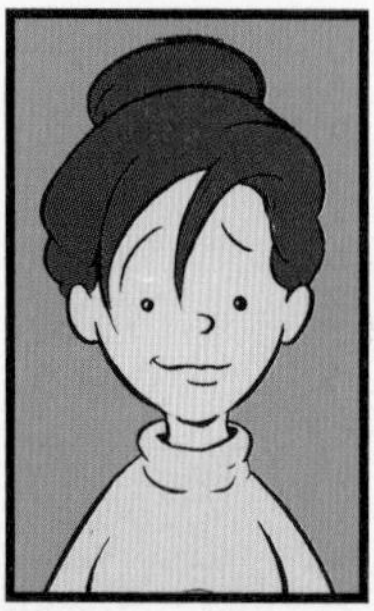

Amelia's Mom (Mary):
Starting a new life in Pennsylvania with Amelia after the divorce.

Amelia's Dad:
Still lives in New York, and
misses Amelia terribly.

G.A.S.P.
Gathering Of Awesome Super Pals.
The superhero club Reggie founded.

Park View Terrace Ninjas:
Club across town and nemesis
to G.A.S.P.

Kyle:
The main ninja. Kind of a jerk
but not without charm.

Joan:
Former Park View Terrace Ninja
(nemesis of G.A.S.P.), now friends
with Amelia and company.

Tweenie Zeenie:
A local kid-run magazine and Web site.

Jimmy Gownley's

AMELIA RULES! ™

Hmm...
Mmm...
Mmm...

THE MEANING OF LIFE...
AND OTHER STUFF

Atheneum Books for Young Readers
New York   London   Toronto   Sydney

ATHENEUM BOOKS FOR YOUNG READERS
An imprint of Simon & Schuster Children's Publishing Division
1230 Avenue of the Americas, New York, New York 10020
For information about special discounts for bulk purchases, please contact Simon & Schuster Special
Sales at 1-866-506-1949 or business@simonandschuster.com.
The Simon & Schuster Speakers Bureau can bring authors to your live event.
For more information or to book an event, contact the Simon & Schuster Speakers Bureau
at 1-866-248-3049 or visit our website at www.simonspeakers.com.
Also available in an Atheneum Books for Young Readers paperback edition
Book design by Sonia Chaghatzbanian
The text for this book is hand-lettered.
The illustrations for this book are digitally rendered.
Manufactured in China
0711 GFC
First Edition
2   4   6   8   10   9   7   5   3   1
Library of Congress Cataloging-in-Publication Data
Gownley, Jimmy.
The meaning of life . . . and other stuff / [Jimmy Gownley]. – 1st ed.
p. cm. – (Jimmy Gownley's Amelia rules! ; 7)
Summary: While trying to figure out the meaning of life, Amelia learns that even when the
world is scary and life is as mystifying as ever, some things, such as friends, do last.
ISBN 978-1-4169-8613-3 (hardcover) – ISBN 978-1-4169-8612-6 (pbk.)
1. Graphic novels. [1. Graphic novels. 2. Meaning (Philosophy)–Fiction.
3. Interpersonal relations–Fiction. 4. Friendship–Fiction.] I. Title.
PZ7.7.G69Me 2011
741.5'973–dc23   2011018407

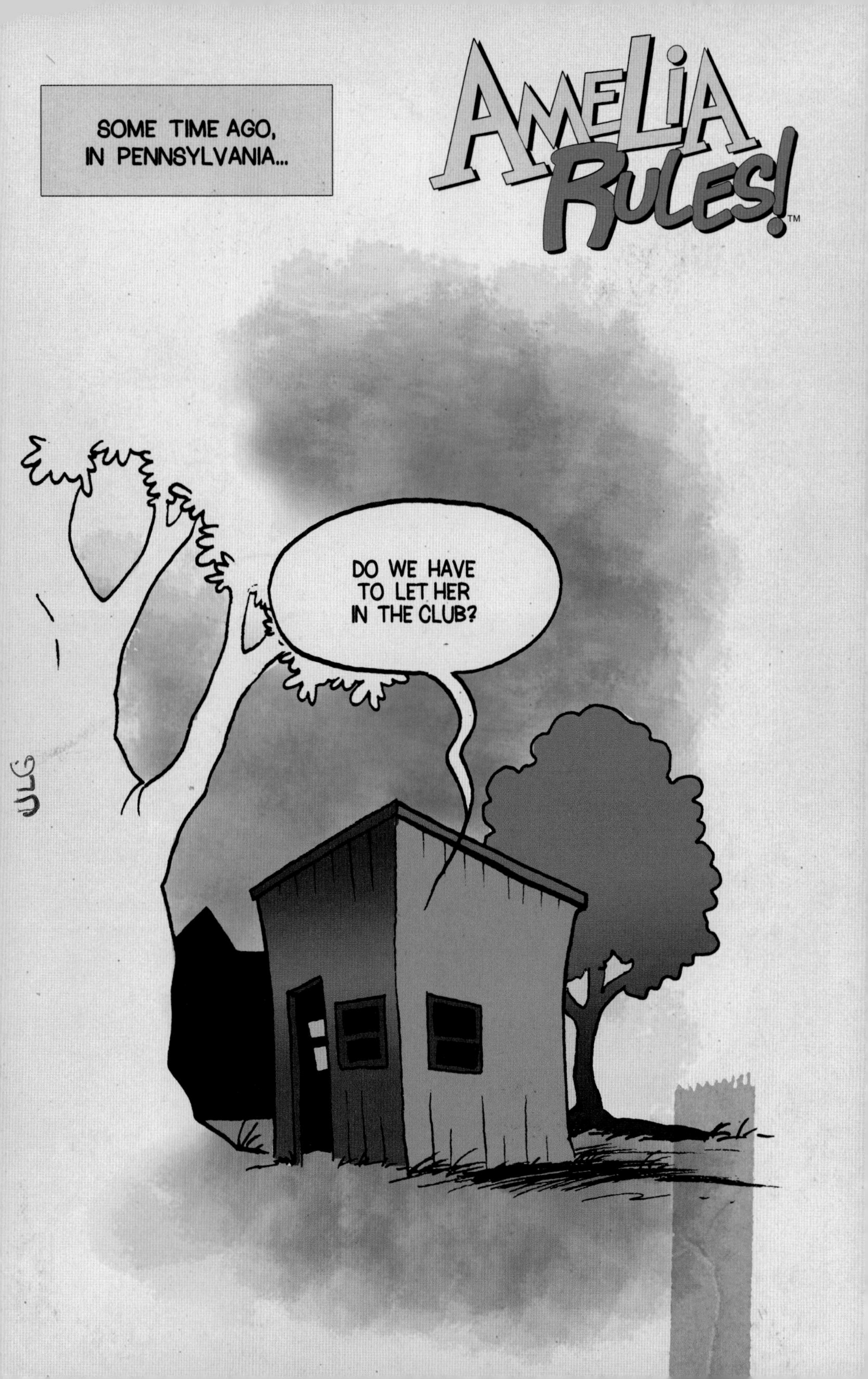
SOME TIME AGO, IN PENNSYLVANIA...
AMELIA RULES!™
DO WE HAVE TO LET HER IN THE CLUB?

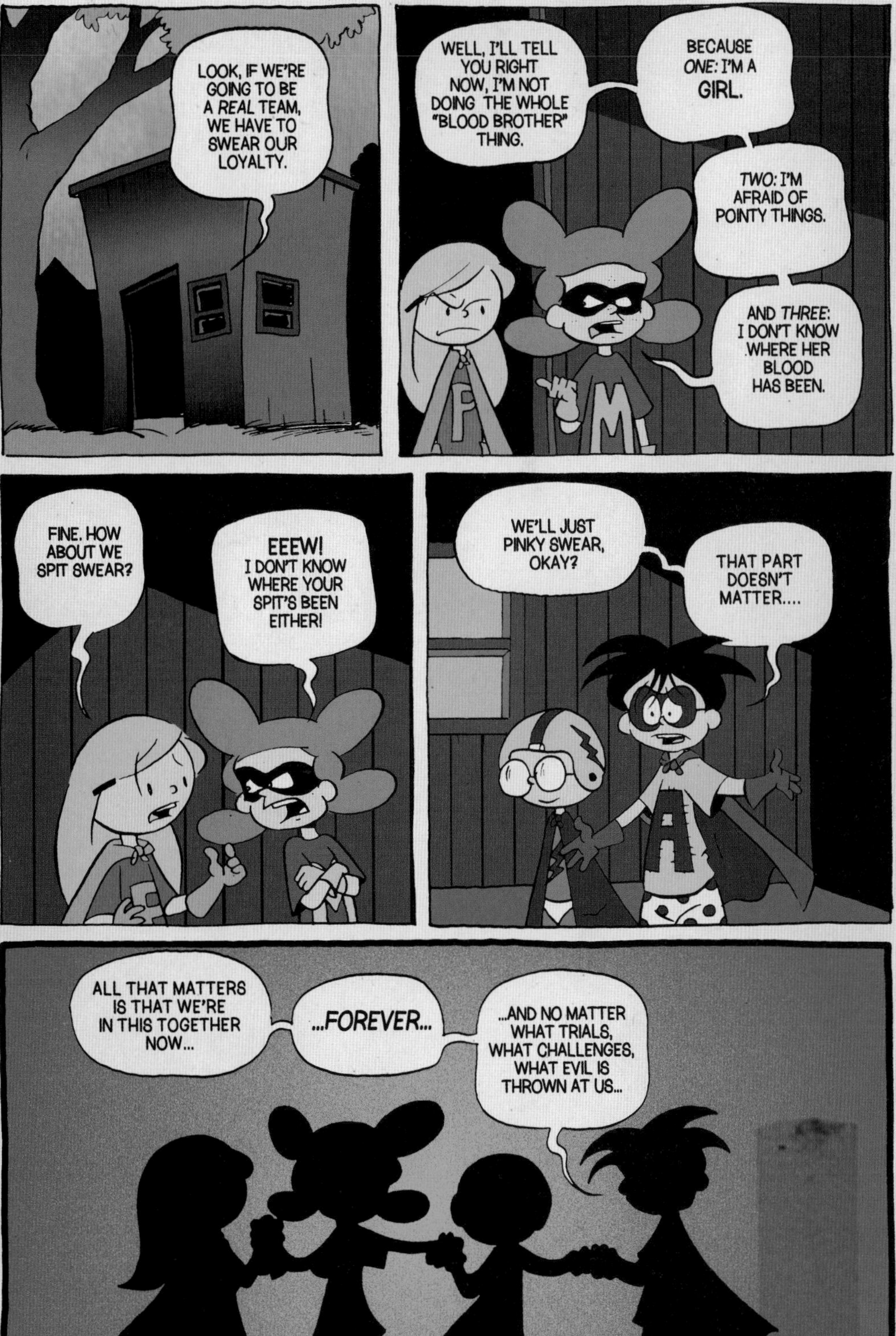

LOOK, IF WE'RE GOING TO BE A *REAL* TEAM, WE HAVE TO SWEAR OUR LOYALTY.
WELL, I'LL TELL YOU RIGHT NOW, I'M NOT DOING THE WHOLE "BLOOD BROTHER" THING.
BECAUSE *ONE:* I'M A GIRL.
TWO: I'M AFRAID OF POINTY THINGS.
AND *THREE*: I DON'T KNOW WHERE HER BLOOD HAS BEEN.
FINE. HOW ABOUT WE SPIT SWEAR?
EEEW! I DON'T KNOW WHERE YOUR SPIT'S BEEN EITHER!
WE'LL JUST PINKY SWEAR, OKAY?
THAT PART DOESN'T MATTER....
ALL THAT MATTERS IS THAT WE'RE IN THIS TOGETHER NOW...
...*FOREVER*...
...AND NO MATTER WHAT TRIALS, WHAT CHALLENGES, WHAT EVIL IS THROWN AT US...

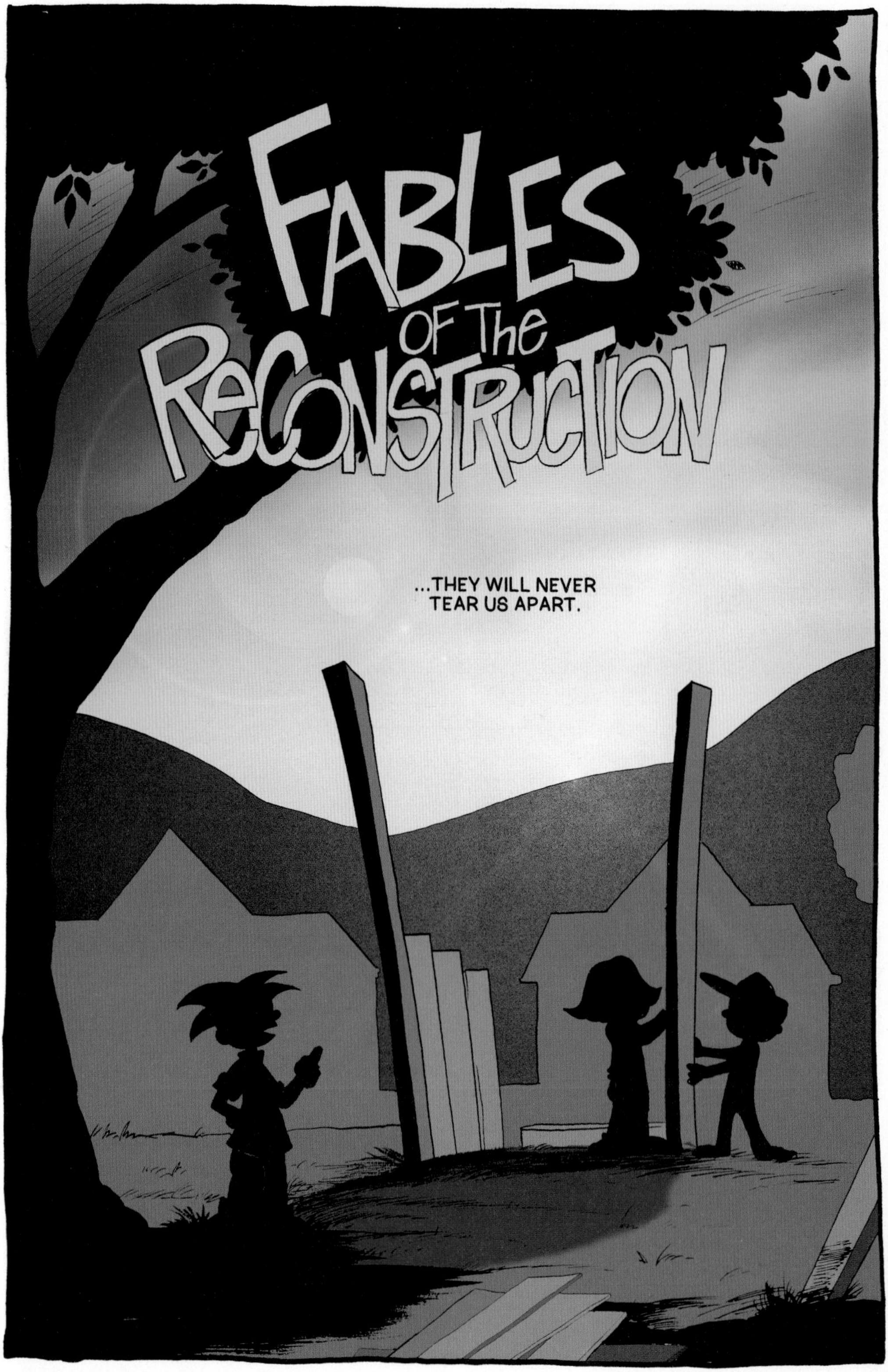
FABLES OF THE RECONSTRUCTION
...THEY WILL NEVER TEAR US APART.

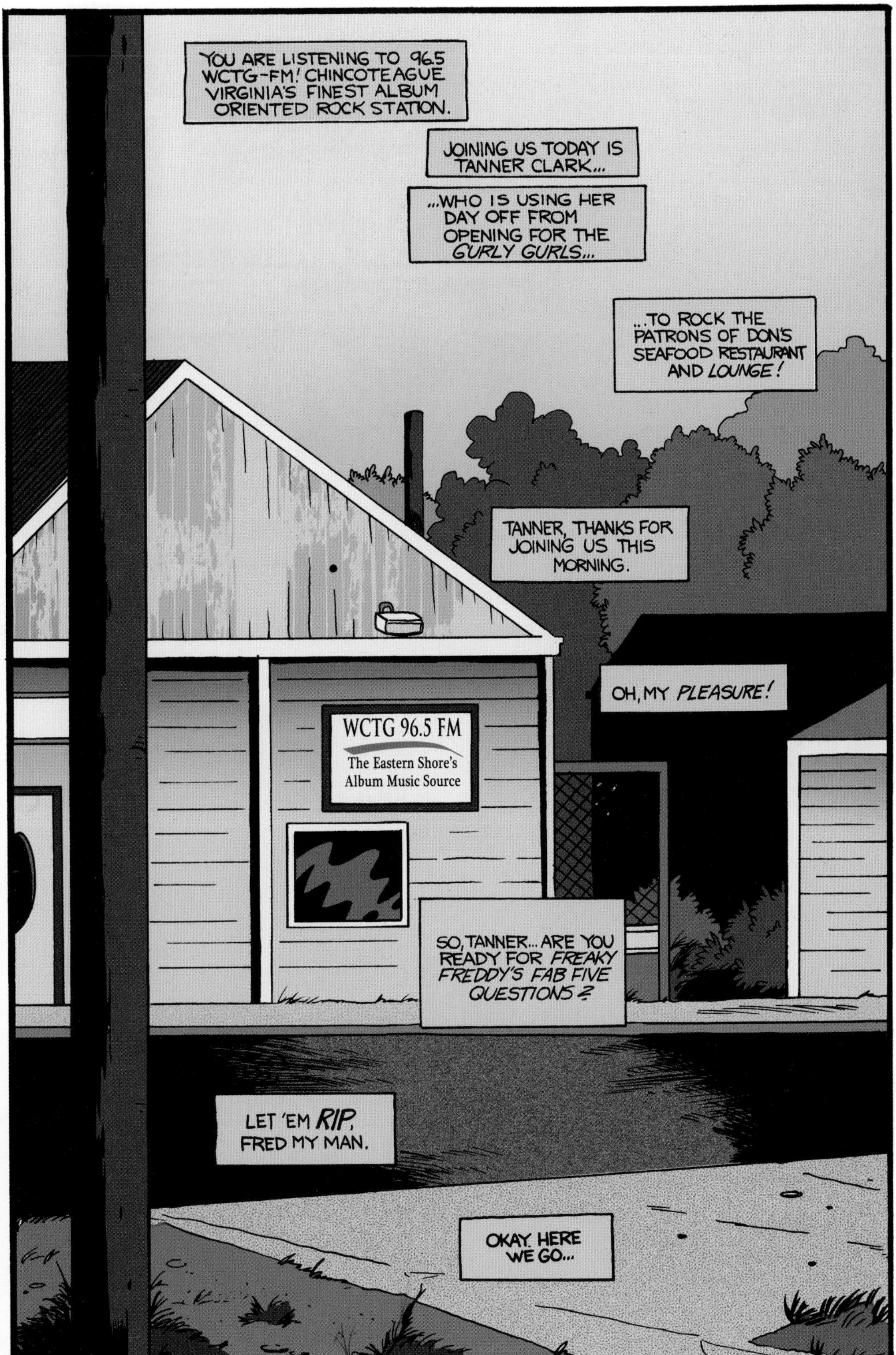
YOU ARE LISTENING TO 96.5 WCTG-FM! CHINCOTEAGUE VIRGINIA'S FINEST ALBUM ORIENTED ROCK STATION.
JOINING US TODAY IS TANNER CLARK...
...WHO IS USING HER DAY OFF FROM OPENING FOR THE *GURLY GURLS*...
...TO ROCK THE PATRONS OF DON'S SEAFOOD RESTAURANT AND *LOUNGE*!
TANNER, THANKS FOR JOINING US THIS MORNING.
OH, MY *PLEASURE*!
WCTG 96.5 FM
The Eastern Shore's Album Music Source
SO, TANNER... ARE YOU READY FOR *FREAKY FREDDY'S FAB FIVE QUESTIONS*?
LET 'EM *RIP*, FRED MY MAN.
OKAY. HERE WE GO...

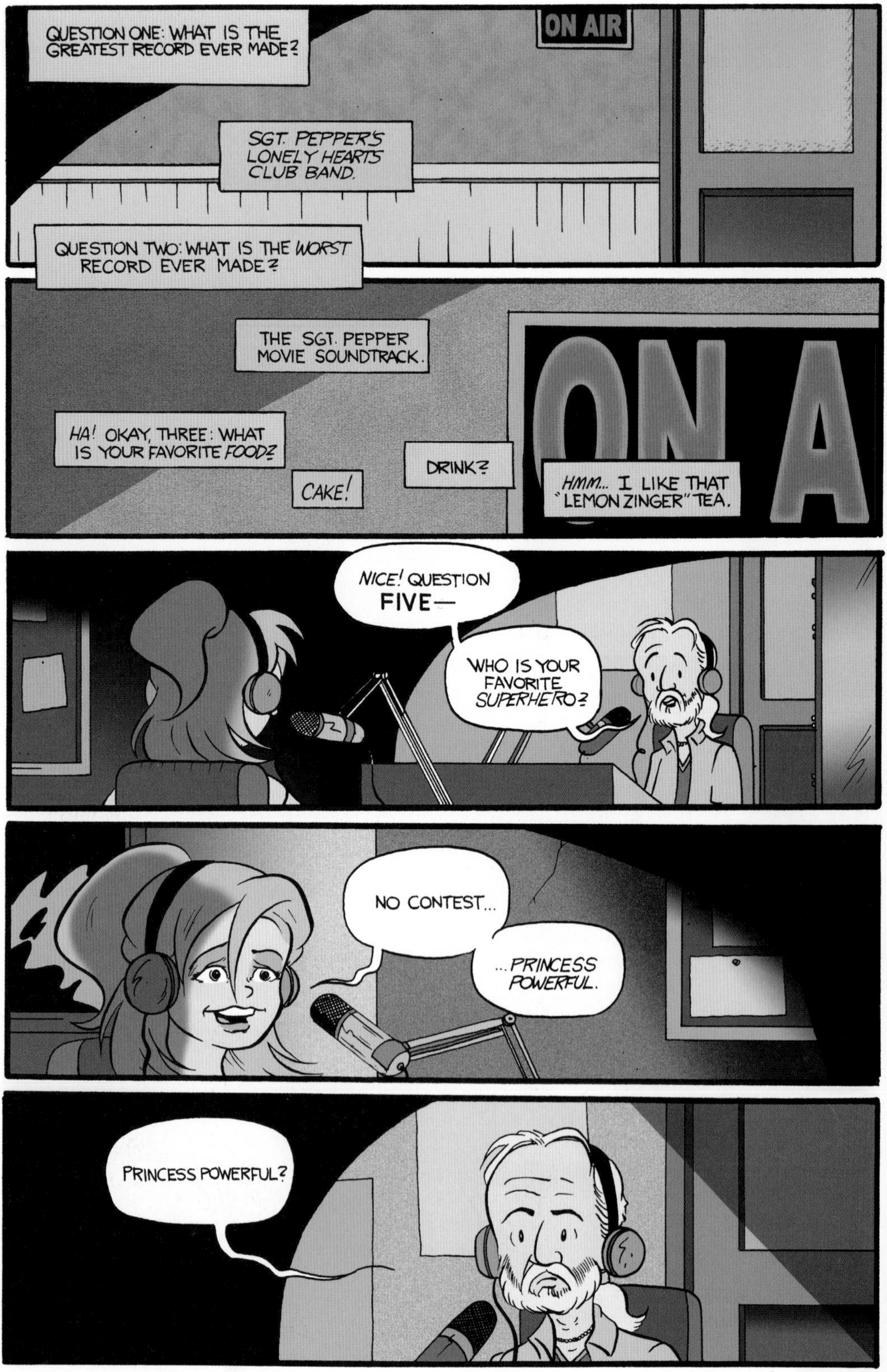
QUESTION ONE: WHAT IS THE GREATEST RECORD EVER MADE?
SGT. PEPPER'S LONELY HEARTS CLUB BAND.
QUESTION TWO: WHAT IS THE WORST RECORD EVER MADE?
ON AIR
THE SGT. PEPPER MOVIE SOUNDTRACK.
HA! OKAY, THREE: WHAT IS YOUR FAVORITE FOOD?
CAKE!
DRINK?
HMM... I LIKE THAT "LEMON ZINGER" TEA.
NICE! QUESTION FIVE—
WHO IS YOUR FAVORITE SUPERHERO?
NO CONTEST...
...PRINCESS POWERFUL.
PRINCESS POWERFUL?

...NEVER HEARD OF HER.

Hmm...
Mmm...
Mmm... ♪

HUH...

WHHOOOAA...

GOOD JOB, GUYS!

REEEEEALLY NICE WORK!

IT'S LOOKING ALMOST AS *BAD* AS THE *ORIGINAL!*

LOOK, JUST TAKE OFF THAT STUPID CAPE AND GIVE US A *HAND.*

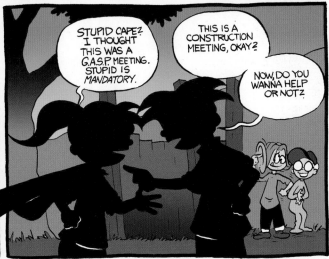

STUPID CAPE? I THOUGHT THIS WAS A G.A.S.P. MEETING. STUPID IS *MANDATORY.*

THIS IS A CONSTRUCTION MEETING, OKAY?

NOW, DO YOU WANNA HELP OR NOT?

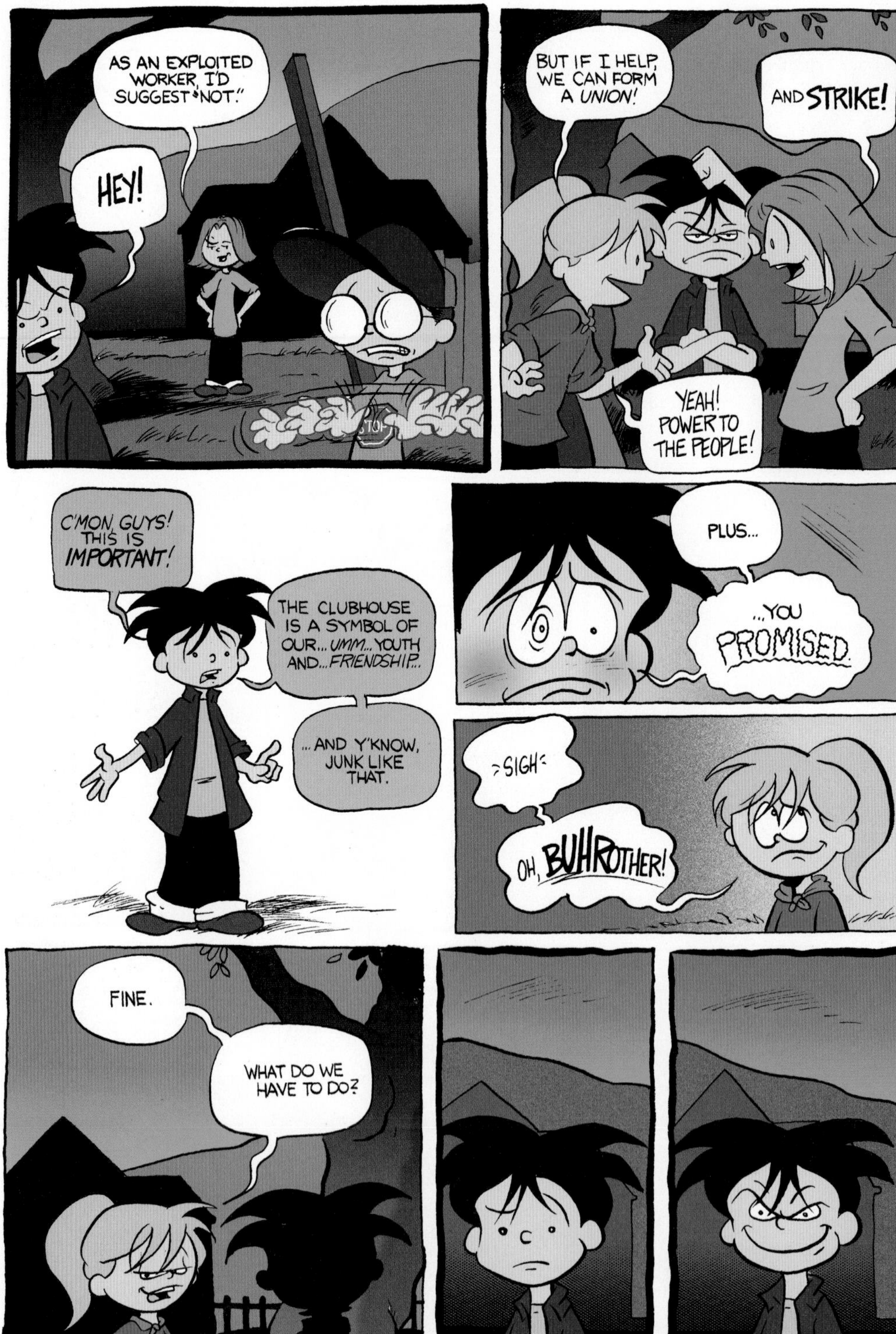

AS AN EXPLOITED WORKER, I'D SUGGEST "NOT."
HEY!
BUT IF I HELP, WE CAN FORM A UNION!
AND STRIKE!
YEAH! POWER TO THE PEOPLE!
C'MON, GUYS! THIS IS IMPORTANT!
THE CLUBHOUSE IS A SYMBOL OF OUR... UMM... YOUTH AND... FRIENDSHIP...
... AND Y'KNOW, JUNK LIKE THAT.
PLUS...
...YOU PROMISED.
SIGH
OH, BUHROTHER!
FINE.
WHAT DO WE HAVE TO DO?

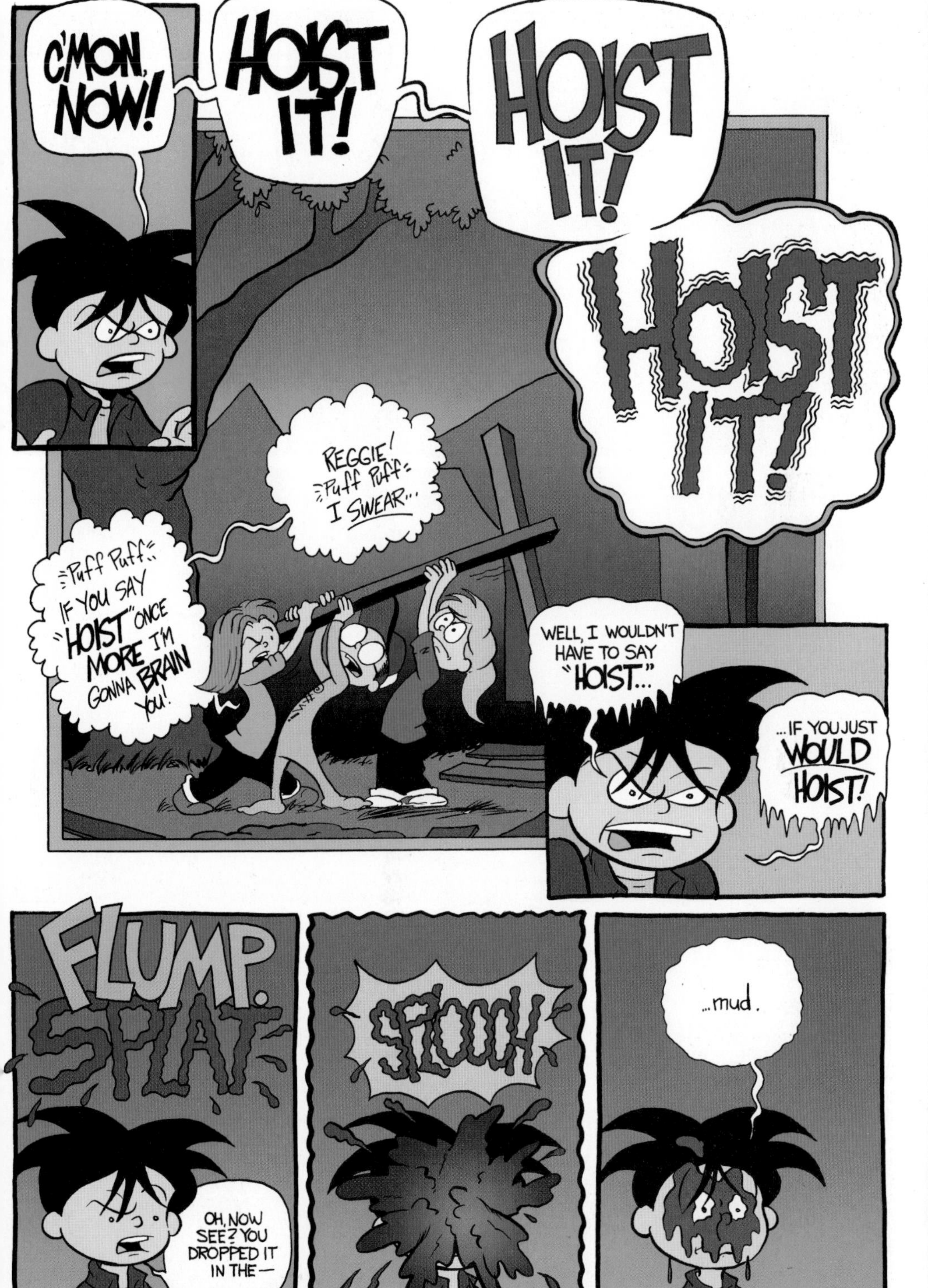

C'MON, NOW!
HOIST IT!
HOIST IT!
HOIST IT!
REGGIE! Puff Puff I SWEAR...
Puff Puff IF YOU SAY "HOIST" ONCE MORE I'M GONNA BRAIN YOU!
WELL, I WOULDN'T HAVE TO SAY "HOIST."...
...IF YOU JUST WOULD HOIST!
FLUMP.
SPLAT
OH, NOW SEE? YOU DROPPED IT IN THE—
SPLOOCH
...mud.

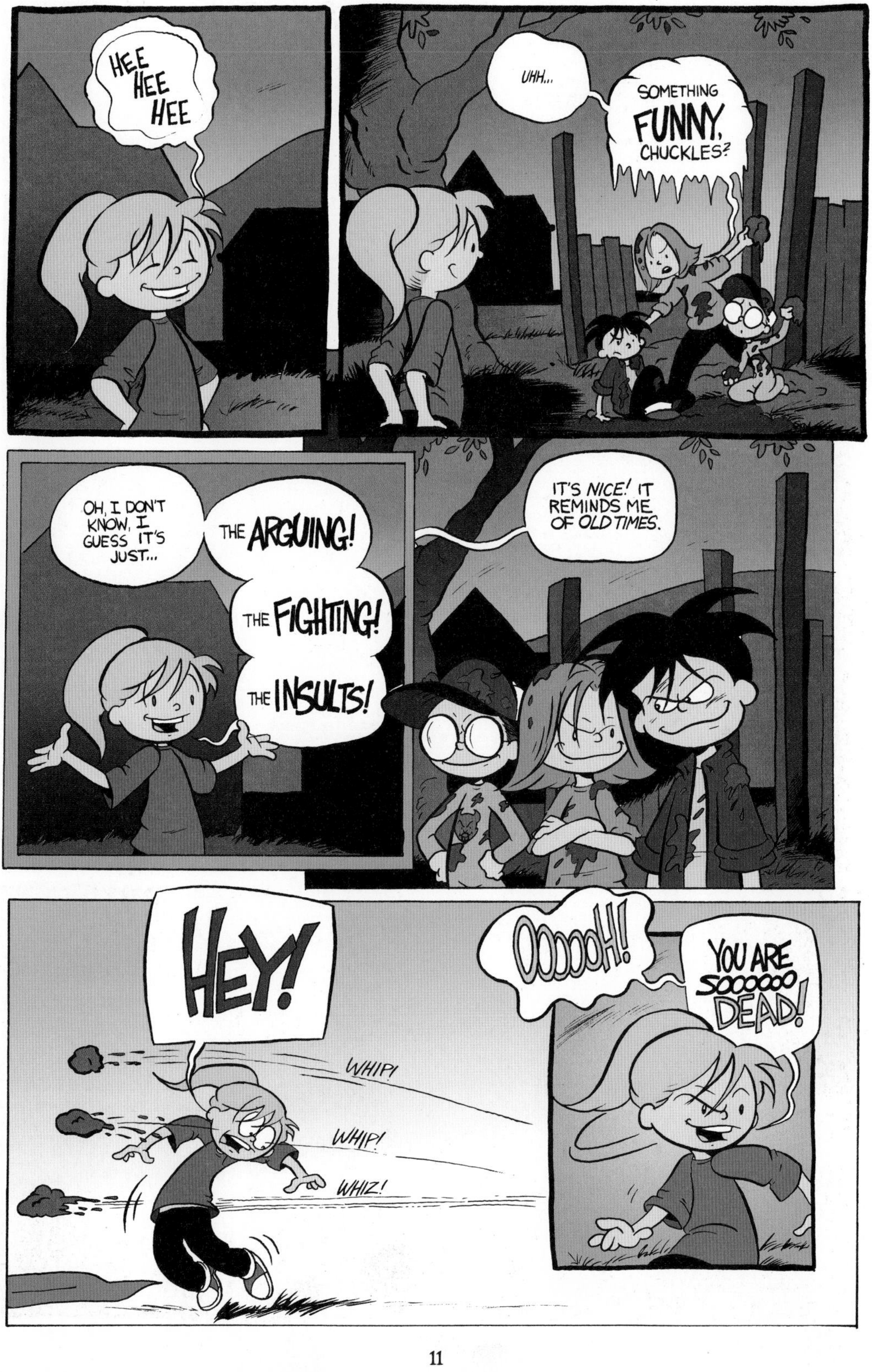
HEE HEE HEE
UHH...
SOMETHING FUNNY, CHUCKLES?
OH, I DON'T KNOW, I GUESS IT'S JUST...
THE ARGUING!
THE FIGHTING!
THE INSULTS!
IT'S NICE! IT REMINDS ME OF OLD TIMES.
HEY!
WHIP!
WHIP!
WHIZ!
OOOOOH!
YOU ARE SOOOOOO DEAD!

IT HAD BEEN A *REALLY* LONG TIME SINCE WE... I DON'T KNOW... ***PLAYED!*** AND I HAVE TO TELL YOU, I FELT LIKE A *KID* AGAIN. (YEAH, I KNOW I'M STILL A KID, I JUST FELT LIKE A *LITTLER* KID, Y'KNOW?)

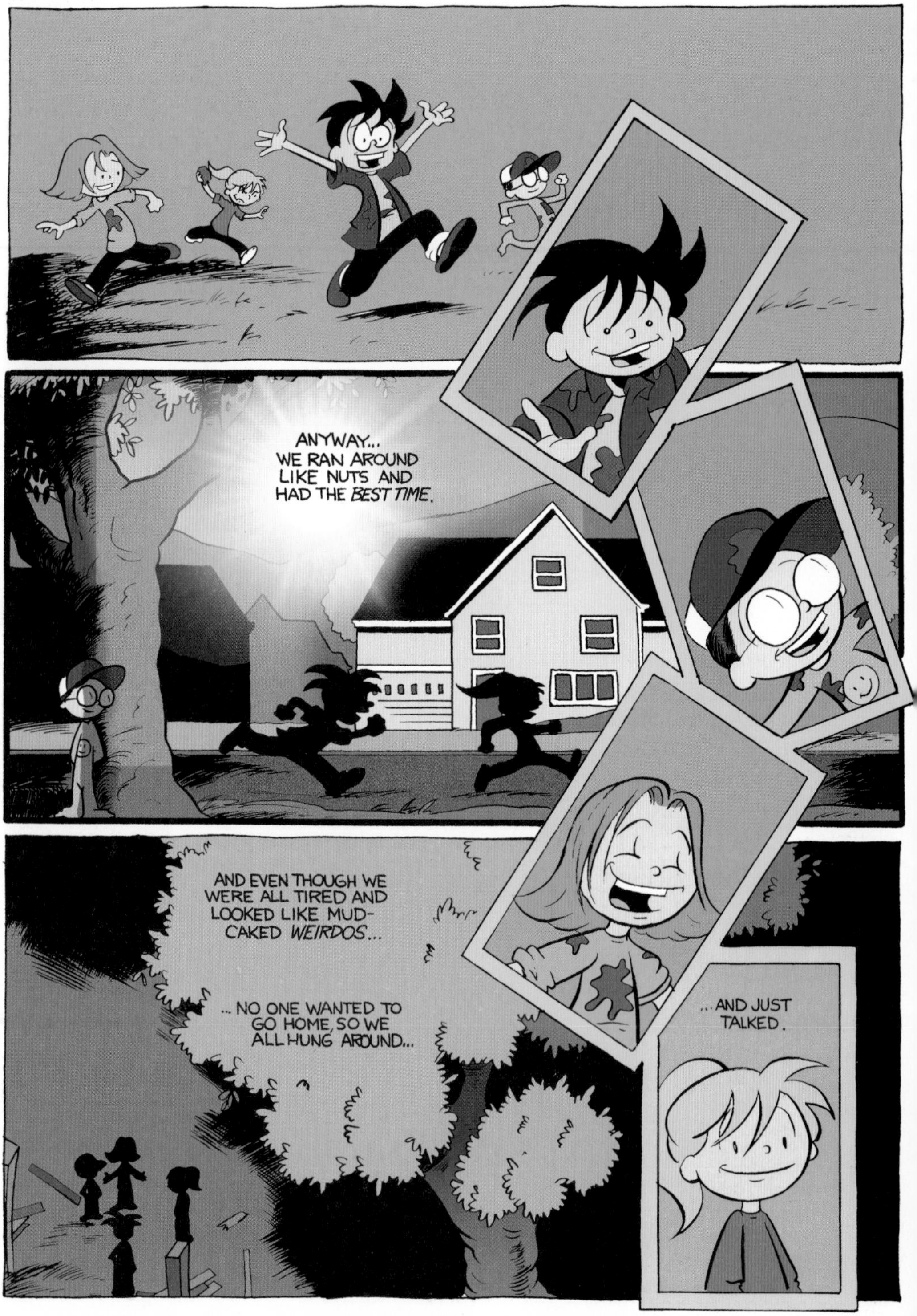

ANYWAY... WE RAN AROUND LIKE NUTS AND HAD THE *BEST TIME*.
AND EVEN THOUGH WE WERE ALL TIRED AND LOOKED LIKE MUD-CAKED *WEIRDOS*...
...NO ONE WANTED TO GO HOME, SO WE ALL HUNG AROUND...
...AND JUST TALKED.

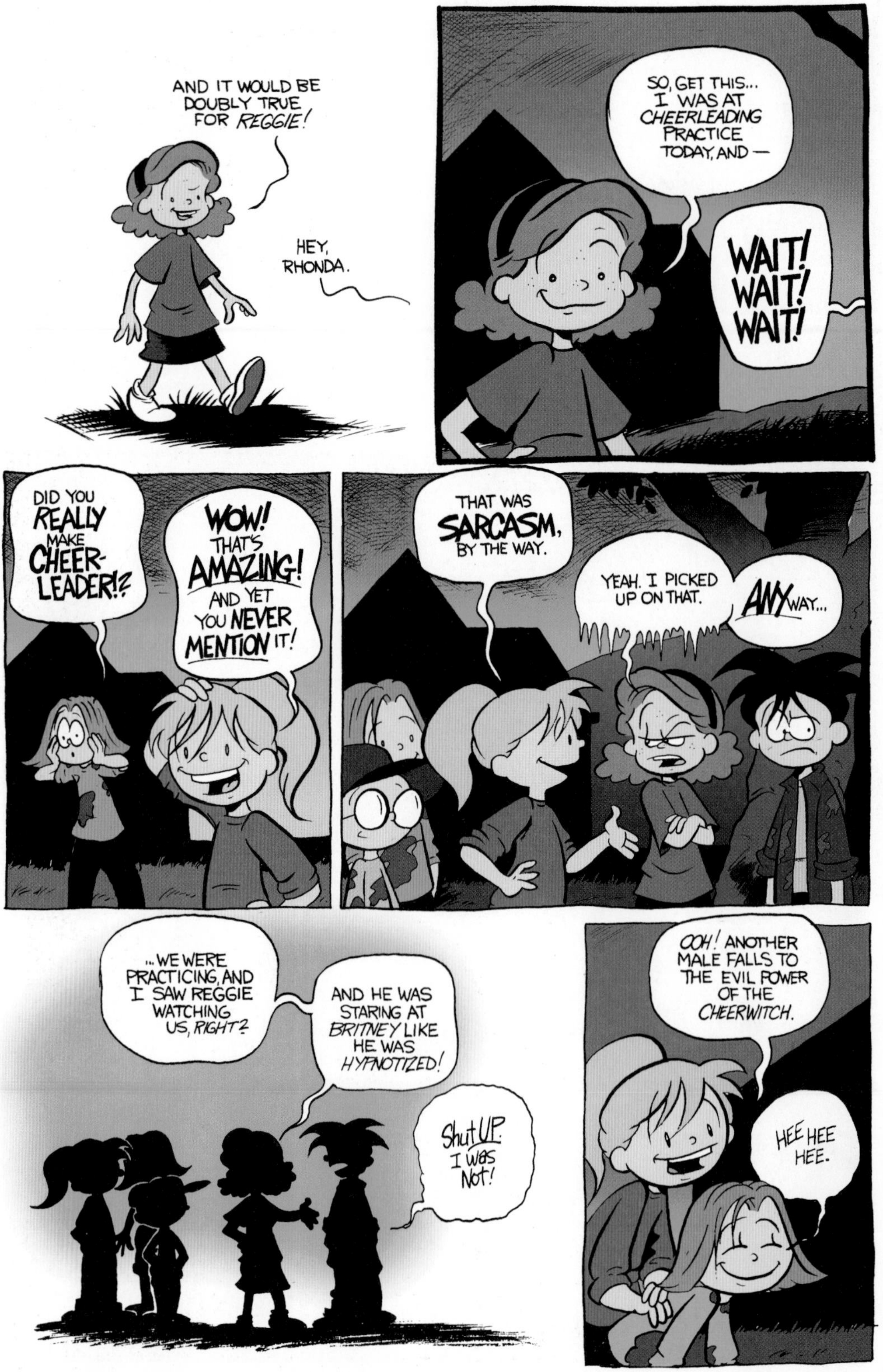
AND IT WOULD BE DOUBLY TRUE FOR *REGGIE!*
HEY, RHONDA.
SO, GET THIS... I WAS AT *CHEERLEADING* PRACTICE TODAY, AND —
WAIT! WAIT! WAIT!
DID YOU **REALLY** MAKE **CHEER-LEADER!?**
WOW! THAT'S **AMAZING!** AND YET YOU **NEVER MENTION** IT!
THAT WAS **SARCASM,** BY THE WAY.
YEAH. I PICKED UP ON THAT.
ANYWAY...
...WE WERE PRACTICING, AND I SAW REGGIE WATCHING US, *RIGHT?*
AND HE WAS STARING AT *BRITNEY* LIKE HE WAS *HYPNOTIZED!*
Shut UP. I was Not!
OOH! ANOTHER MALE FALLS TO THE EVIL POWER OF THE *CHEERWITCH.*
HEE HEE HEE.

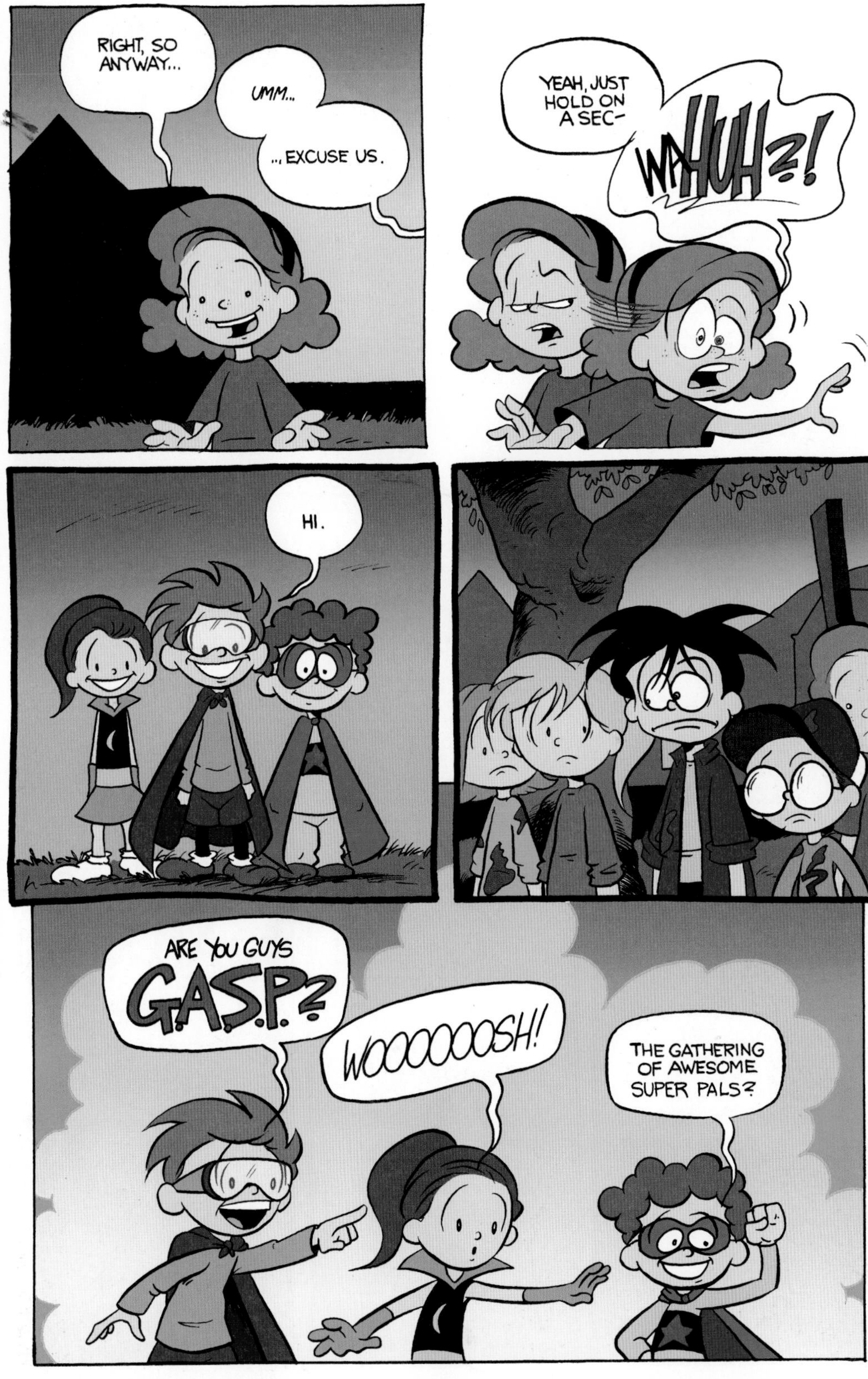

RIGHT, SO ANYWAY...
UMM...
..., EXCUSE US.
YEAH, JUST HOLD ON A SEC-
WAHUH?!
HI.
ARE YOU GUYS G.A.S.P.?
WOOOOOOOSH!
THE GATHERING OF AWESOME SUPER PALS?

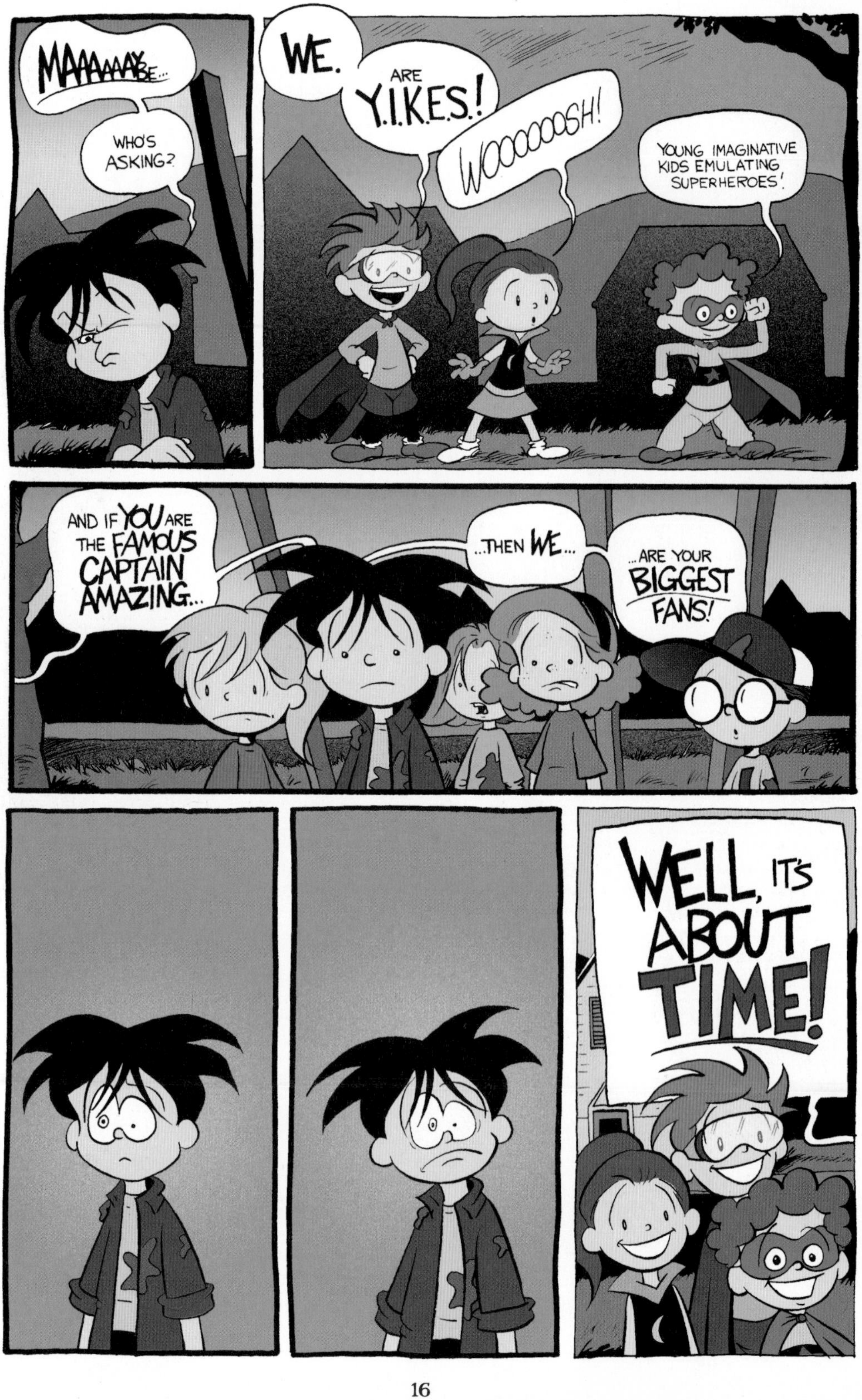
MAAAAAAYBE...
WHO'S ASKING?
WE.
ARE Y.I.K.E.S.!
WOOOOOOSH!
YOUNG IMAGINATIVE KIDS EMULATING SUPERHEROES!
AND IF YOU ARE THE FAMOUS CAPTAIN AMAZING...
...THEN WE...
...ARE YOUR BIGGEST FANS!
WELL, IT'S ABOUT TIME!

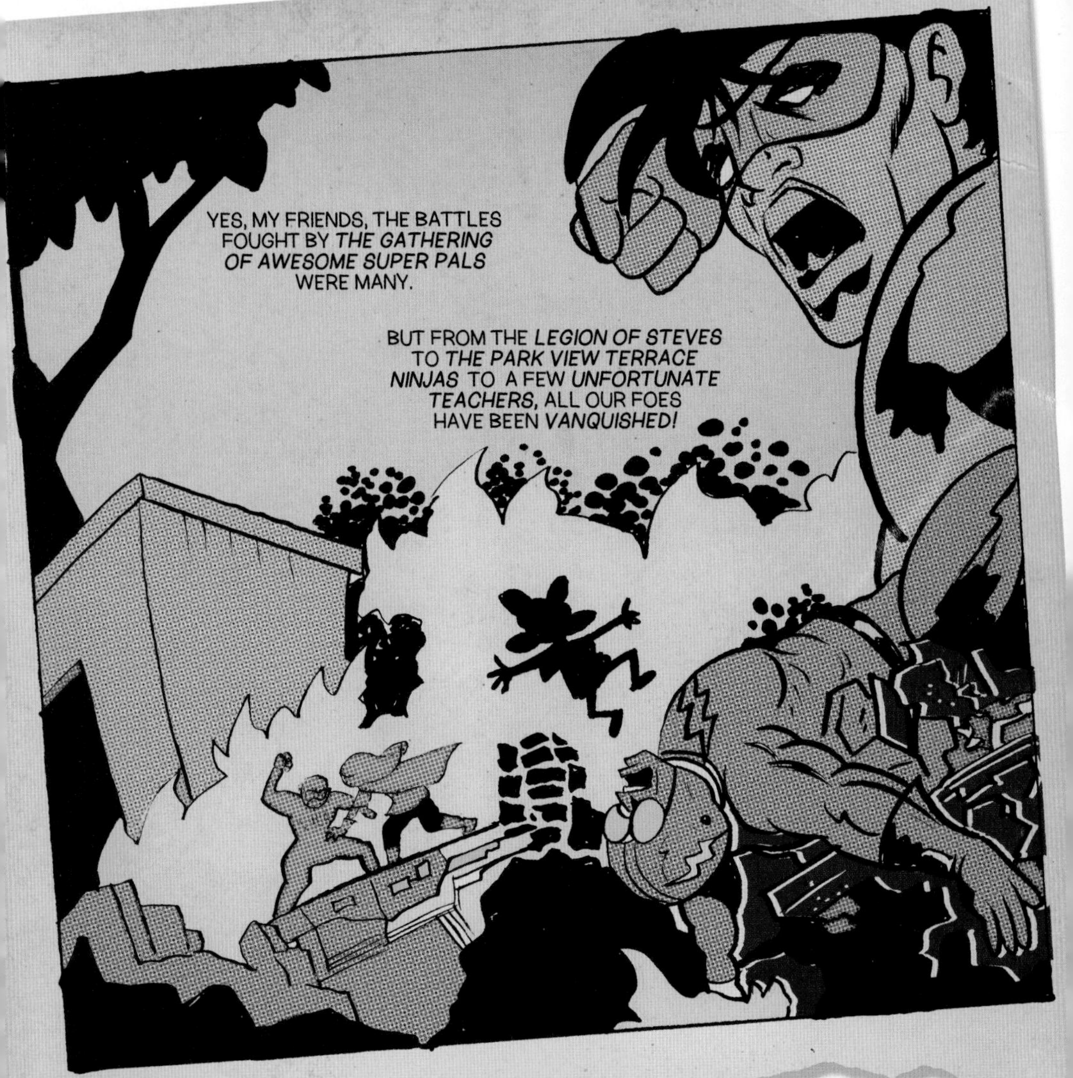
YES, MY FRIENDS, THE BATTLES FOUGHT BY THE GATHERING OF AWESOME SUPER PALS WERE MANY.
BUT FROM THE LEGION OF STEVES TO THE PARK VIEW TERRACE NINJAS TO A FEW UNFORTUNATE TEACHERS, ALL OUR FOES HAVE BEEN VANQUISHED!

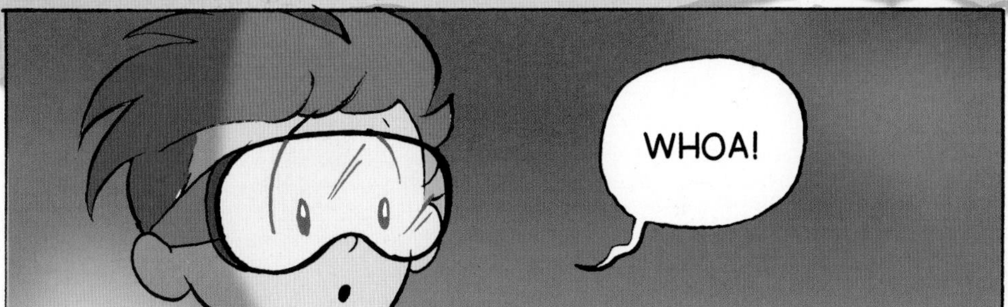
WHOA!

18

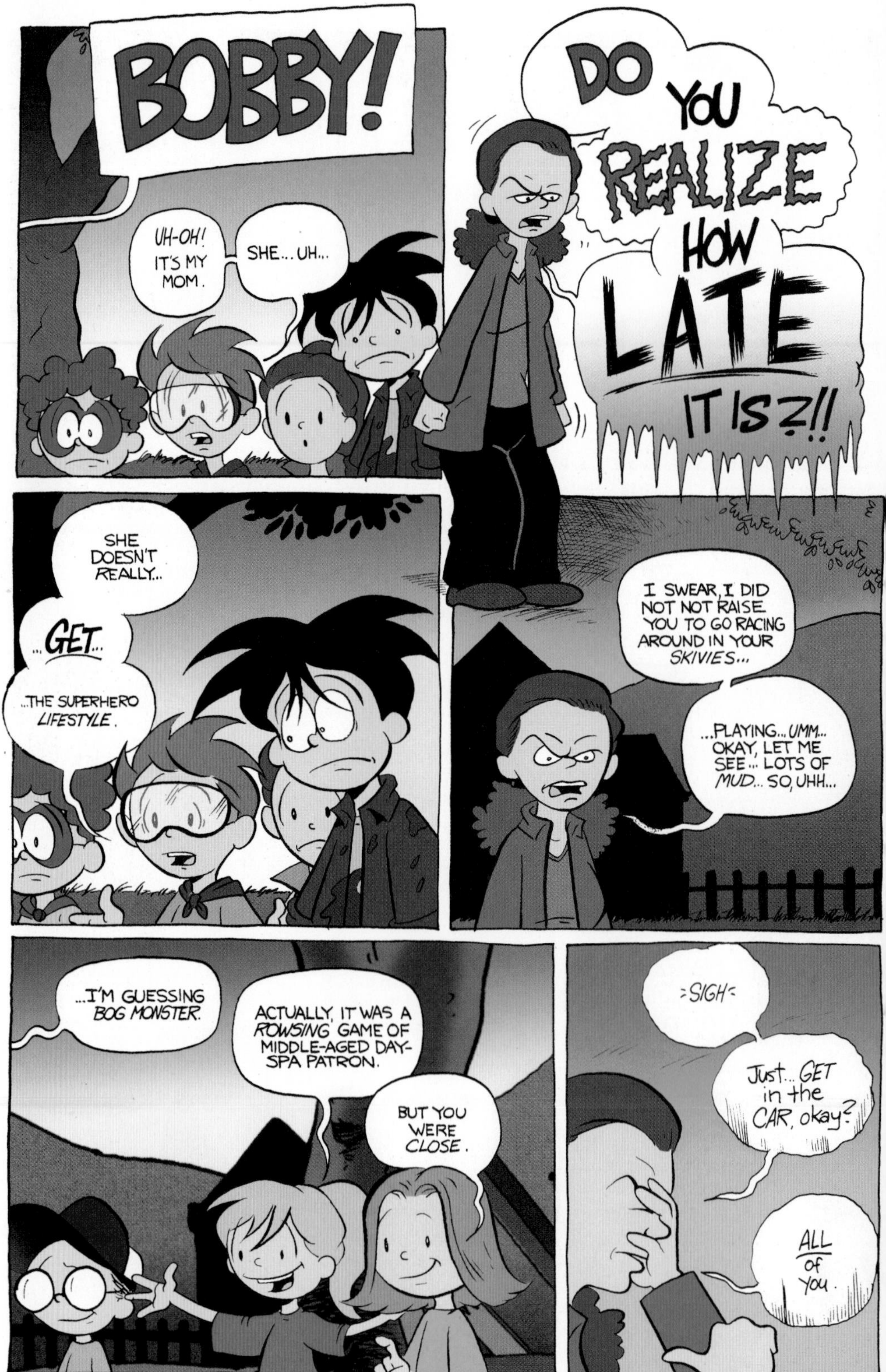
BOBBY!
UH-OH! IT'S MY MOM.
SHE... UH...
DO YOU REALIZE HOW LATE IT IS?!!
SHE DOESN'T REALLY...
...GET...
...THE SUPERHERO LIFESTYLE.
I SWEAR, I DID NOT NOT RAISE YOU TO GO RACING AROUND IN YOUR SKIVIES...
...PLAYING... UMM... OKAY, LET ME SEE... LOTS OF MUD... SO, UHH...
...I'M GUESSING BOG MONSTER.
ACTUALLY, IT WAS A ROWSING GAME OF MIDDLE-AGED DAY-SPA PATRON.
BUT YOU WERE CLOSE.
=SIGH=
Just... GET in the CAR, okay?
ALL of You.

I SWEAR...

I SHOULD'VE SEEN THIS COMING **YEARS** AGO.

YOUR **FATHER** HAD TENDENCIES.

AS SOON AS I SAW THAT *GREEN LANTERN* TATTOO, I SHOULD HAVE *RUN* FOR THE *HILLS*.

WELL, *THAT* WAS—

SHH!

QUIET! I'M THINKING.

SEE? I TOLD YOU HE COULD DO IT. YOU OWE ME A *BUCK*.

AWW, SHOOT.

OKAY, STEPHEN HAWKING, WHAT ARE YOU THINKING ABOUT?

I... I THINK... "MAYBE WE'VE BEEN LOOKING AT THINGS THE *WRONG WAY*.

YEAH!

THAT'S *IT!*

21

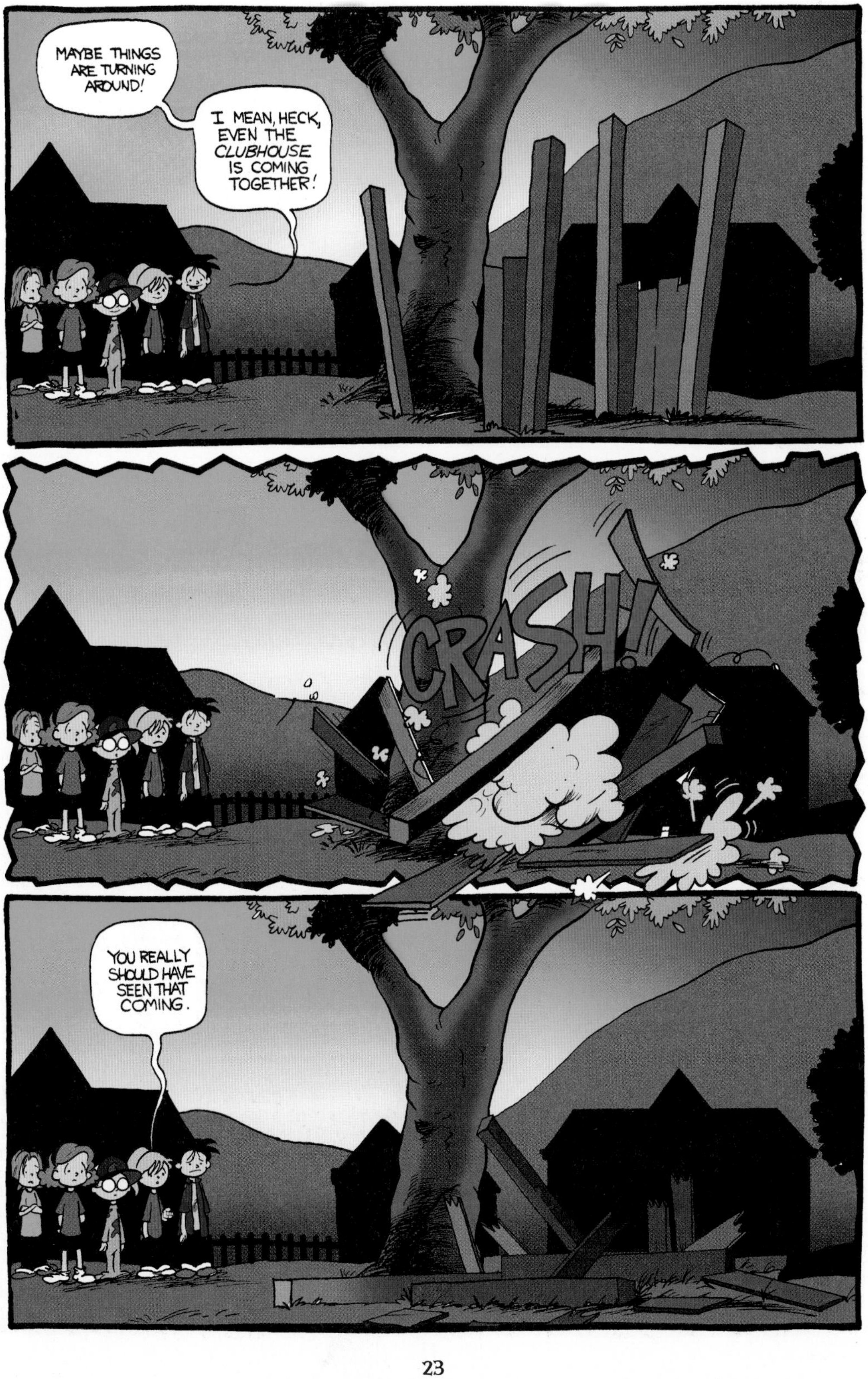
MAYBE THINGS ARE TURNING AROUND!
I MEAN, HECK, EVEN THE *CLUBHOUSE* IS COMING TOGETHER!
CRASH!
YOU REALLY SHOULD HAVE SEEN THAT COMING.

SO WE WERE ALL LYING AROUND ON THESE RAFTS, JUST FLOATING IN THIS BIG BEAUTIFUL SWIMMING POOL.

IT WAS REAL PEACEFUL AND QUIET, AND EVERYONE WAS HAVING A GOOD TIME.

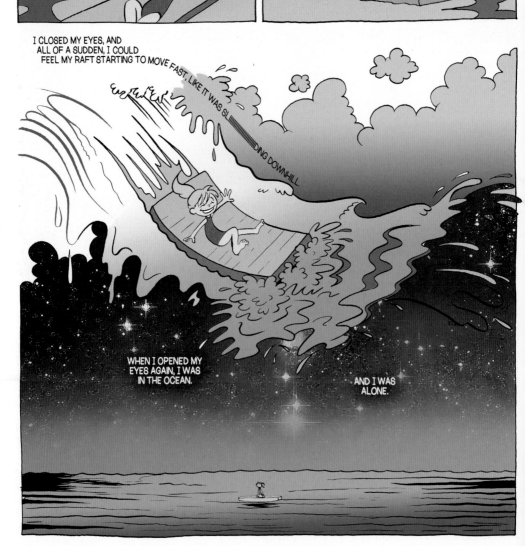

I CLOSED MY EYES, AND ALL OF A SUDDEN, I COULD FEEL MY RAFT STARTING TO MOVE FAST, LIKE IT WAS SLIIIIIIIIIIIDING DOWNHILL.

WHEN I OPENED MY EYES AGAIN, I WAS IN THE OCEAN.

AND I WAS ALONE.

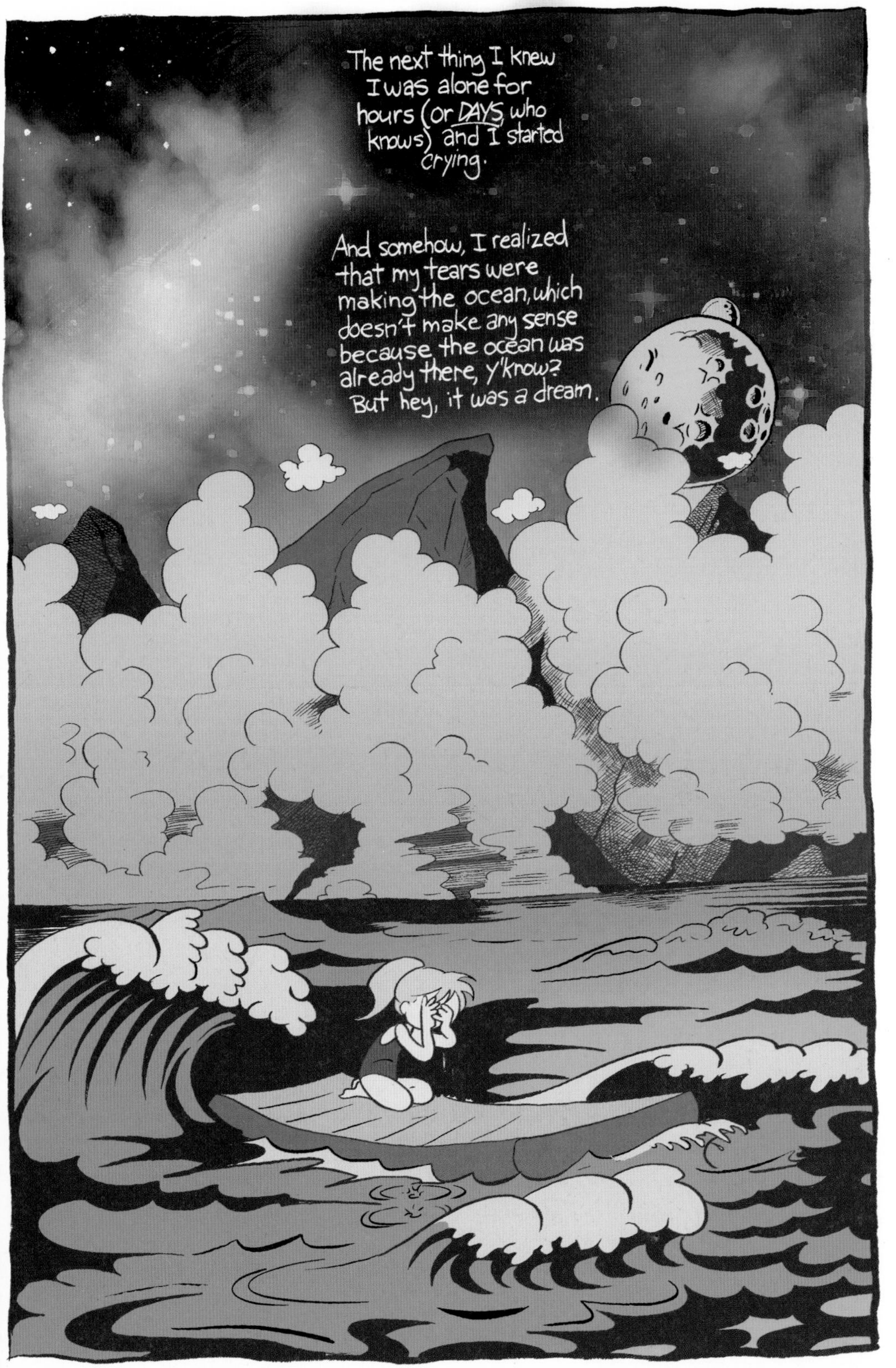
The next thing I knew I was alone for hours (or DAYS, who knows) and I started crying.
And somehow, I realized that my tears were making the ocean, which doesn't make any sense because the ocean was already there, y'know? But hey, it was a dream.

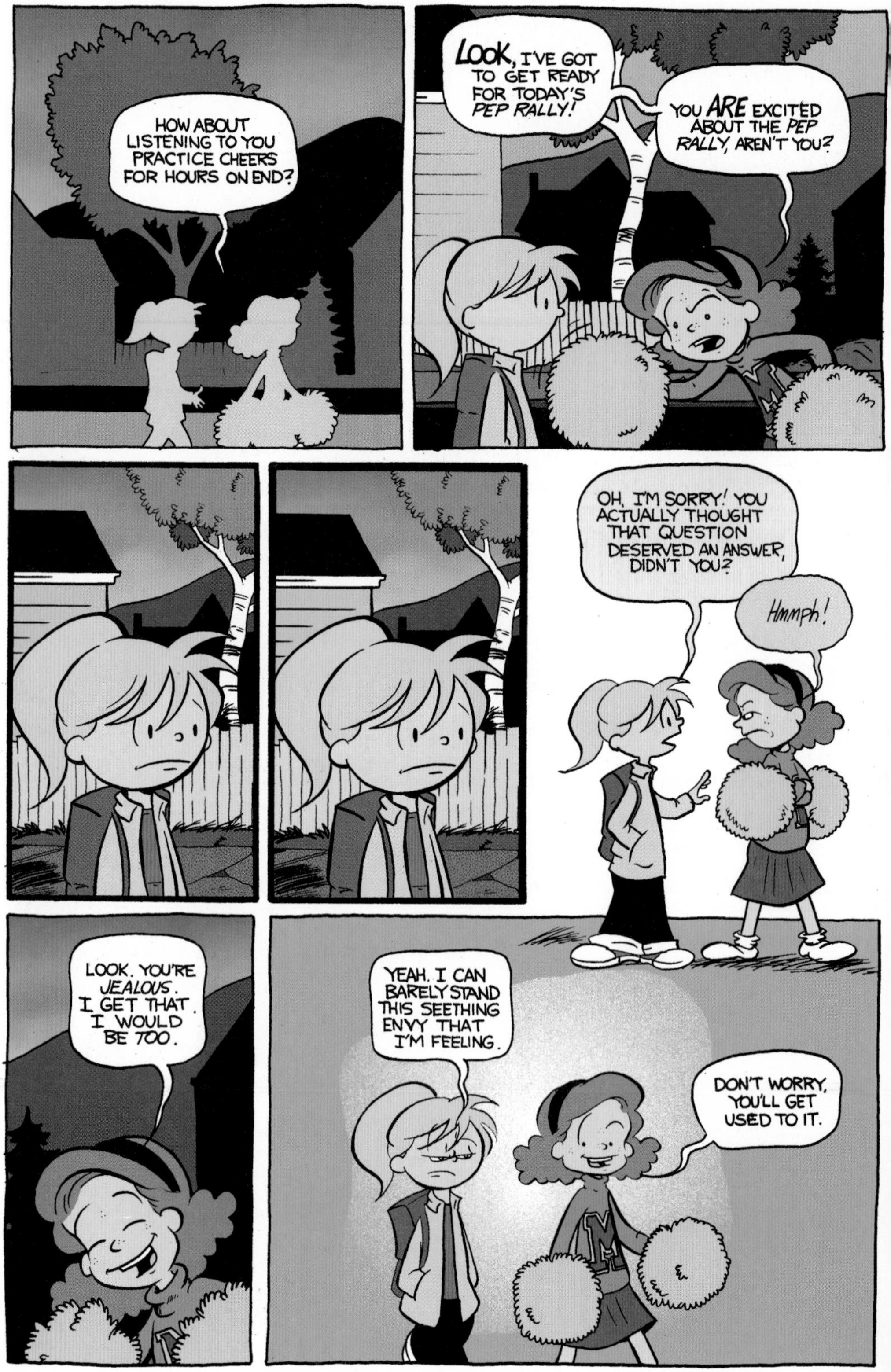
HOW ABOUT LISTENING TO YOU PRACTICE CHEERS FOR HOURS ON END?
LOOK, I'VE GOT TO GET READY FOR TODAY'S PEP RALLY!
YOU ARE EXCITED ABOUT THE PEP RALLY, AREN'T YOU?
OH, I'M SORRY! YOU ACTUALLY THOUGHT THAT QUESTION DESERVED AN ANSWER, DIDN'T YOU?
Hmmph!
LOOK. YOU'RE JEALOUS. I GET THAT. I WOULD BE TOO.
YEAH. I CAN BARELY STAND THIS SEETHING ENVY THAT I'M FEELING.
DON'T WORRY, YOU'LL GET USED TO IT.

AND BEFORE YOU KNOW IT, YOU'LL BE INFUSED WITH SCHOOL SPIRIT.

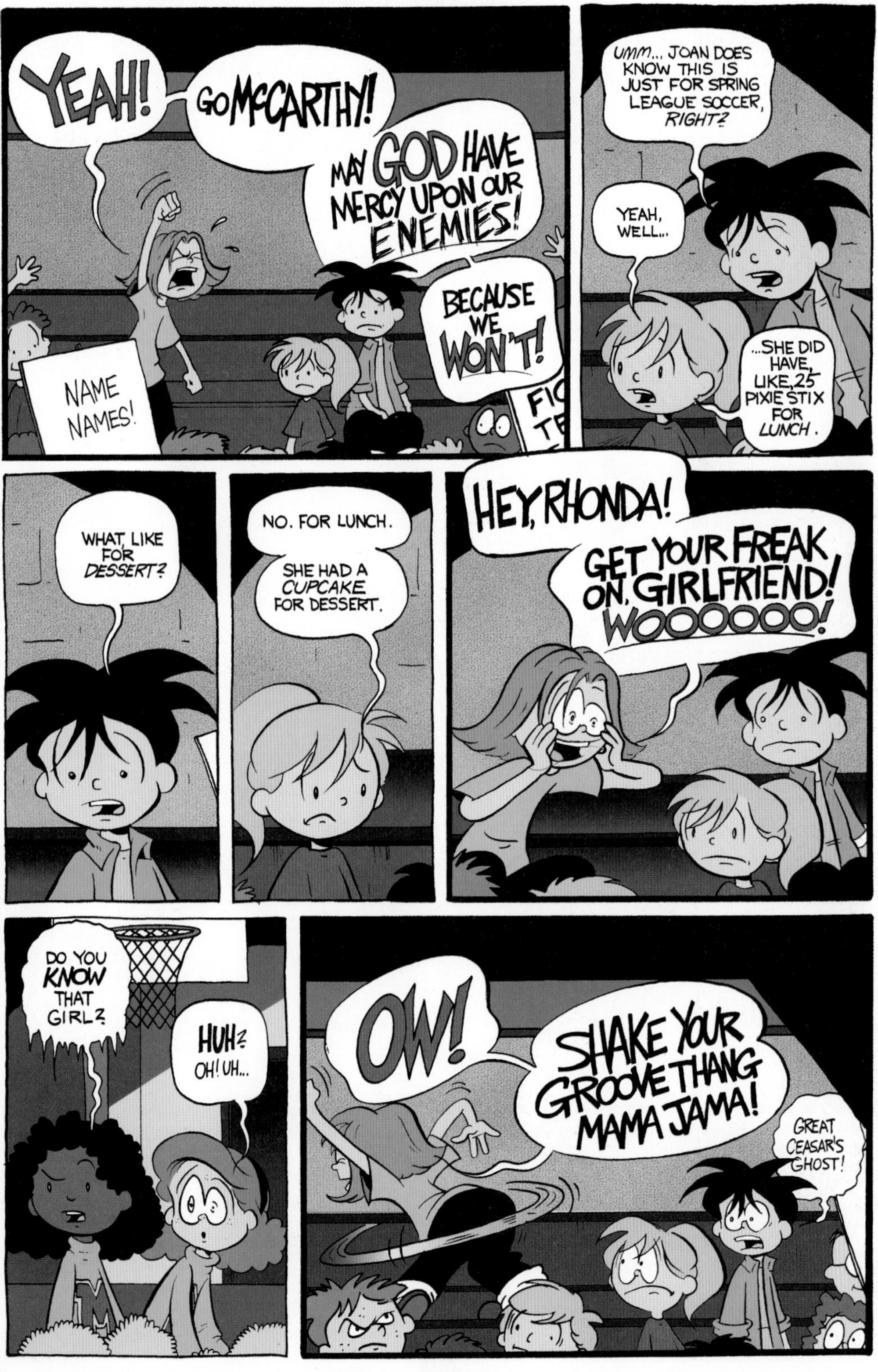

YEAH!
GO McCARTHY!
MAY GOD HAVE MERCY UPON OUR ENEMIES!
BECAUSE WE WON'T!
NAME NAMES!
UMM... JOAN DOES KNOW THIS IS JUST FOR SPRING LEAGUE SOCCER, RIGHT?
YEAH, WELL...
...SHE DID HAVE, LIKE, 25 PIXIE STIX FOR LUNCH.
WHAT, LIKE FOR DESSERT?
NO. FOR LUNCH.
SHE HAD A CUPCAKE FOR DESSERT.
HEY, RHONDA!
GET YOUR FREAK ON, GIRLFRIEND! WOOOOOO!
DO YOU KNOW THAT GIRL?
HUH? OH! UH...
OW!
SHAKE YOUR GROOVE THANG MAMA JAMA!
GREAT CEASAR'S GHOST!

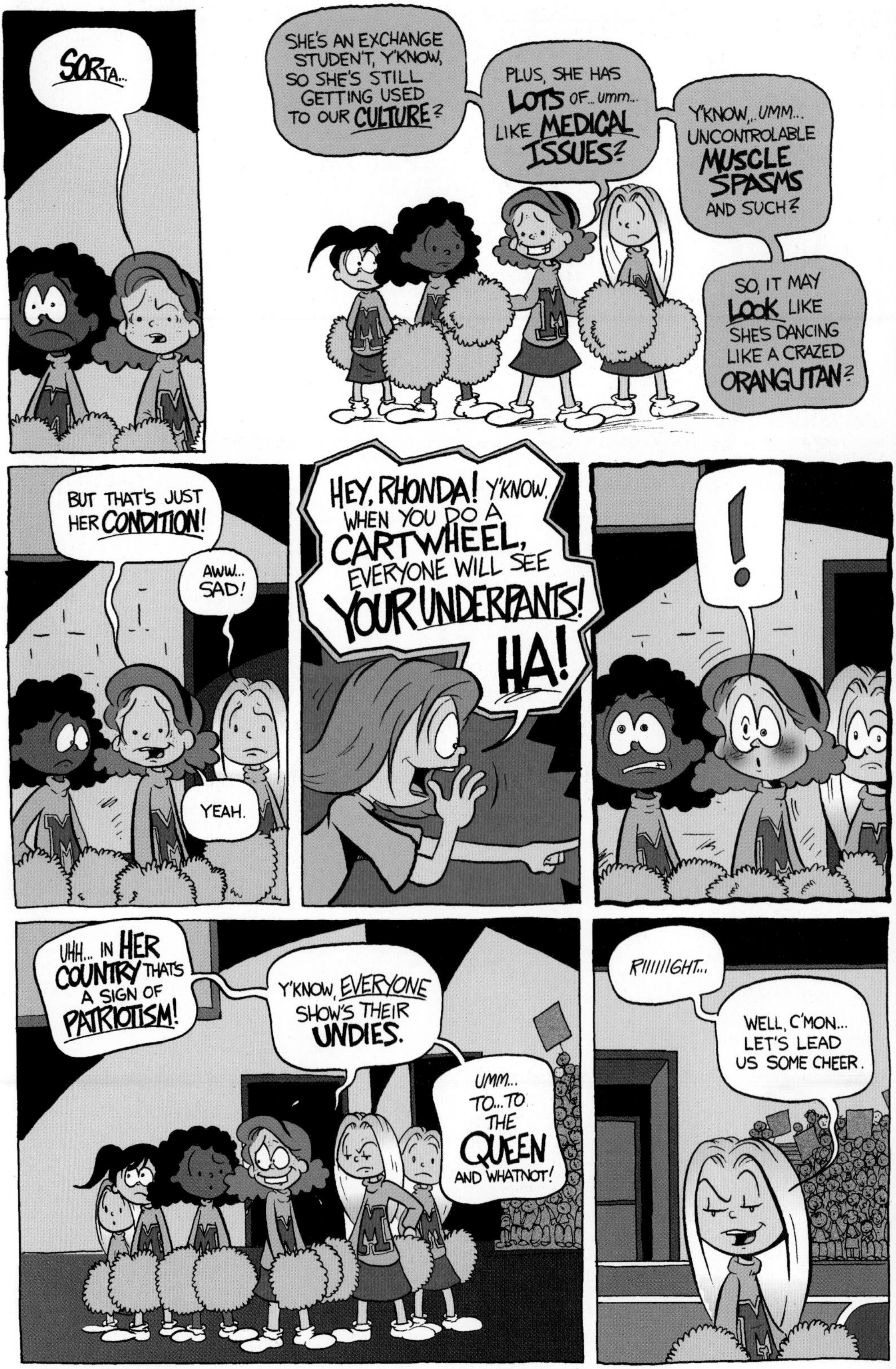
SORTA...
SHE'S AN EXCHANGE STUDENT, Y'KNOW, SO SHE'S STILL GETTING USED TO OUR CULTURE?
PLUS, SHE HAS LOTS OF.. umm... LIKE MEDICAL ISSUES?
Y'KNOW,.. UMM... UNCONTROLABLE MUSCLE SPASMS AND SUCH?
SO, IT MAY LOOK LIKE SHE'S DANCING LIKE A CRAZED ORANGUTAN?
BUT THAT'S JUST HER CONDITION!
AWW... SAD!
YEAH.
HEY, RHONDA! Y'KNOW, WHEN YOU DO A CARTWHEEL, EVERYONE WILL SEE YOUR UNDERPANTS!
HA!
!
UHH... IN HER COUNTRY THAT'S A SIGN OF PATRIOTISM!
Y'KNOW, EVERYONE SHOW'S THEIR UNDIES.
UMM... TO...TO THE QUEEN AND WHATNOT!
RIIIIIGHT...
WELL, C'MON... LET'S LEAD US SOME CHEER.

2228403

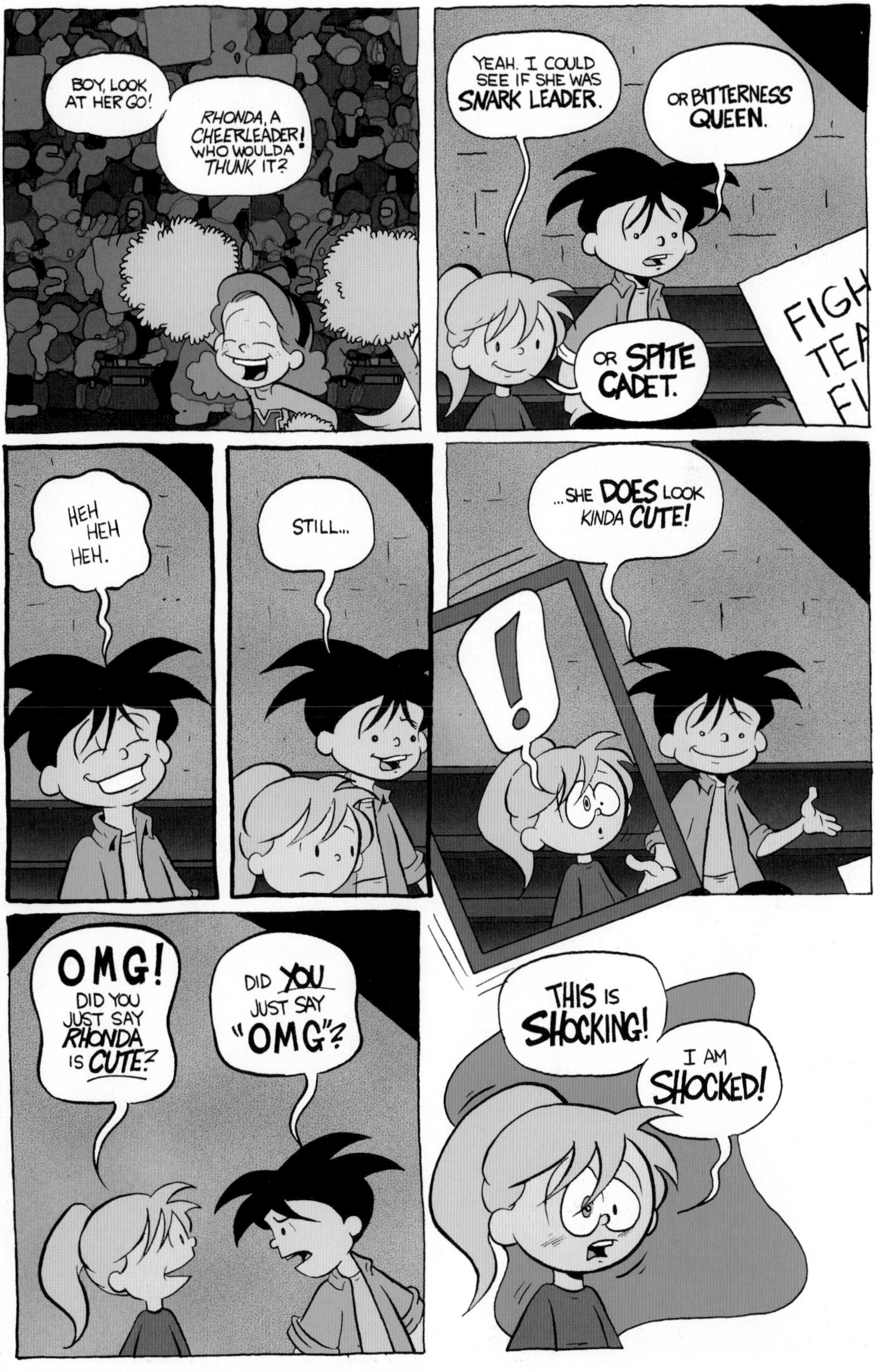
BOY, LOOK AT HER GO!
RHONDA, A CHEERLEADER! WHO WOULDA THUNK IT?
YEAH. I COULD SEE IF SHE WAS SNARK LEADER.
OR BITTERNESS QUEEN.
OR SPITE CADET.
FIGH
TEA
FI
HEH HEH HEH.
STILL...
...SHE DOES LOOK KINDA CUTE!
!
OMG! DID YOU JUST SAY RHONDA IS CUTE?
DID YOU JUST SAY "OMG"?
THIS IS SHOCKING!
I AM SHOCKED!

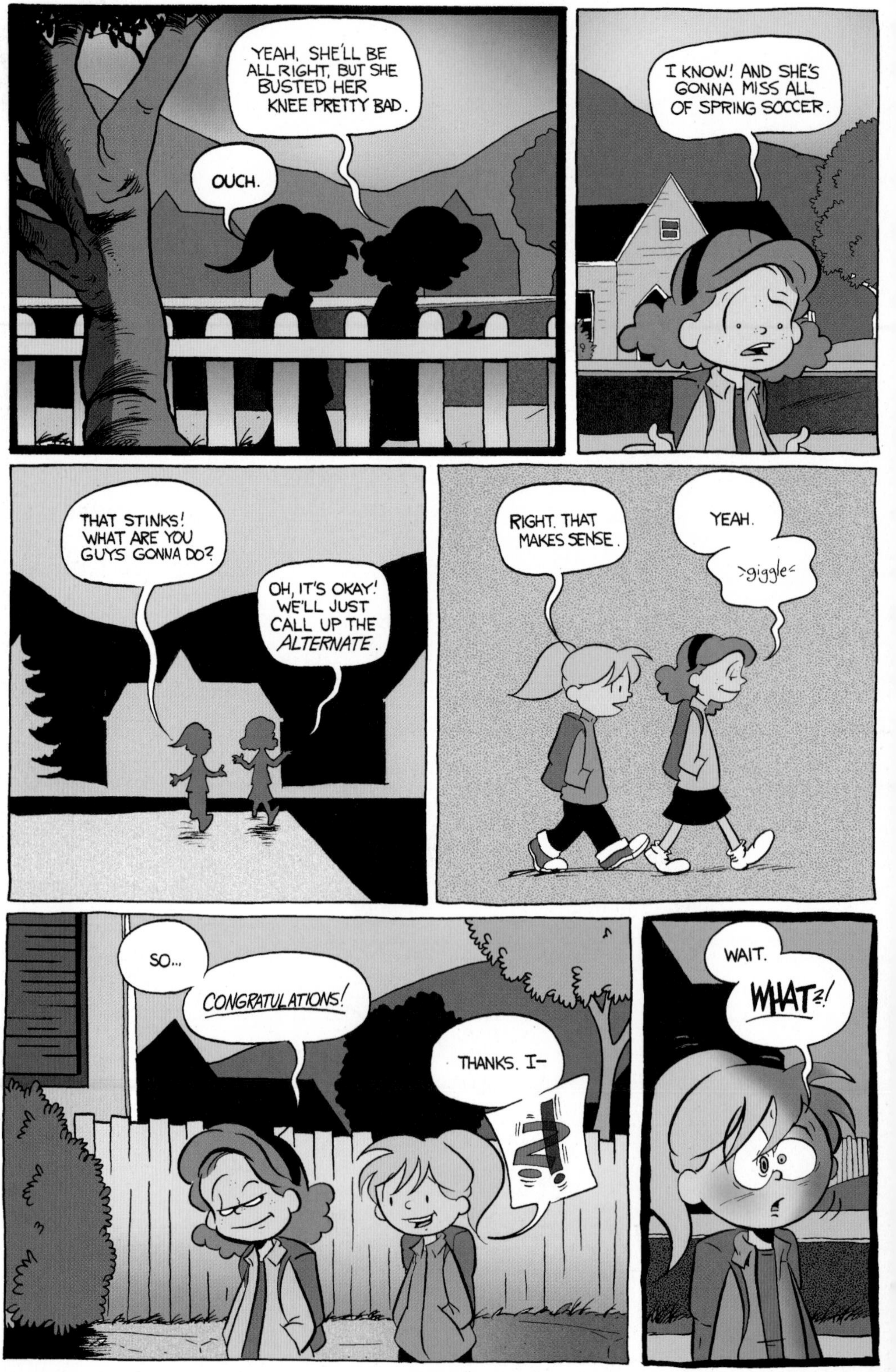
YEAH, SHE'LL BE ALL RIGHT, BUT SHE BUSTED HER KNEE PRETTY BAD.
OUCH.
I KNOW! AND SHE'S GONNA MISS ALL OF SPRING SOCCER.
THAT STINKS! WHAT ARE YOU GUYS GONNA DO?
OH, IT'S OKAY! WE'LL JUST CALL UP THE *ALTERNATE*.
RIGHT. THAT MAKES SENSE.
YEAH.
>giggle<
SO...
CONGRATULATIONS!
THANKS. I-
?!
WAIT.
WHAT?!

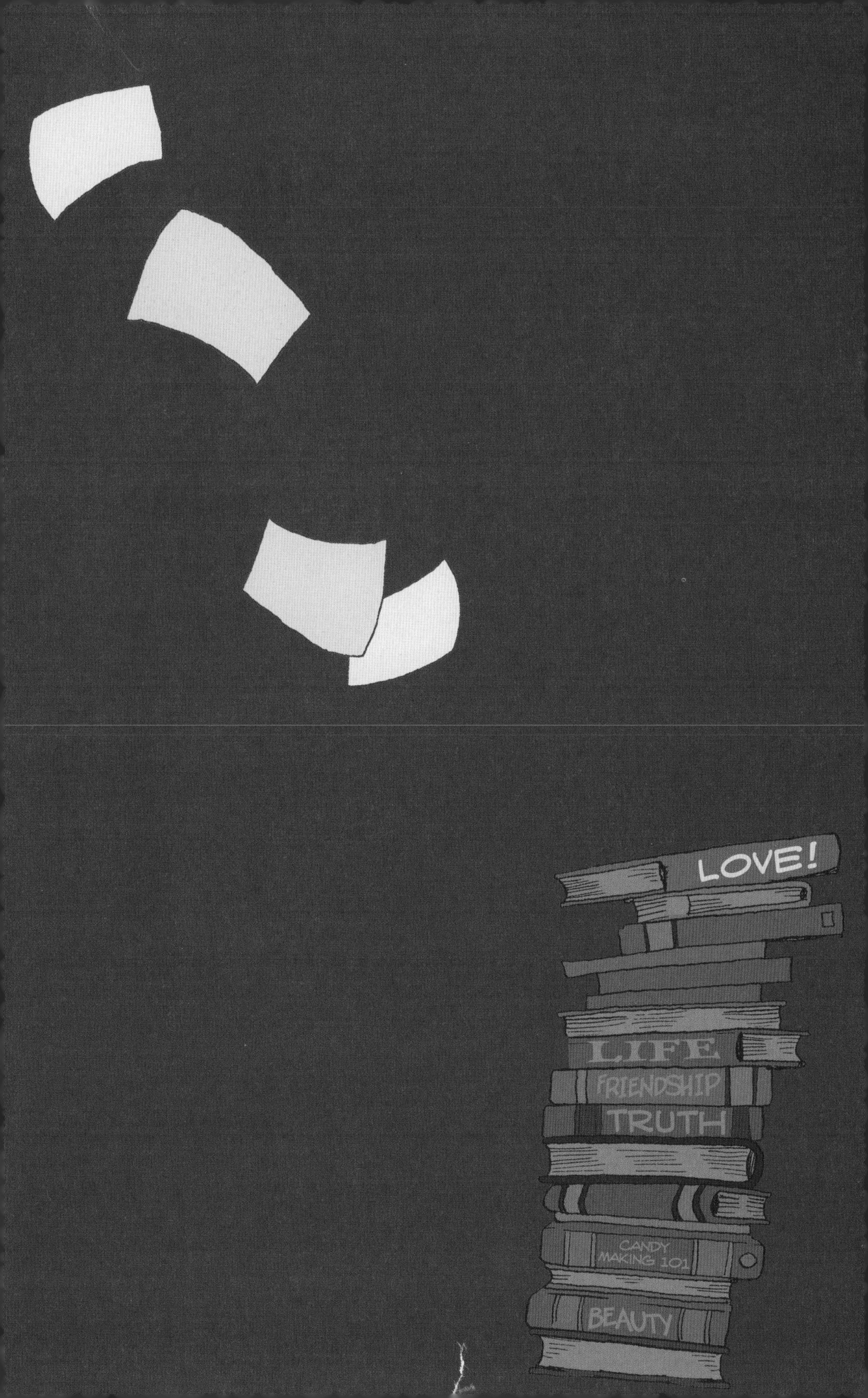
LOVE!
LIFE
FRIENDSHIP
TRUTH
CANDY MAKING 101
BEAUTY

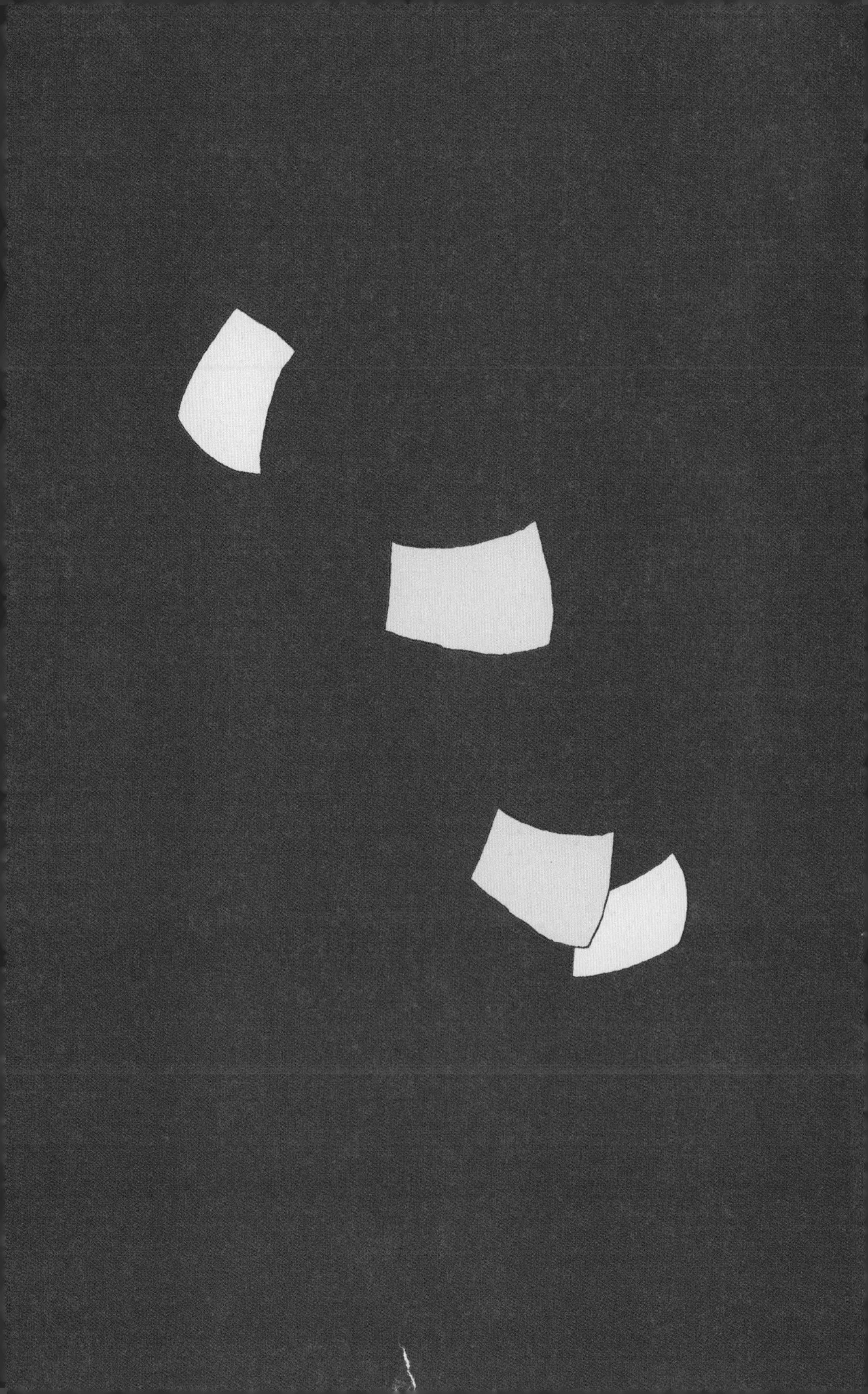

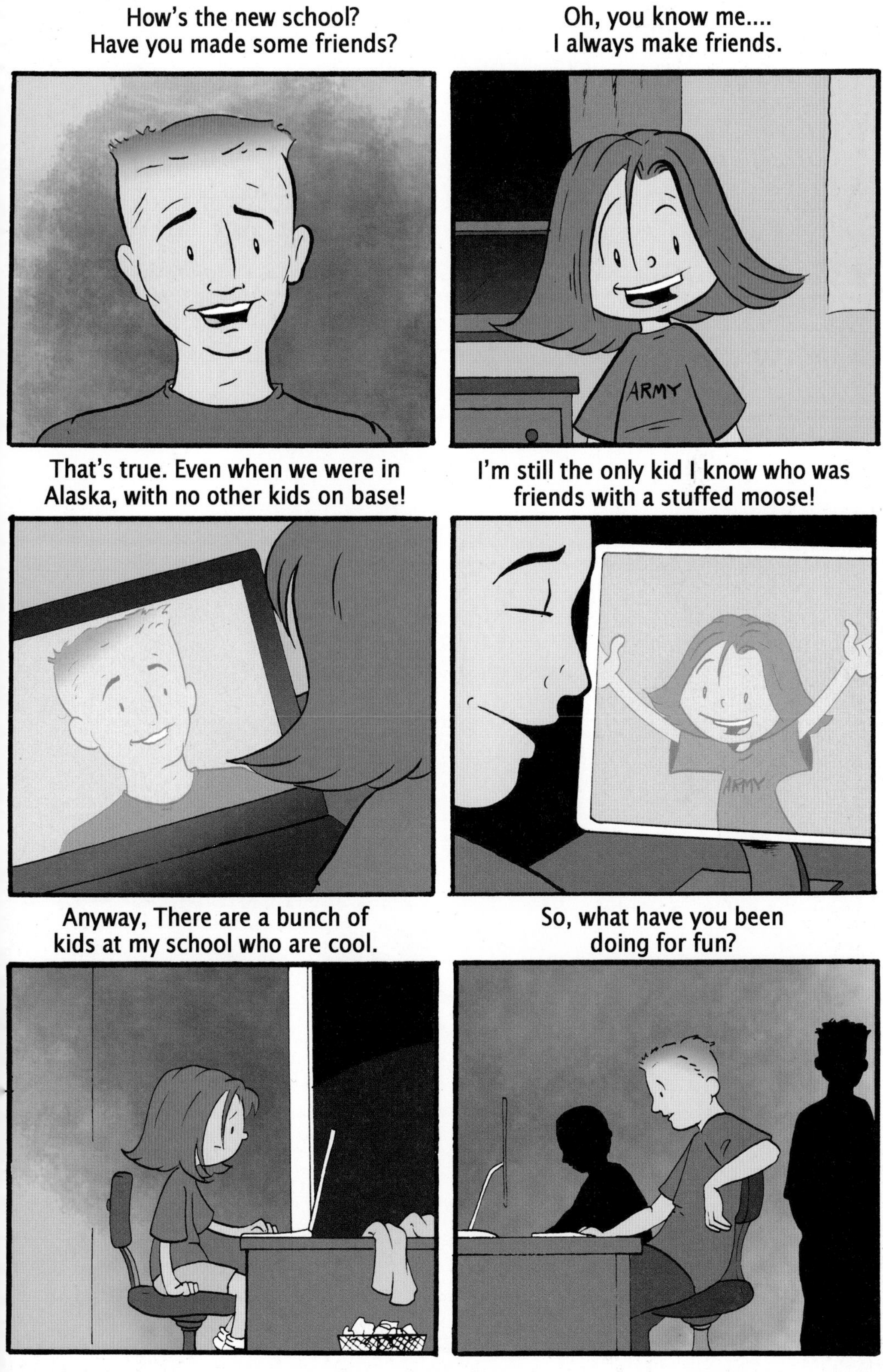
How's the new school? Have you made some friends?
Oh, you know me.... I always make friends.
ARMY
That's true. Even when we were in Alaska, with no other kids on base!
I'm still the only kid I know who was friends with a stuffed moose!
ARMY
Anyway, There are a bunch of kids at my school who are cool.
So, what have you been doing for fun?

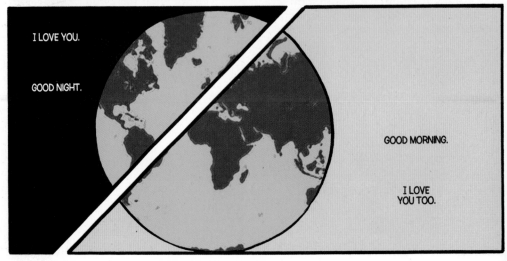

38

AND OVER THERE IS THE OL' FIVE-AND-DIME STORE.

THERE'S AN OLD FIVE-AND-DIME STORE, REALLY?

HARRY'S 5 AND

1926

WELL, YOU DIDN'T EXPECT A NEW FIVE-AND-DIME, DID YOU?

GOOD POINT.

SIGH AND DOWN THERE IS THE SCHOOL.

GREAT!

SO, SHOW ME THE LOCAL HOUSE O' LEARNIN'.

SORRY, I TRY NOT TO GET WITHIN A HUNDRED YARDS OF THE SCHOOL ON A SATURDAY.

IT'S AGAINST MY BELIEFS.

YOUR BELIEFS?

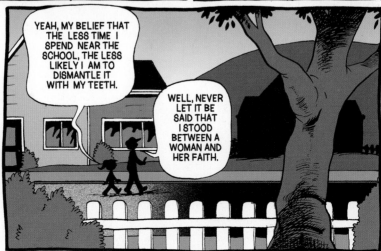

YEAH, MY BELIEF THAT THE LESS TIME I SPEND NEAR THE SCHOOL, THE LESS LIKELY I AM TO DISMANTLE IT WITH MY TEETH.

WELL, NEVER LET IT BE SAID THAT I STOOD BETWEEN A WOMAN AND HER FAITH.

UMM... SPEAKING OF *SCHOOL*... I NEED A FAVOR.

WELL, MOM AND I NEED A FAVOR, ACTUALLY.

OH! OKAY, WHAT'S UP?

OKAY, WELL, THERE ARE THESE MEETINGS, SEE...

...WITH THE... UH...PRINCIPAL.

OKAY... MEETINGS WITH THE PRINCIPAL...

YEAH. *ANY*WAY...

THERE WAS THIS SORT OF... INCIDENT...

...EARLIER IN THE YEAR?

AN INCIDENT?

A *RIOT?!*

ALMOST! I SAID, "*ALMOST* A *RIOT*."

GEEZ, DAD, *RELAX!*

AN *OUTBURST*, REALLY...

AN *ALTERCATION*...

YOU COULD ALMOST SAY A *RIOT*, I GUESS.

SO PRINCIPAL WRIGHT HAS BEEN MAKING MOM AND ME GO TO THESE MEETINGS, Y'KNOW? TO MAKE SURE I'M TOWING THE LINE.

I SEE.

SO, ANYWAY, MOM WANTS YOU TO START COMING ALONG...

...SINCE APPARENTLY I GET INTO TROUBLE BECAUSE I'M "OF YOUR ILK."

HA!

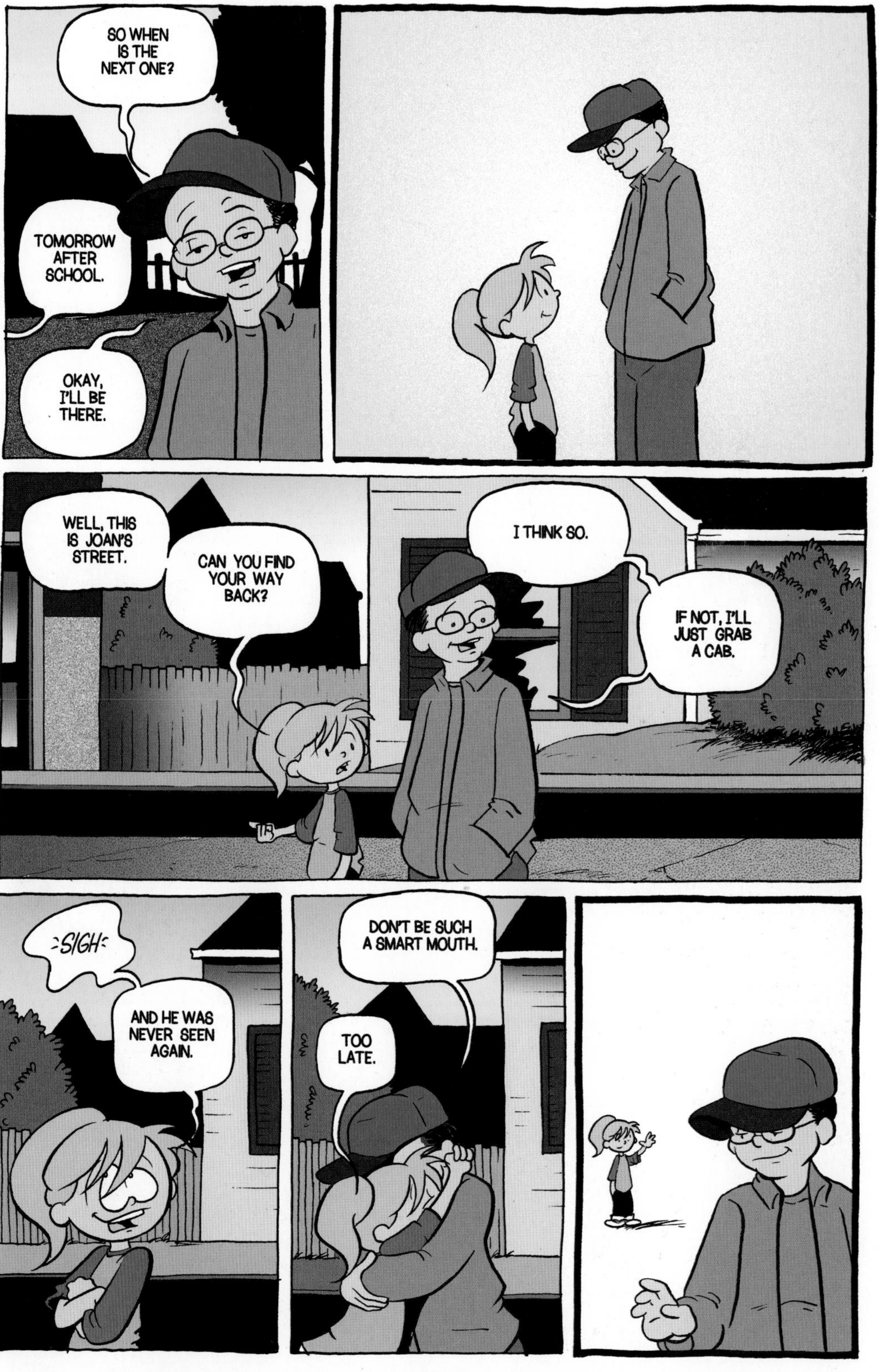
SO WHEN IS THE NEXT ONE?
TOMORROW AFTER SCHOOL.
OKAY, I'LL BE THERE.
WELL, THIS IS JOAN'S STREET.
CAN YOU FIND YOUR WAY BACK?
I THINK SO.
IF NOT, I'LL JUST GRAB A CAB.
SIGH
AND HE WAS NEVER SEEN AGAIN.
DON'T BE SUCH A SMART MOUTH.
TOO LATE.

I LOVE JOAN DRISCOLL.

SHE'S FUN AND CRAZY AND TOUGH AND SUPER, *SUPER* WEIRD.

I FEEL LIKE I COULD TALK TO HER ABOUT *ANYTHING*.

WELL, ALMOST ANYTHING.

HER DAD'S IN THE ARMY. A FEW MONTHS AGO, HE WAS SENT AWAY...TO FIGHT, I GUESS.

JOAN DOESN'T TALK ABOUT IT MUCH, WHICH IS OKAY, I GUESS.

IF SHE DID, I WOULDN'T KNOW WHAT TO SAY.

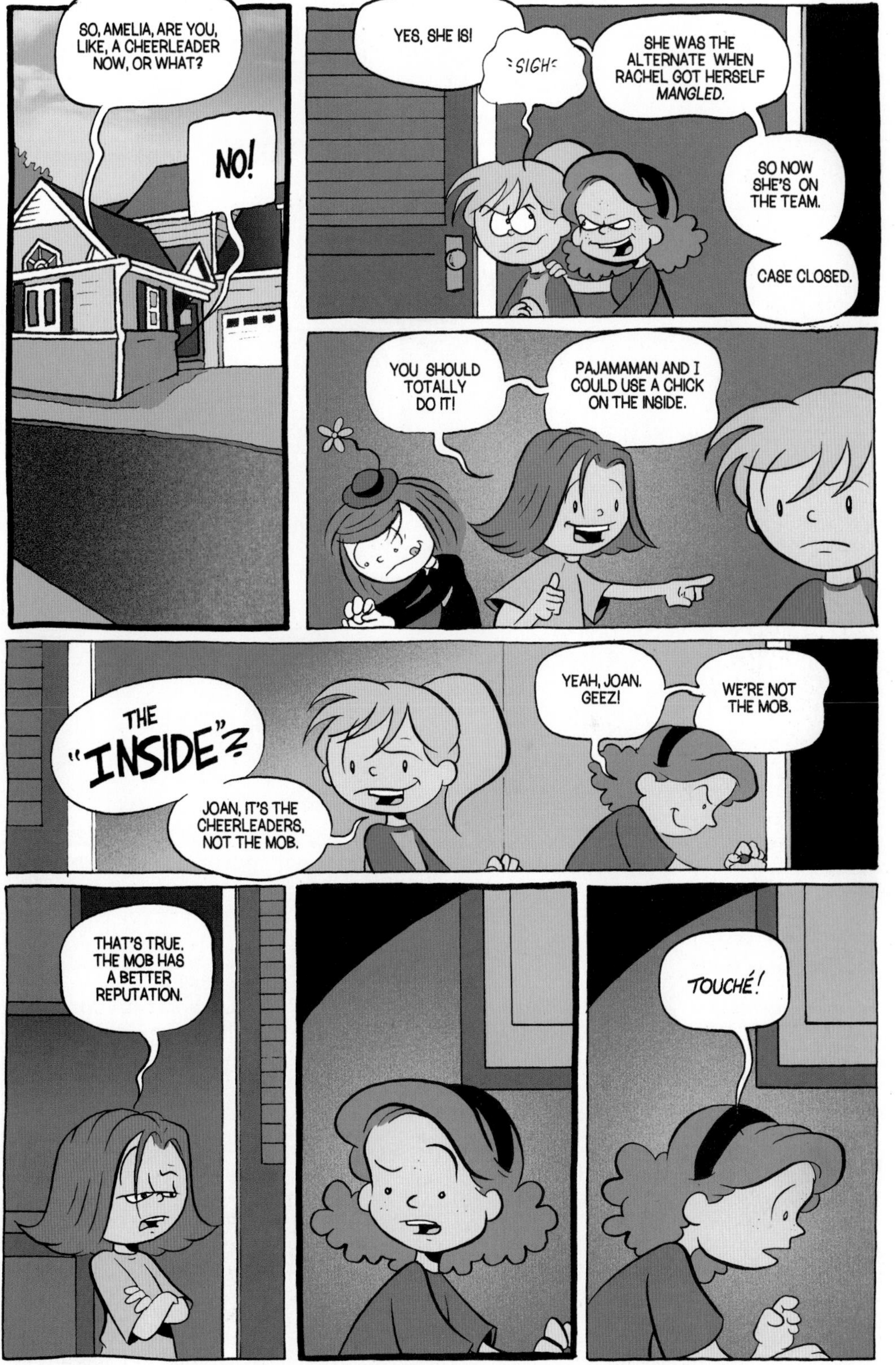
SO, AMELIA, ARE YOU, LIKE, A CHEERLEADER NOW, OR WHAT?
NO!
YES, SHE IS!
SIGH
SHE WAS THE ALTERNATE WHEN RACHEL GOT HERSELF *MANGLED.*
SO NOW SHE'S ON THE TEAM.
CASE CLOSED.
YOU SHOULD TOTALLY DO IT!
PAJAMAMAN AND I COULD USE A CHICK ON THE INSIDE.
THE "INSIDE"?
JOAN, IT'S THE CHEERLEADERS, NOT THE MOB.
YEAH, JOAN. GEEZ!
WE'RE NOT THE MOB.
THAT'S TRUE. THE MOB HAS A BETTER REPUTATION.
TOUCHÉ!

47

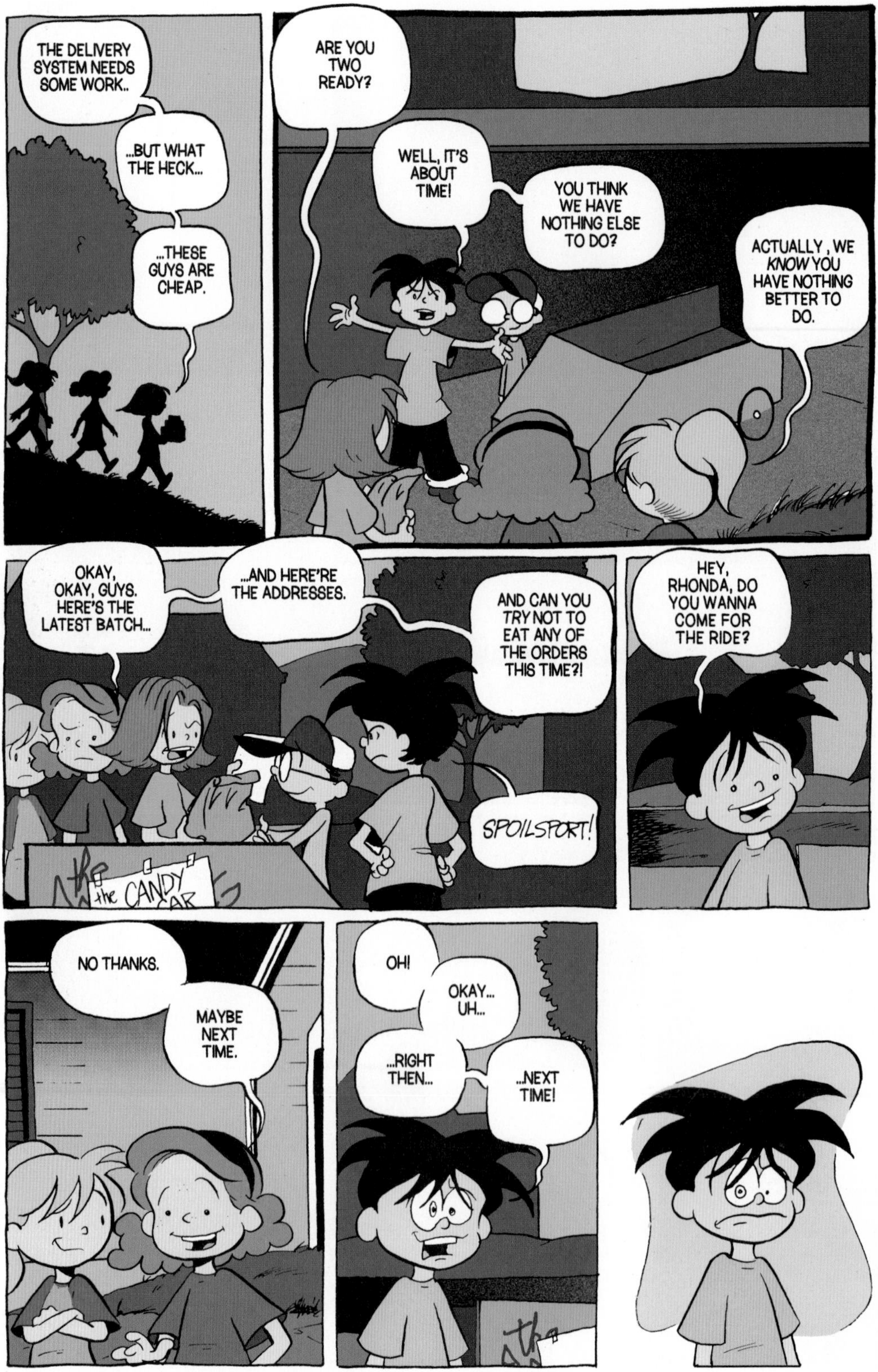
THE DELIVERY SYSTEM NEEDS SOME WORK..
...BUT WHAT THE HECK...
...THESE GUYS ARE CHEAP.
ARE YOU TWO READY?
WELL, IT'S ABOUT TIME!
YOU THINK WE HAVE NOTHING ELSE TO DO?
ACTUALLY, WE *KNOW* YOU HAVE NOTHING BETTER TO DO.
OKAY, OKAY, GUYS. HERE'S THE LATEST BATCH...
...AND HERE'RE THE ADDRESSES.
AND CAN YOU *TRY* NOT TO EAT ANY OF THE ORDERS THIS TIME?!
SPOILSPORT!
the CANDY CAR
HEY, RHONDA, DO YOU WANNA COME FOR THE RIDE?
NO THANKS.
MAYBE NEXT TIME.
OH!
OKAY... UH...
...RIGHT THEN...
...NEXT TIME!

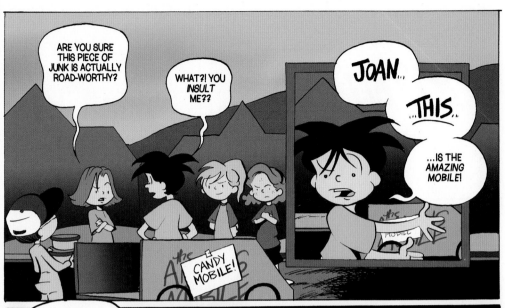

OF COURSE, I SHOULD HAVE REMEMBERED THAT RHONDA WAS NEVER GOOD AT TAKING A HINT!

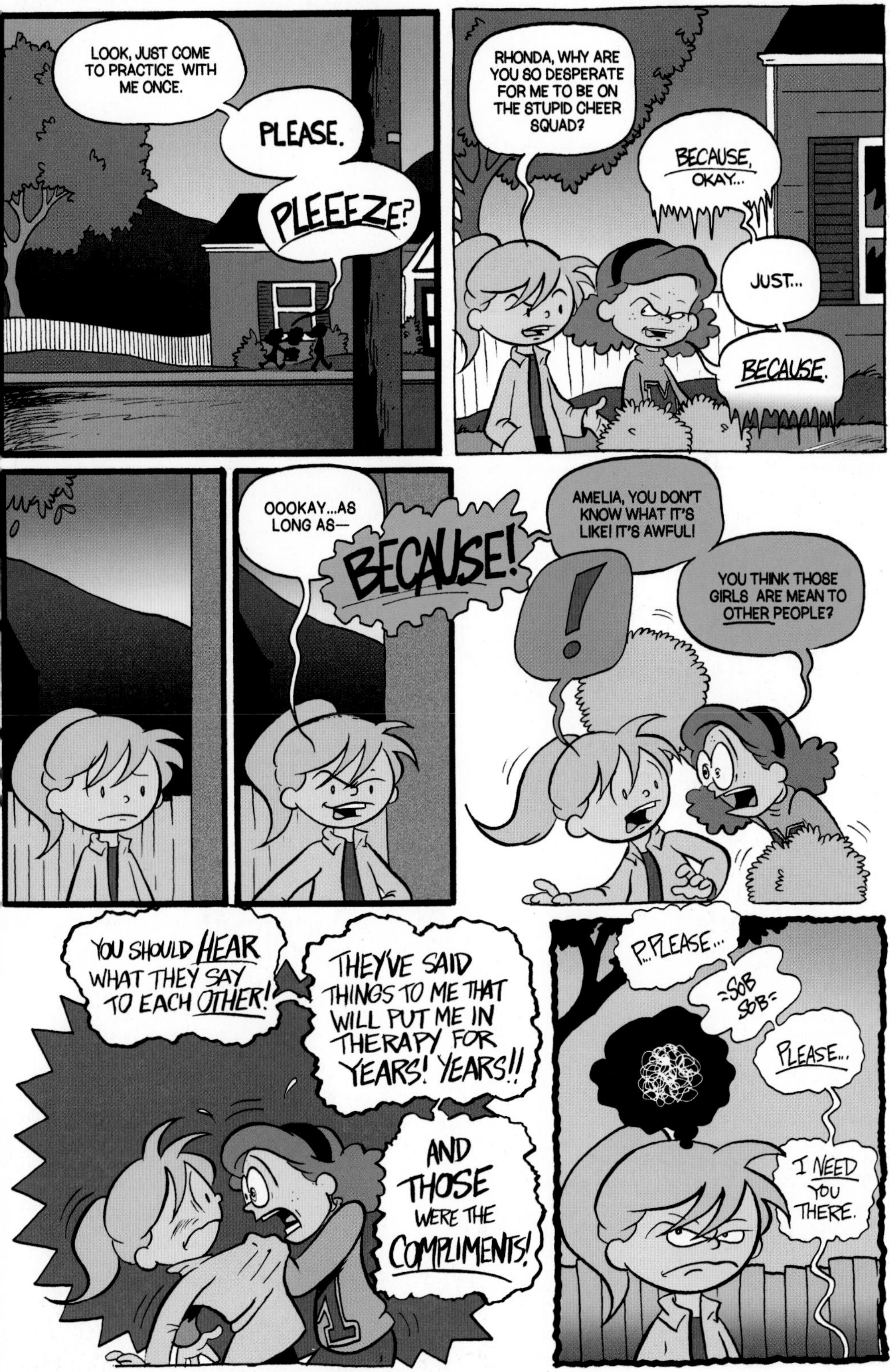
LOOK, JUST COME TO PRACTICE WITH ME ONCE.
PLEASE.
PLEEEZE?
RHONDA, WHY ARE YOU SO DESPERATE FOR ME TO BE ON THE STUPID CHEER SQUAD?
BECAUSE, OKAY...
JUST...
BECAUSE.
OOOKAY...AS LONG AS—
BECAUSE!
AMELIA, YOU DON'T KNOW WHAT IT'S LIKE! IT'S AWFUL!
!
YOU THINK THOSE GIRLS ARE MEAN TO OTHER PEOPLE?
YOU SHOULD HEAR WHAT THEY SAY TO EACH OTHER!
THEY'VE SAID THINGS TO ME THAT WILL PUT ME IN THERAPY FOR YEARS! YEARS!!
AND THOSE WERE THE COMPLIMENTS!
P...PLEASE...
SOB SOB
PLEASE...
I NEED YOU THERE.

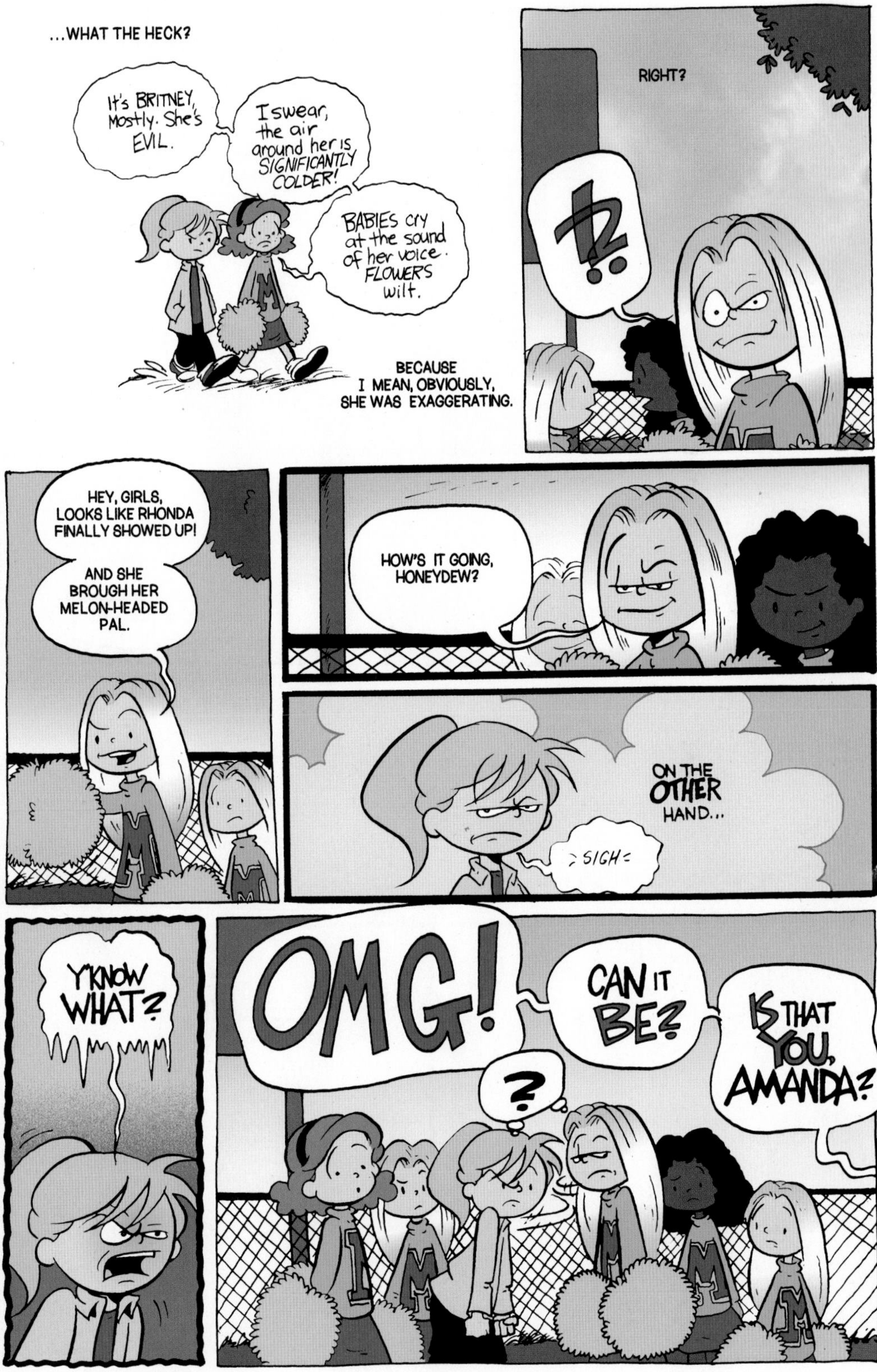
...WHAT THE HECK?
It's BRITNEY, Mostly. She's EVIL.
I swear, the air around her is SIGNIFICANTLY COLDER!
BABIES cry at the sound of her voice. FLOWERS wilt.
BECAUSE I MEAN, OBVIOUSLY, SHE WAS EXAGGERATING.
RIGHT?
?!
HEY, GIRLS, LOOKS LIKE RHONDA FINALLY SHOWED UP!
AND SHE BROUGH HER MELON-HEADED PAL.
HOW'S IT GOING, HONEYDEW?
ON THE OTHER HAND...
SIGH
Y'KNOW WHAT?
OMG!
CAN IT BE?
IS THAT YOU, AMANDA?
?

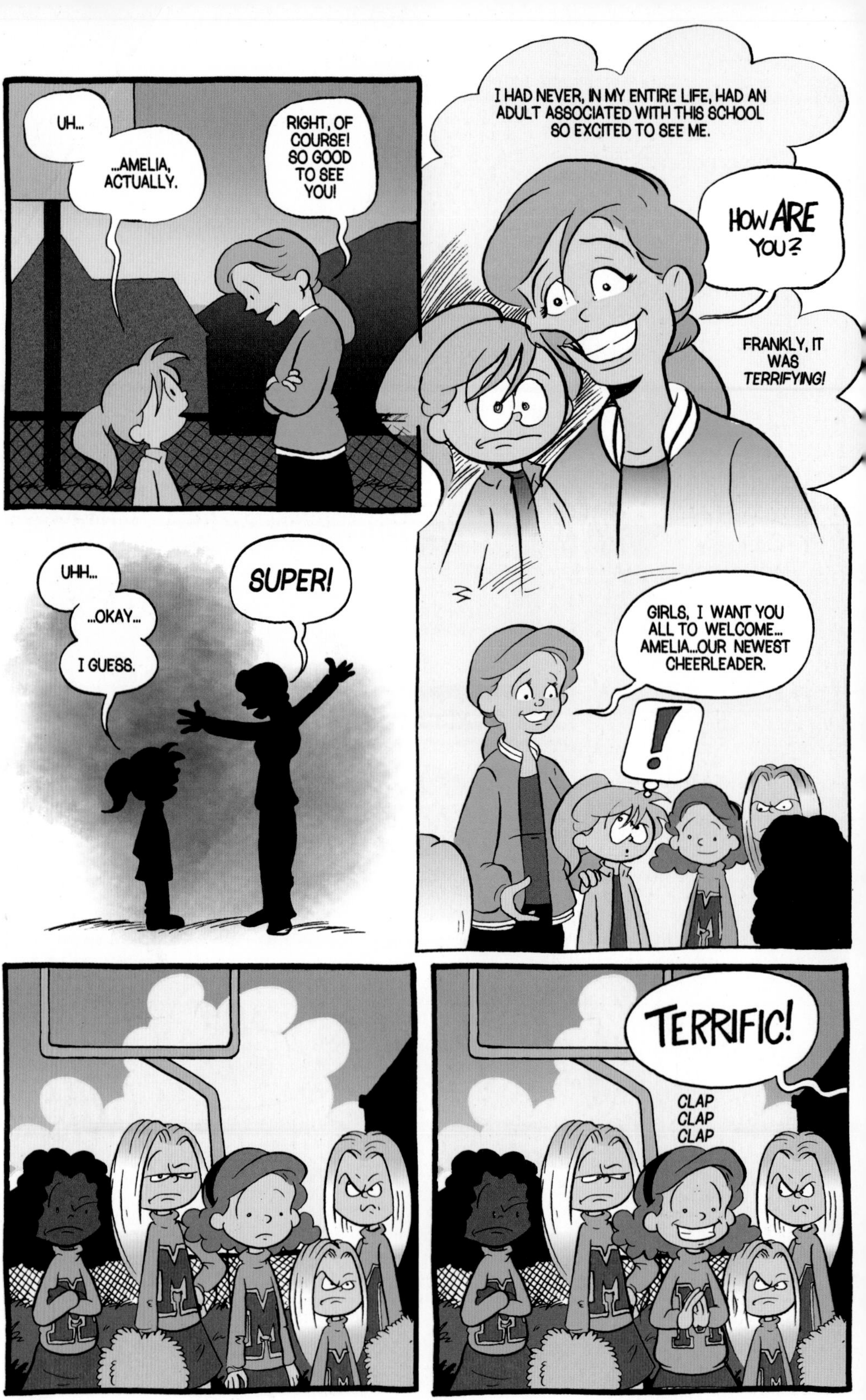
UH...
...AMELIA, ACTUALLY.
RIGHT, OF COURSE! SO GOOD TO SEE YOU!
I HAD NEVER, IN MY ENTIRE LIFE, HAD AN ADULT ASSOCIATED WITH THIS SCHOOL SO EXCITED TO SEE ME.
HOW ARE YOU?
FRANKLY, IT WAS TERRIFYING!
UHH...
...OKAY...
I GUESS.
SUPER!
GIRLS, I WANT YOU ALL TO WELCOME... AMELIA...OUR NEWEST CHEERLEADER.
!
TERRIFIC!
CLAP CLAP CLAP

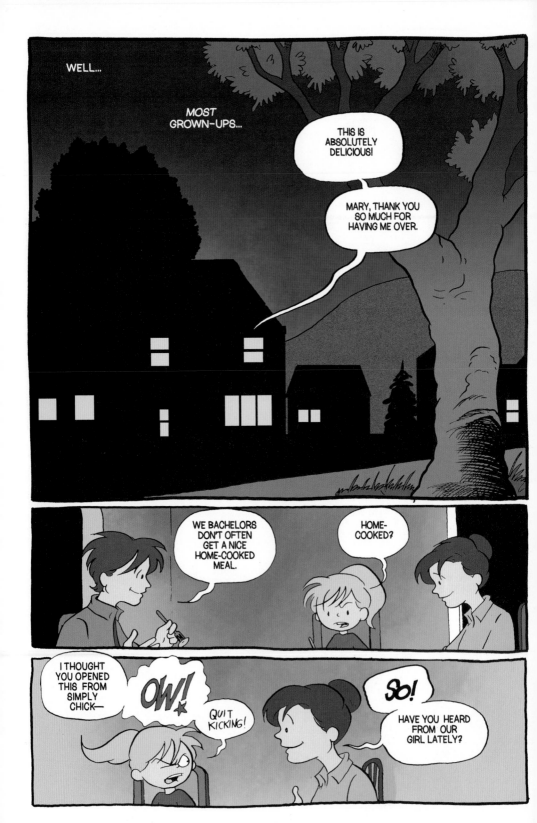

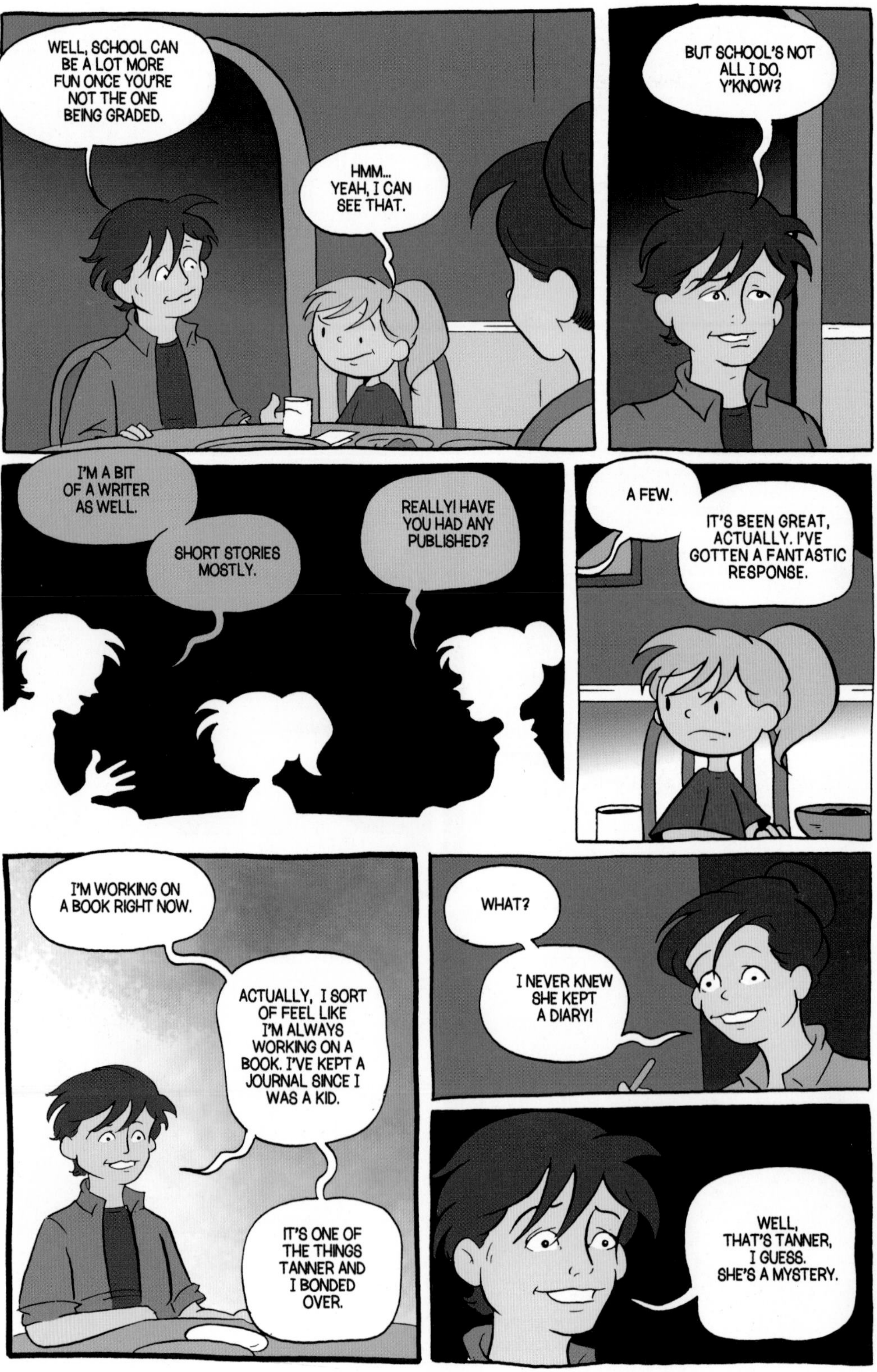
WELL, SCHOOL CAN BE A LOT MORE FUN ONCE YOU'RE NOT THE ONE BEING GRADED.
HMM... YEAH, I CAN SEE THAT.
BUT SCHOOL'S NOT ALL I DO, Y'KNOW?
I'M A BIT OF A WRITER AS WELL.
SHORT STORIES MOSTLY.
REALLY! HAVE YOU HAD ANY PUBLISHED?
A FEW.
IT'S BEEN GREAT, ACTUALLY. I'VE GOTTEN A FANTASTIC RESPONSE.
I'M WORKING ON A BOOK RIGHT NOW.
ACTUALLY, I SORT OF FEEL LIKE I'M ALWAYS WORKING ON A BOOK. I'VE KEPT A JOURNAL SINCE I WAS A KID.
IT'S ONE OF THE THINGS TANNER AND I BONDED OVER.
WHAT?
I NEVER KNEW SHE KEPT A DIARY!
WELL, THAT'S TANNER, I GUESS. SHE'S A MYSTERY.

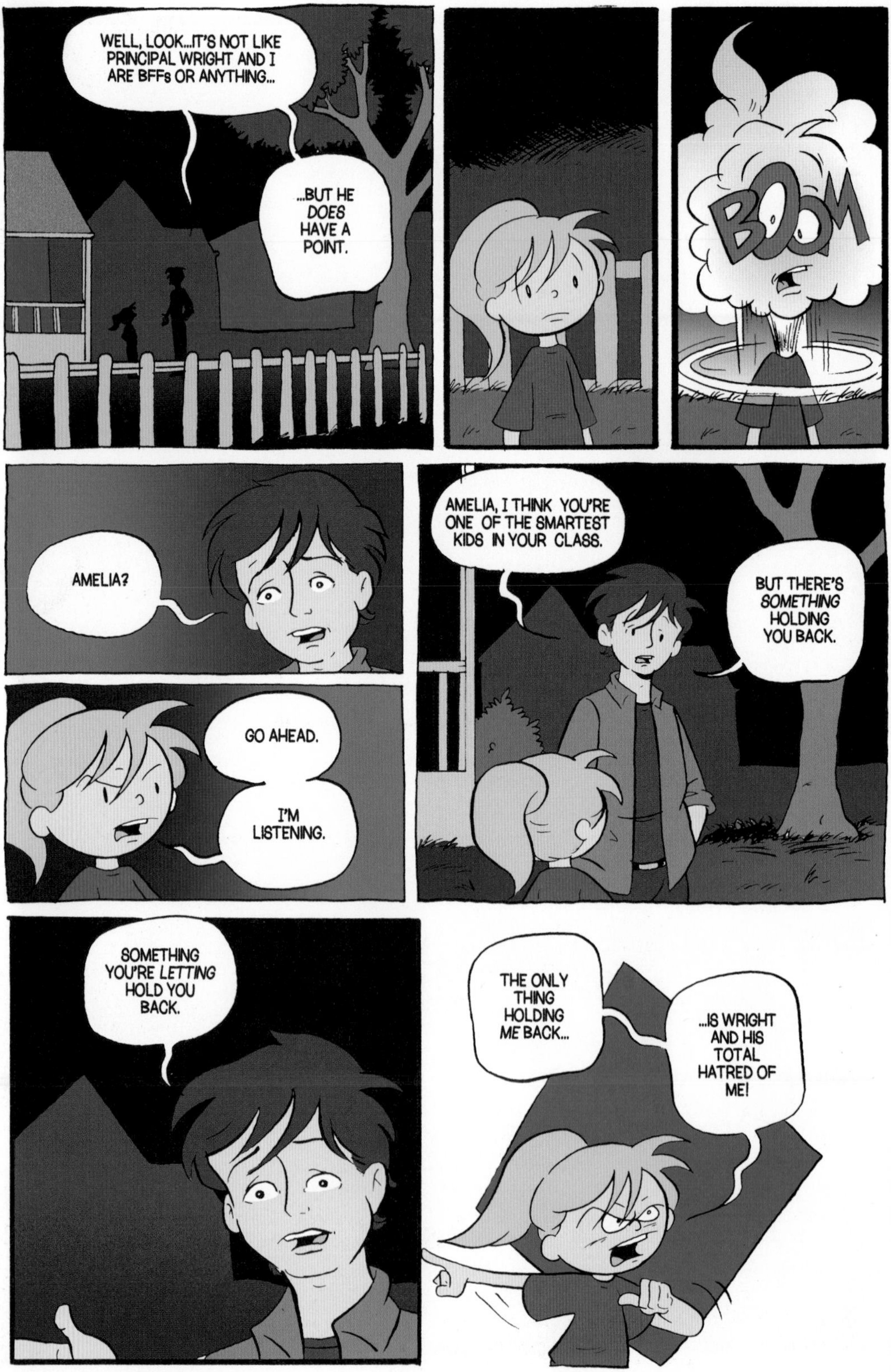
WELL, LOOK...IT'S NOT LIKE PRINCIPAL WRIGHT AND I ARE BFFs OR ANYTHING...
...BUT HE *DOES* HAVE A POINT.
BOOM
AMELIA?
AMELIA, I THINK YOU'RE ONE OF THE SMARTEST KIDS IN YOUR CLASS.
BUT THERE'S *SOMETHING* HOLDING YOU BACK.
GO AHEAD.
I'M LISTENING.
SOMETHING YOU'RE *LETTING* HOLD YOU BACK.
THE ONLY THING HOLDING *ME* BACK...
...IS WRIGHT AND HIS TOTAL HATRED OF ME!

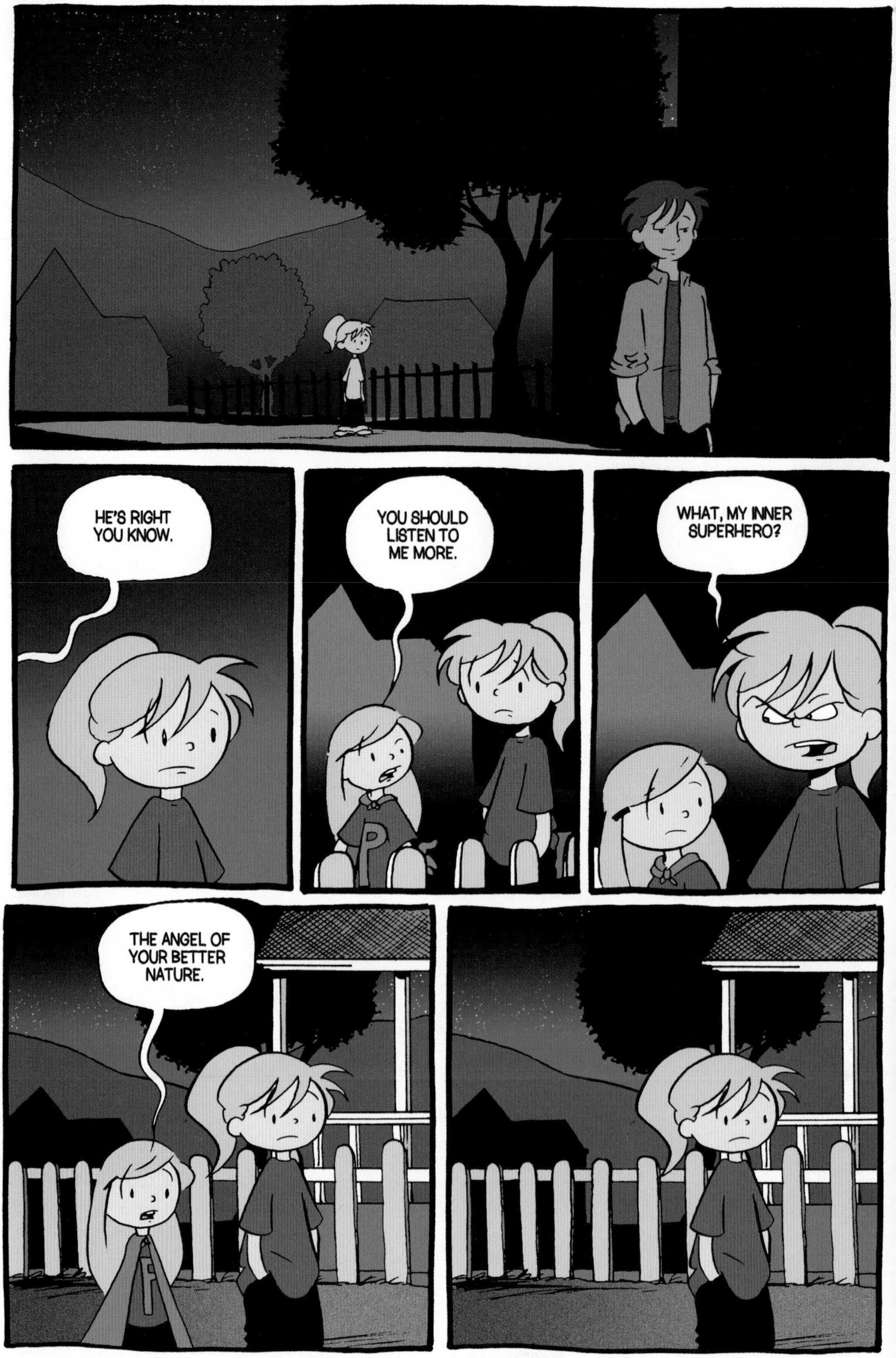
HE'S RIGHT YOU KNOW.
YOU SHOULD LISTEN TO ME MORE.
WHAT, MY INNER SUPERHERO?
THE ANGEL OF YOUR BETTER NATURE.

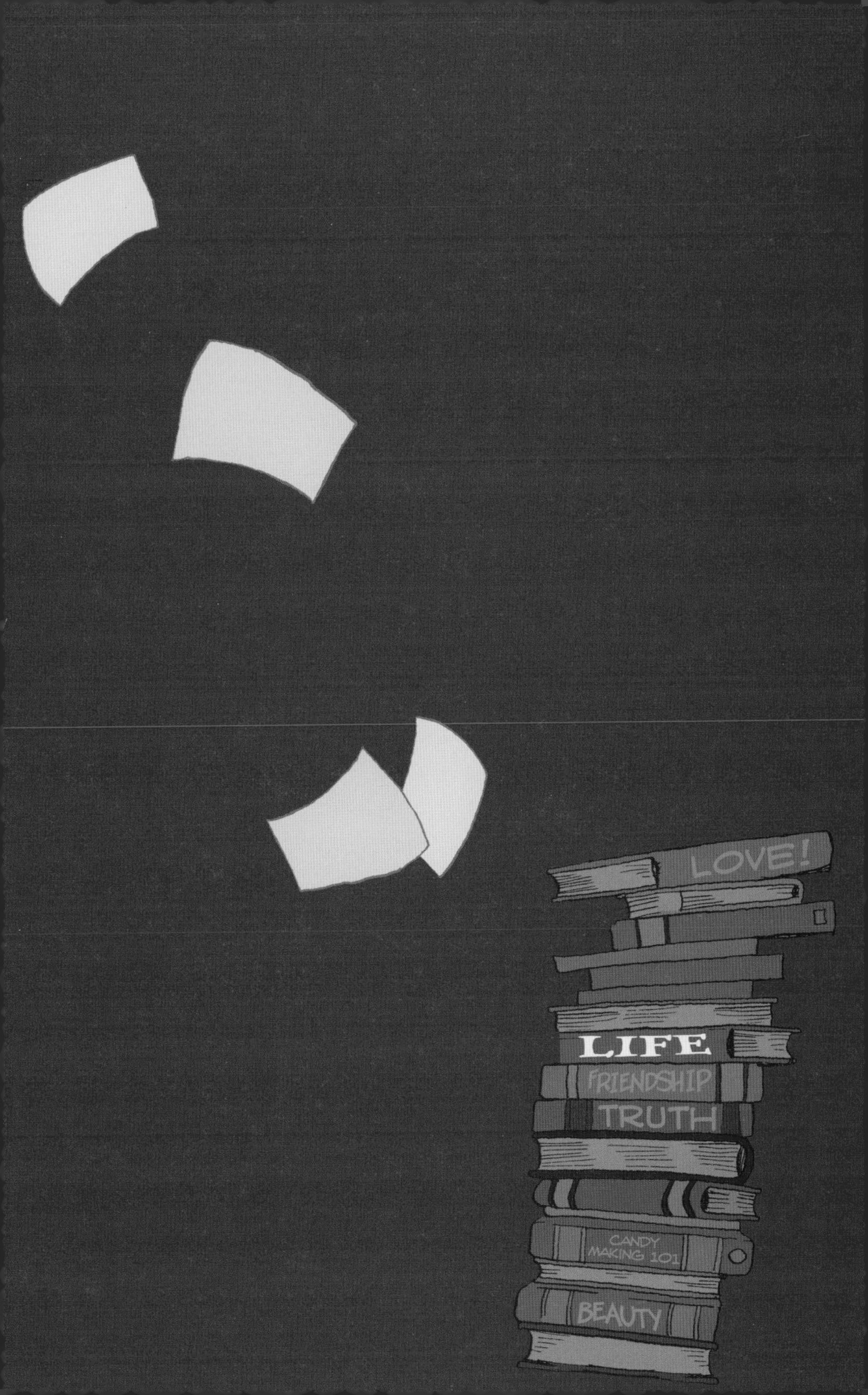
LOVE!
LIFE
FRIENDSHIP
TRUTH
CANDY MAKING 101
BEAUTY

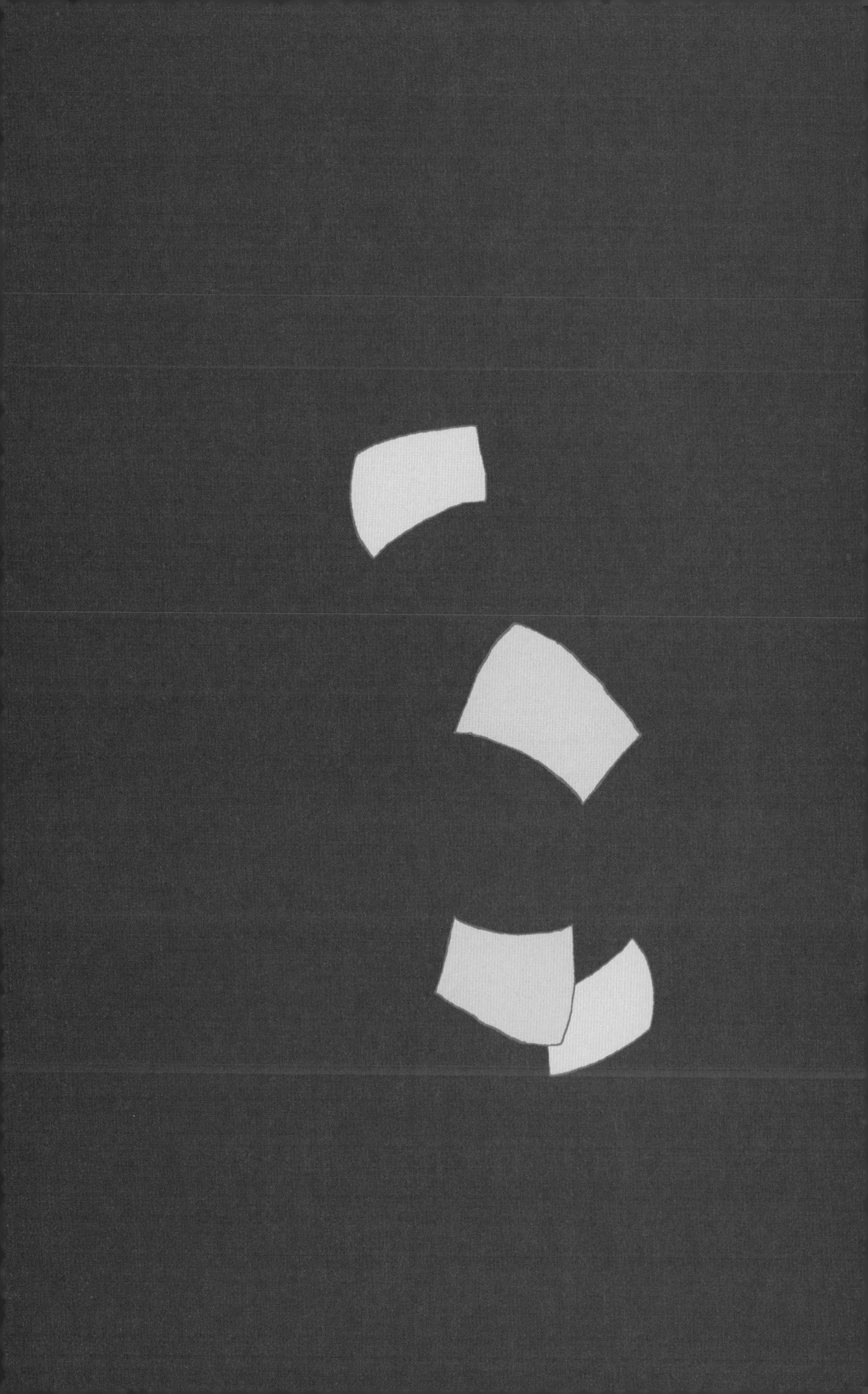

71

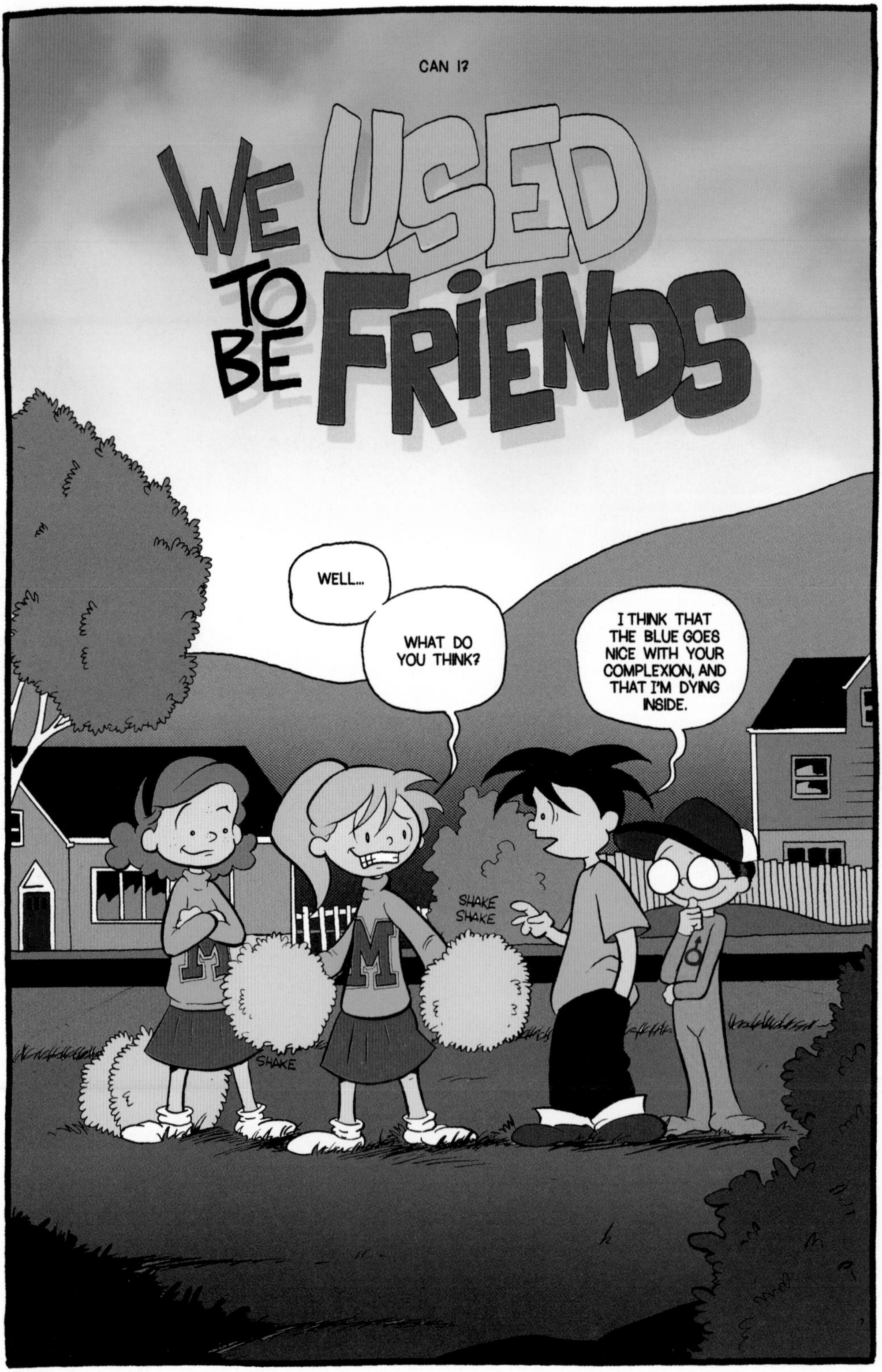
CAN I?
WE USED TO BE FRIENDS
WELL...
WHAT DO YOU THINK?
SHAKE SHAKE
SHAKE
I THINK THAT THE BLUE GOES NICE WITH YOUR COMPLEXION, AND THAT I'M DYING INSIDE.

C'MON, REGGIE, YOU SHOULD BE HAPPY FOR HER.

SHE HAS THE HONOR OF WEARING AN OFFICIAL McCARTHY MAVERICKS CHEERLEADER UNIFORM.

THE ONLY UNIFORM YOU HAVE HAS THE UNDIES ON THE OUTSIDE.

HEY! THAT UNIFORM INSPIRES FEAR IN THE HEARTS OF NINJAS...

...AND STEVES...

...AND MY MINISTER!

LOOK, ALL I'M SAYING IS

Oh, RHONNNDAAAA

WE'RE TAKING YOUR SISTER TO THE MAAAAALL!

WE NEED TO BUY HER SOMETHING EXPENSIVE!!

OKAYeee I DON'T CARRRE.

OH! I SEE YOUR...

"FRIENDS"...

...ARE HERE.

WELL, TRY NOT TO DO ANYTHING TO HUMILATE THE FAMILEEEEE.

NOoooo PROMISES.

THAT'S ONE THING ABOUT RHONDA'S FAMILY... THEY'RE SO MESSED UP. IT MAKES YOU FORGET YOUR OWN PROBLEMS.

WELL...

FOR A MINUTE OR TWO, ANYWAY.

IT'S TOO MUCH PRESSURE! I FEEL LIKE I'M MAKING A HUGE MISTAKE!

DON'T WORRY, I'LL BE THERE WITH YOU.

RHONDA, I THINK I'M FREAKING OUT!

WHAT? WHY?

WHAT *GOOD* WILL *THAT* DO? YOU'RE AS *BAD* OFF AS *I* AM!!

SHAKE SHAKE SHAKE SHAKE

HOW CAN *YOU* HELP *ME*?!

WELL, AFTER ALL, I AM THE ONE WHO MADE THE SQUAD, RIGHT? I KNOW WHAT I'M DOING.

HUH?

OH! UHH... RIGHT!

OKAY THEN, STICK WITH ME.

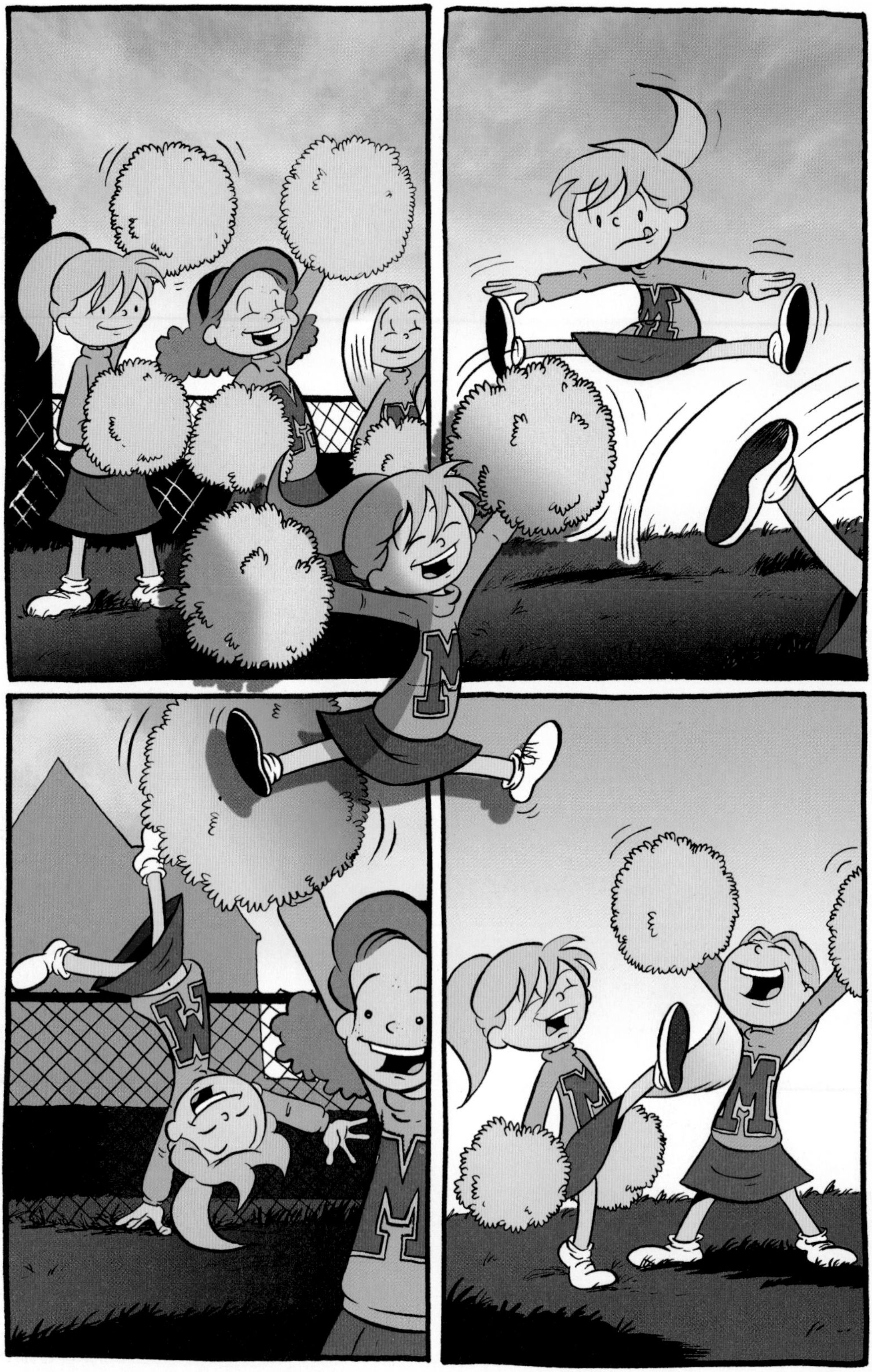

IF THERE IS A THEME TO MY LIFE,
IT'S _THIS_:

"NOTHING LASTS."

NOT FAMILY.

NOT FRIENDS.

NOT HOMES.

NOT HAPPINESS.

NOT LOVE.

NOT HOPE.

NOT PEACE.

NOT ANYTHING.

(NOT EVEN BEING
ON THE _STUPID_
CHEERLEADING
SQUAD.)

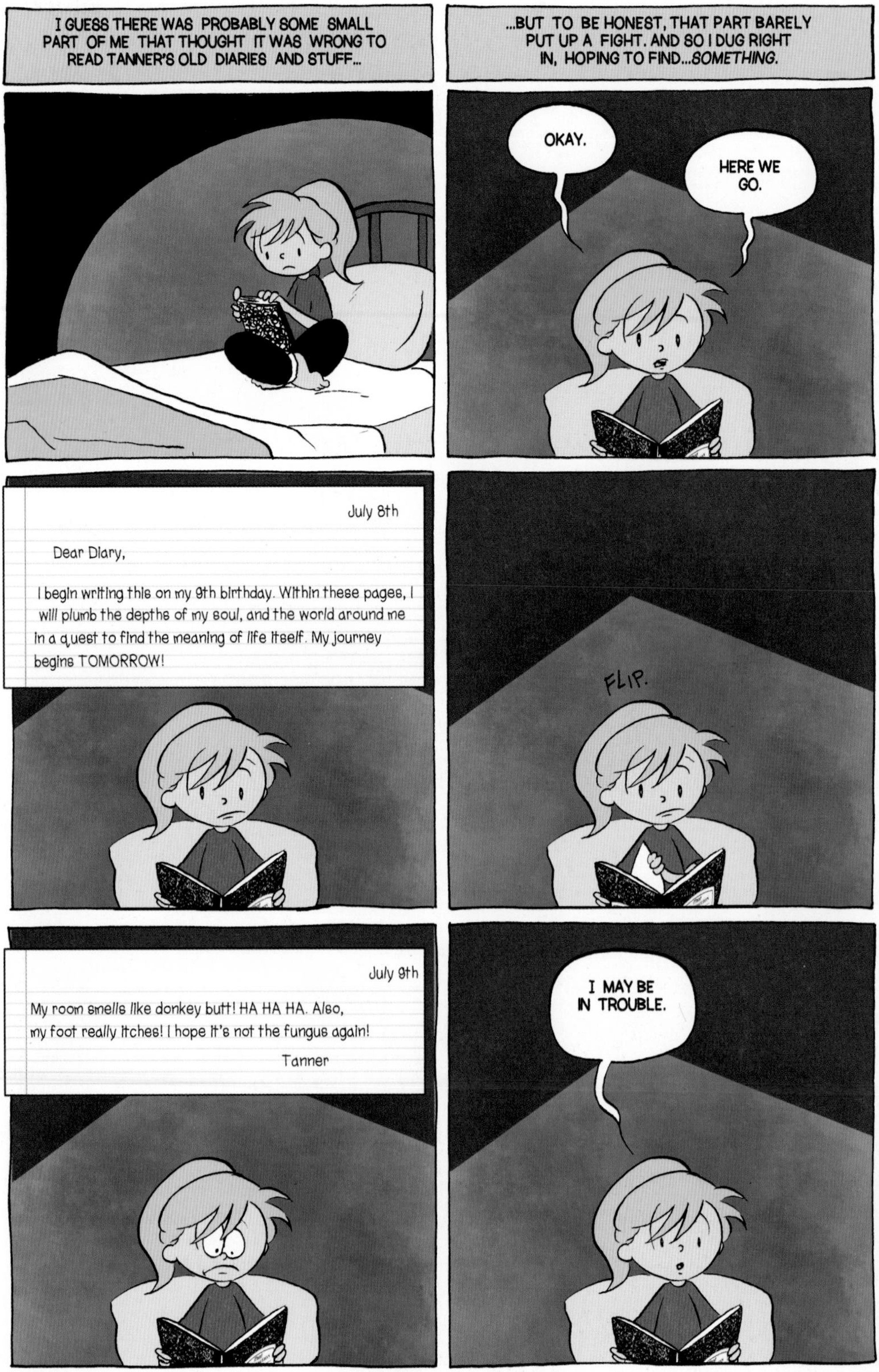
I GUESS THERE WAS PROBABLY SOME SMALL PART OF ME THAT THOUGHT IT WAS WRONG TO READ TANNER'S OLD DIARIES AND STUFF...
...BUT TO BE HONEST, THAT PART BARELY PUT UP A FIGHT. AND SO I DUG RIGHT IN, HOPING TO FIND...*SOMETHING.*
OKAY.
HERE WE GO.
July 8th
Dear Diary,
I begin writing this on my 9th birthday. Within these pages, I will plumb the depths of my soul, and the world around me in a quest to find the meaning of life itself. My journey begins TOMORROW!
FLIP.
July 9th
My room smells like donkey butt! HA HA HA. Also, my foot really itches! I hope it's not the fungus again!
Tanner
I MAY BE IN TROUBLE.

I'm not sure, but I think I hate school. Well, maybe not hate, but it sure is boring.

Today, we were reading one of the Spoingle book. The Spoingle is messed up, man.

Mrs. Hill called on Randy Gallagher to read out loud. UGH! Talk about boring! I think he even put Mrs. Hill to sleep. I thought about screaming at the top of my lungs, just to see what would happen, but I decided against it.

No promises tomorrow though!

The good news is that Mikey (the boy who lives next door to us) said "Hi" to me three times today. I said "Hi" the first TWO of the times, but I don't care.... It still counts! He's so cute, I can barely stand it. I think he likes Mary more though. Big sisters are the WORST! She's never even nice to him. She calls him names I don't even UNDERSTAND!

Tanner

PS: On second thought, I do hate school!

PPS: At recess, Randy Gallagher asked if I wanted to play "doctor." I'm not sure what that means, but I kicked him in the shin, just to be safe.

Tanner

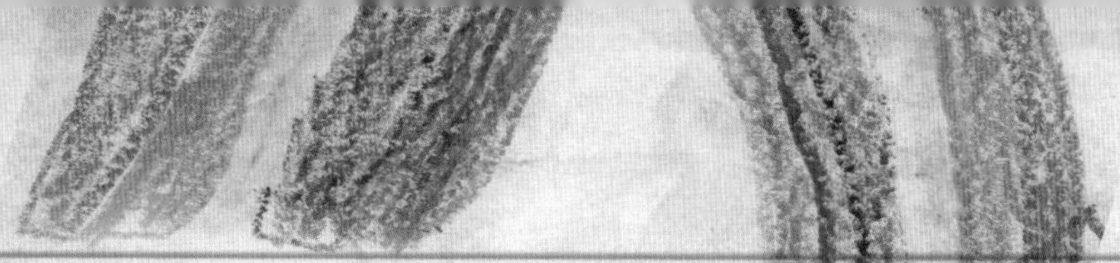

Today was the best and worst day EVER! Randy was bugging me ALL DAY. All he ever does is tease me. It's awful! Mary always says it's 'cause he likes me, but that makes no sense! If you like someone, just say "I like you"! Don't pull their pigtails till they cry. Plus, I get picked on a lot. Half the class calls me a freak, so either they ALL love me or they all really do think I'm a freak. But, you know what, I don't care. Because something awesome happened to me today.

On the way home, Randy was picking on me (of course) and he took my book bag. He was trying to throw it up in a tree! But Mikey saw and came over to stop it. AND GUESS WHAT? Randy beat the snot out of him!

Which I know sounds bad, right? But that means Mikey was willing to get beat up over ME!

Mary is still so dumb! She still thinks that Randy likes me and that Mikey was just being NICE! That makes no SENSE! Mary can be so stoooooooopid! If you like someone, you are nice. If you DON'T like someone, you are mean. END OF STORY!

Tanner

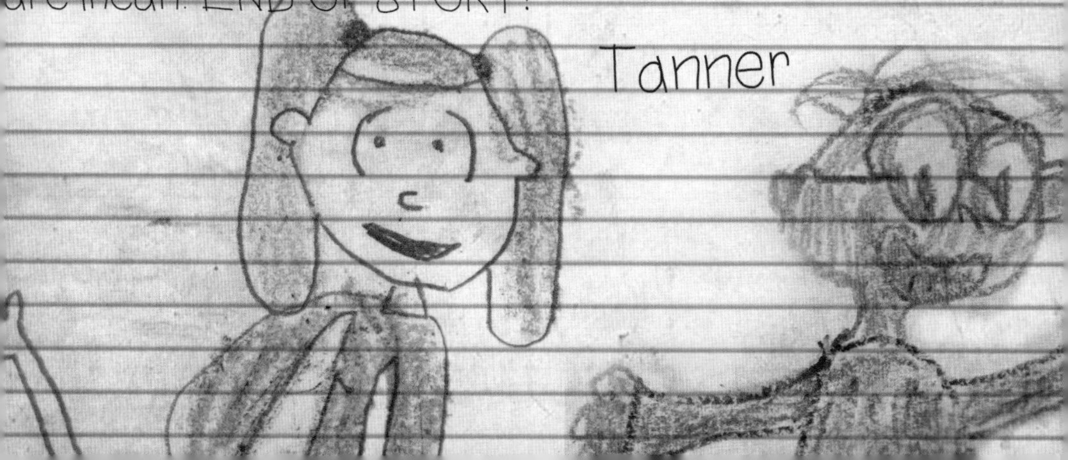

♭Catching Up With... *Tanner Clark*

ANYONE FAMILIAR with the alt rock scene of the past few years knows the name *TANNER CLARK*. Her runaway hit album *Broken Record* and it's ubiquitous single "Gaberdine Prom Queen" made her the voice of a new generation of repressed, unappreciated suburban girls. But suddenly, at the height of her success, she vanished. Rumors of censorship, bankruptcy, and worse followed, but through it all, Clark remained silent. Recently, **On the Scene** caught up with Ms. Clark for a rare phone interview.

On the Scene: So the music world is wondering where you disappeared to.
Tanner Clark: I've been around.

On the Scene: You haven't been visible.
Tanner Clark: Really? I'm invisible? That's so weird! I can usually see myself in the mirror.

On the Scene: I mean, you haven't been performing or recording lately.
Tanner Clark: I performed a song just last night.

On the Scene: In public?
Tanner Clark: To my niece, in her room.

On the Scene: And that's satisfying to you?
Tanner Clark: Sure.

On the Scene: As satisfying as playing to an arena full of fans?
Tanner Clark: In some ways it's more satisfying. I mean, when people show up for a concert, I'm not even sure why they are there, y'know? I don't know what they want from the experience.

On the Scene: But you do know with your niece?
Tanner Clark: Look, it's just that she was sad, y'know? Her life felt out of control, I sang her a song, and she felt better.

On the Scene: And that's all you need?
Tanner Clark: That's all I can give.

On the Scene: Now or forever?
Tanner Clark: I can't answer that right now.

I MEAN, HEY, IT ALMOST SORTA MENTIONED ME!

The enigmatic Tanner Clark at an early club performance

On the Scene: Is there anything else you'd like to say to your fans?
Tanner Clark (long pause): Just...thank you, I guess. I never expected to have an audience or get to make a record....They made that possible...but nothing lasts forever, y'know? I just needed to run away for a while.

On the Scene: So you might be back someday?
Tanner Clark: I wish I could say yes, but I simply don't know.

On the Scene: But in the meantime, you'll play for your niece?
Tanner Clark: Yep.

On the Scene: Do you think, with all your talent, if that's what you gave to the world...one happy kid...would that be enough? I mean, with all you are capable of doing?

Tanner Clark: Not everything needs to be a grand gesture, y'know? And not every problem in life can be fixed with a song or a play or a book. Sometimes it's just the opposite. Sometimes the best way to get someone through the pain of their past or their present is just to be there with them and to hold their hand and wait for the future. ♭

On the Scene

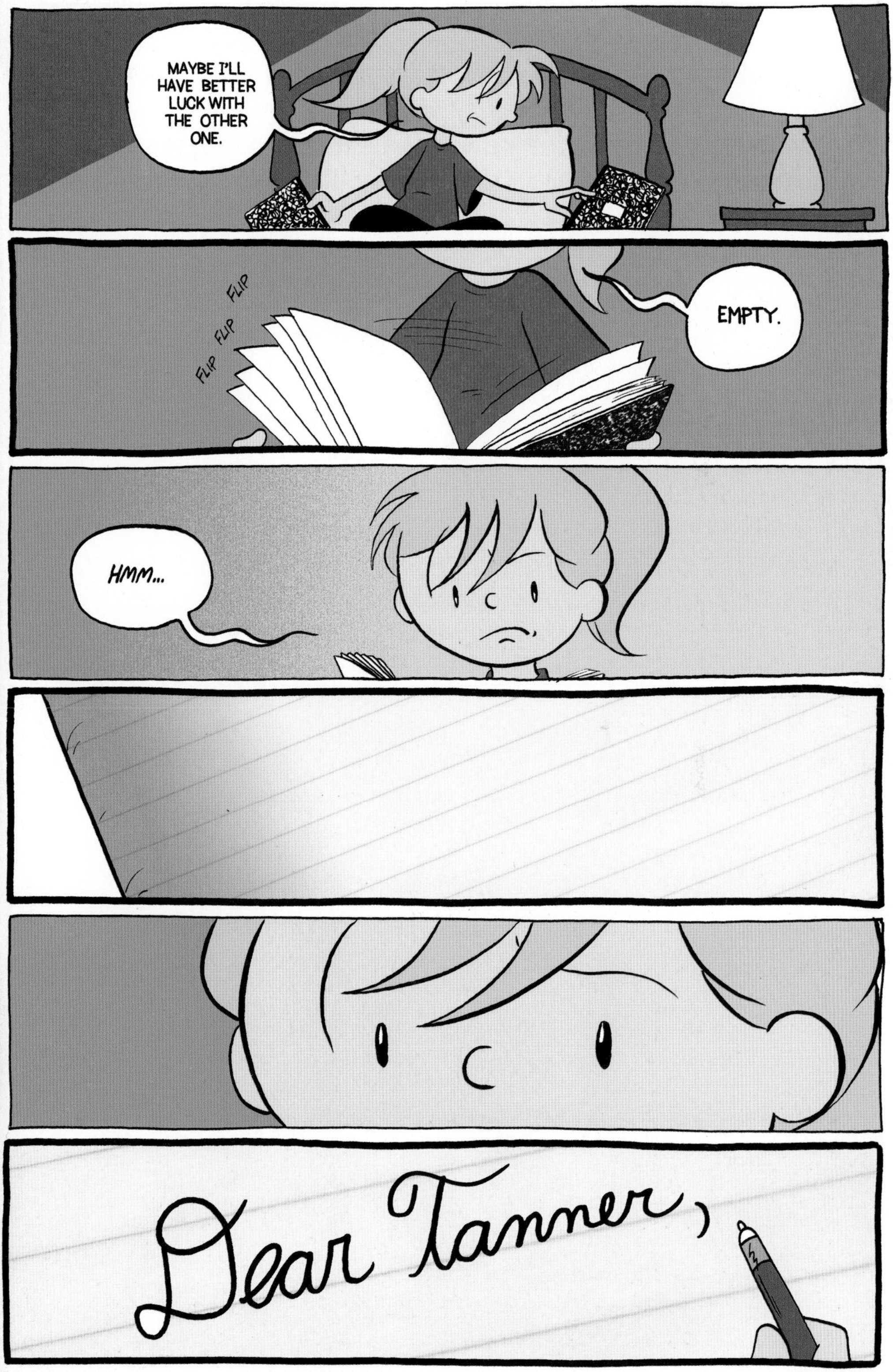
MAYBE I'LL HAVE BETTER LUCK WITH THE OTHER ONE.
FLIP FLIP FLIP
EMPTY.
HMM...
Dear Tanner,

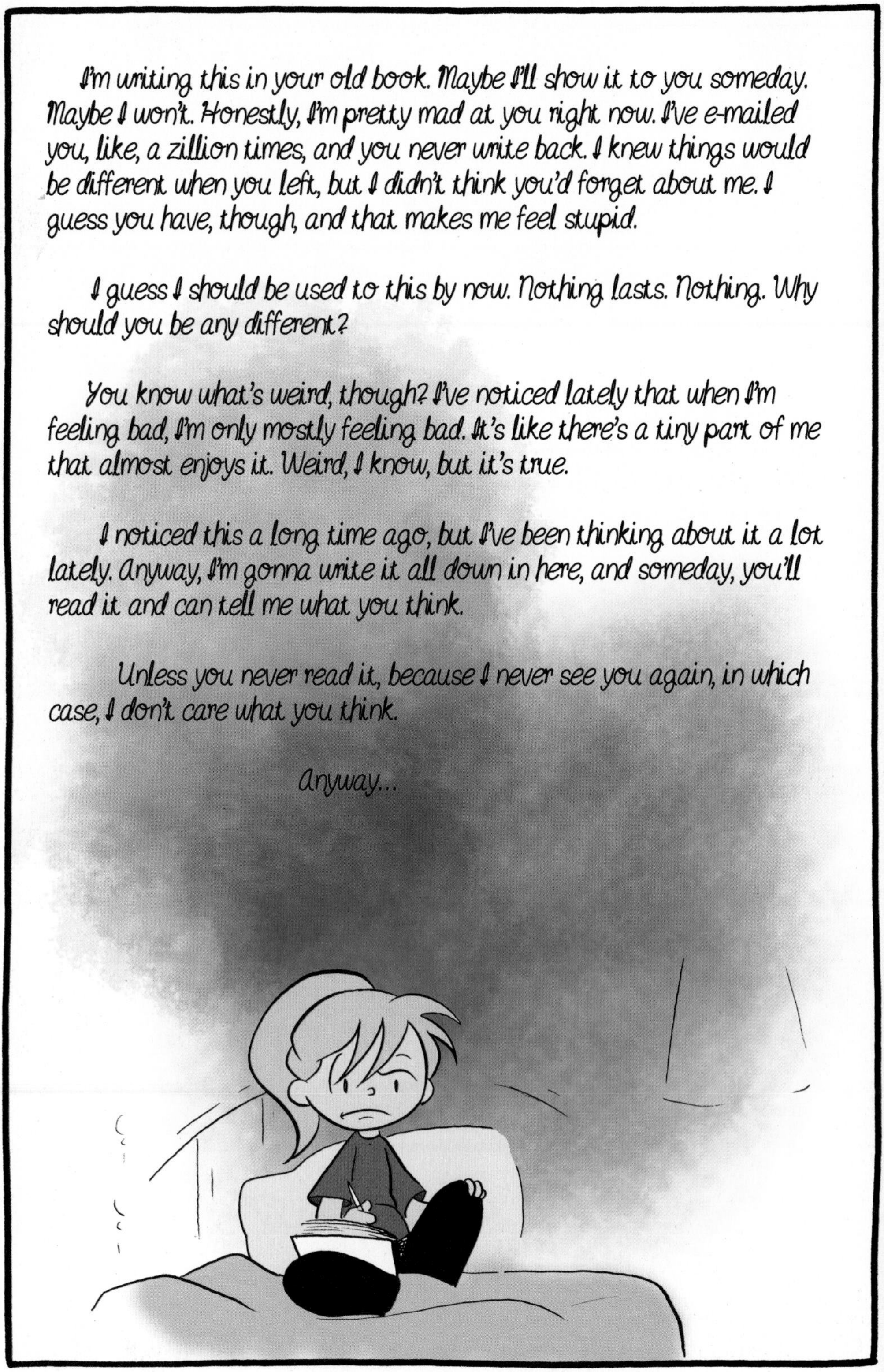
I'm writing this in your old book. Maybe I'll show it to you someday. Maybe I won't. Honestly, I'm pretty mad at you right now. I've e-mailed you, like, a zillion times, and you never write back. I knew things would be different when you left, but I didn't think you'd forget about me. I guess you have, though, and that makes me feel stupid.
I guess I should be used to this by now. Nothing lasts. Nothing. Why should you be any different?
You know what's weird, though? I've noticed lately that when I'm feeling bad, I'm only mostly feeling bad. It's like there's a tiny part of me that almost enjoys it. Weird, I know, but it's true.
I noticed this a long time ago, but I've been thinking about it a lot lately. Anyway, I'm gonna write it all down in here, and someday, you'll read it and can tell me what you think.
Unless you never read it, because I never see you again, in which case, I don't care what you think.
Anyway...

So we're went over to the park. I was alway supposed to tell Mom and Dad if I left the front of the building, but I didn't care.

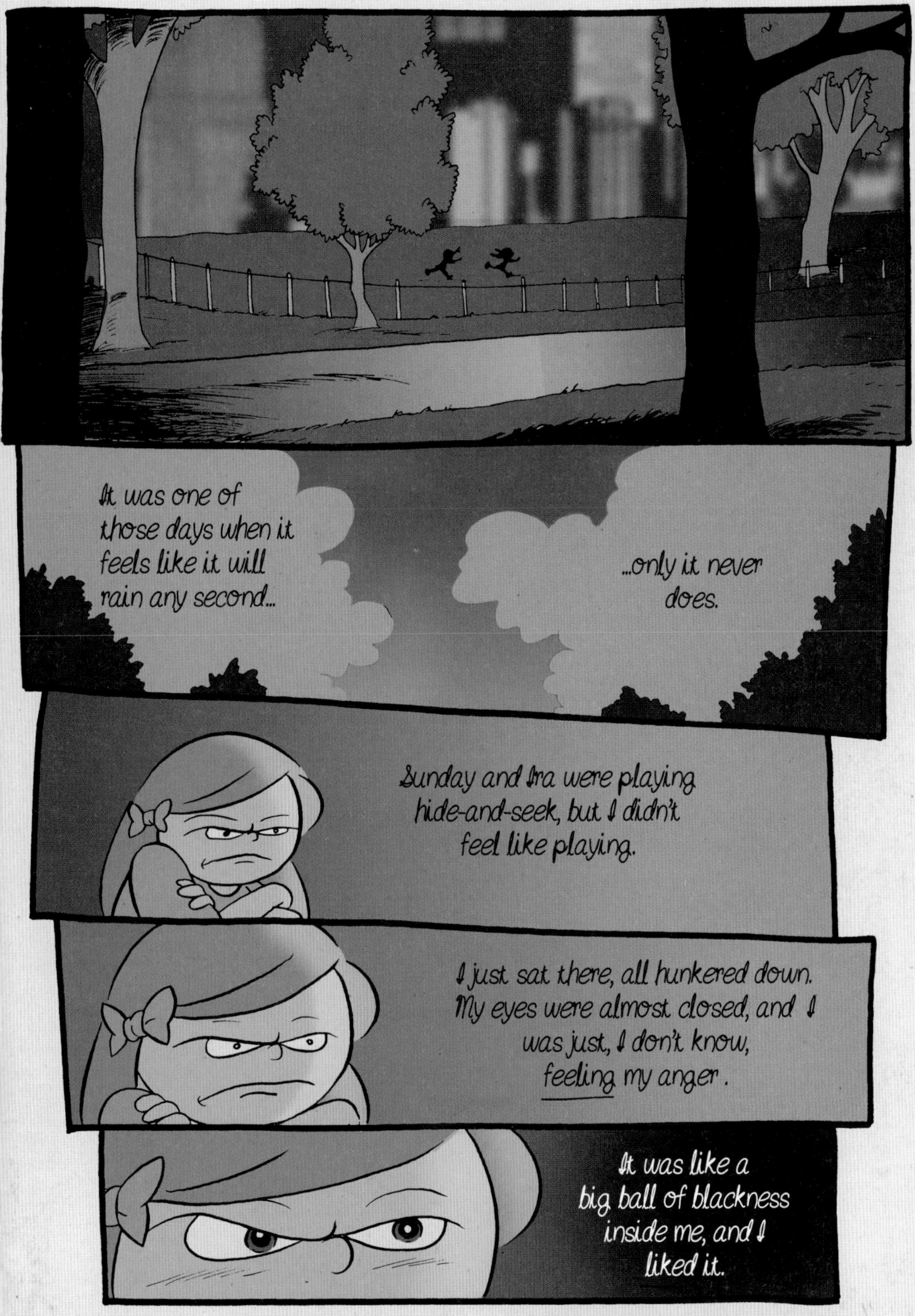
It was one of those days when it feels like it will rain any second...
...only it never does.
Sunday and Ira were playing hide-and-seek, but I didn't feel like playing.
I just sat there, all hunkered down. My eyes were almost closed, and I was just, I don't know, feeling my anger.
It was like a big ball of blackness inside me, and I liked it.

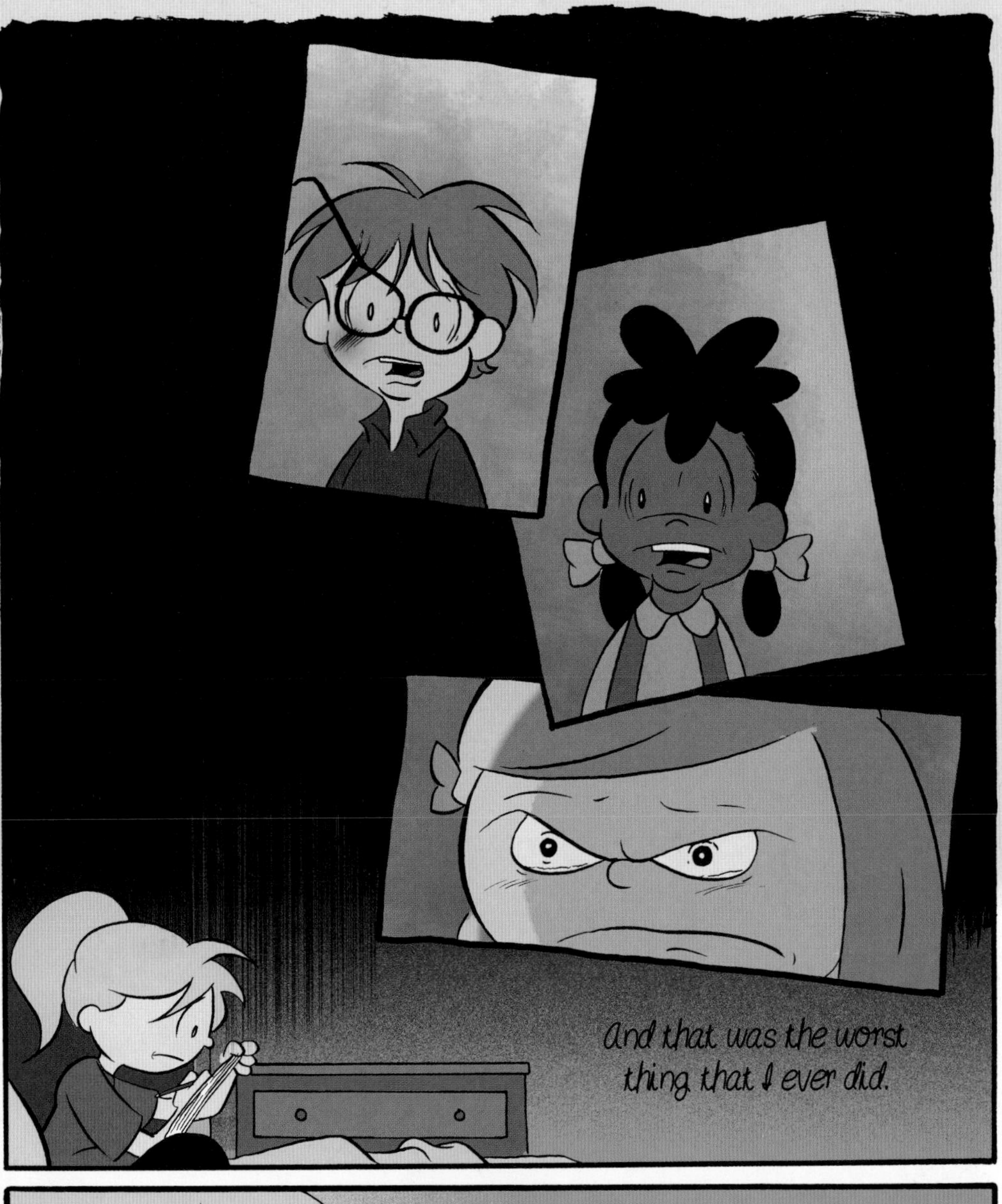
And that was the worst thing that I ever did.

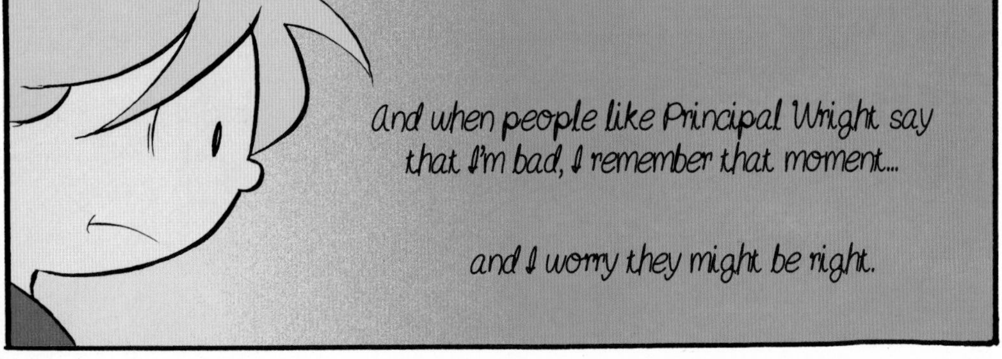
And when people like Principal Wright say that I'm bad, I remember that moment...
and I worry they might be right.

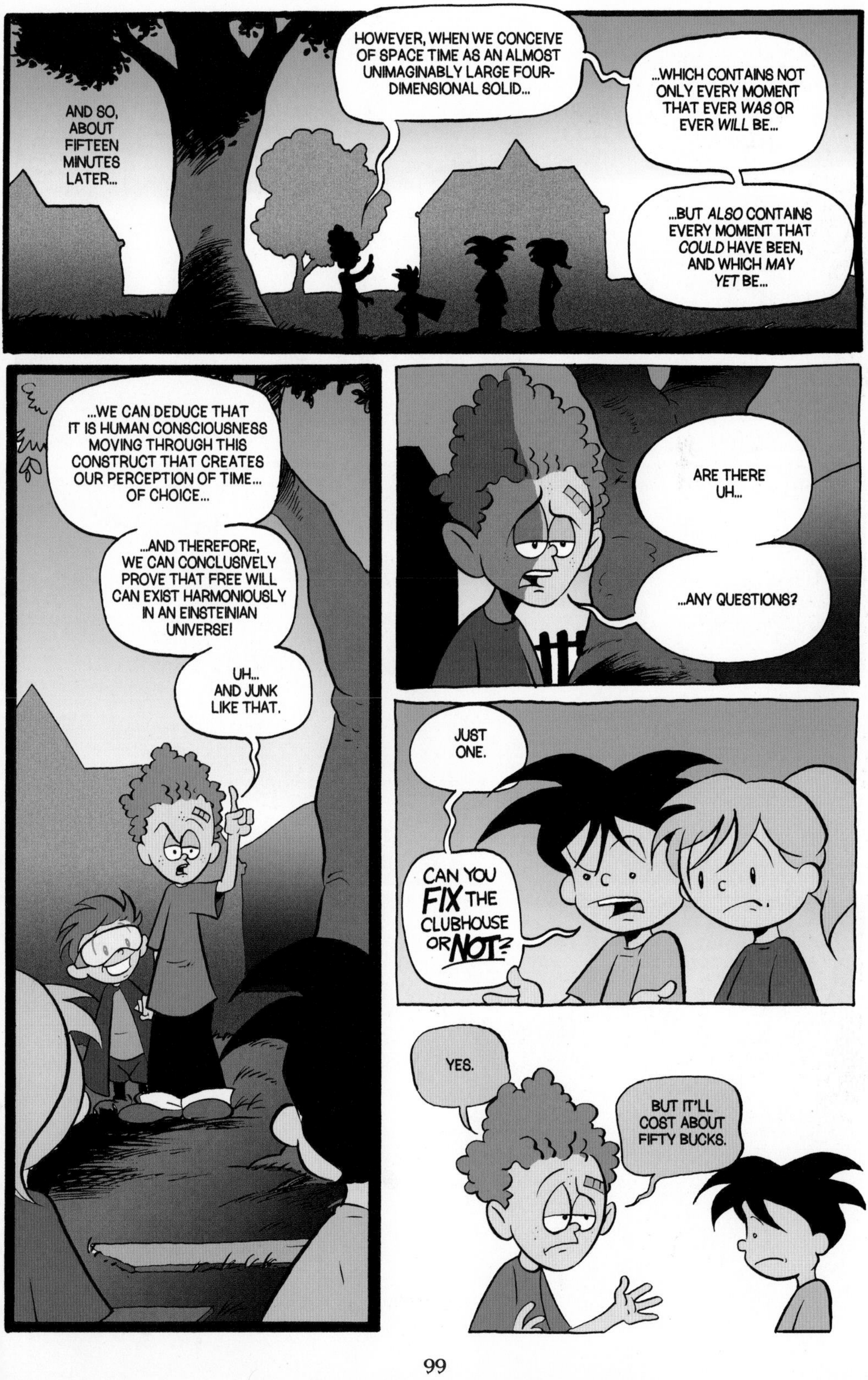
AND SO, ABOUT FIFTEEN MINUTES LATER...
HOWEVER, WHEN WE CONCEIVE OF SPACE TIME AS AN ALMOST UNIMAGINABLY LARGE FOUR-DIMENSIONAL SOLID...
...WHICH CONTAINS NOT ONLY EVERY MOMENT THAT EVER *WAS* OR EVER *WILL* BE...
...BUT *ALSO* CONTAINS EVERY MOMENT THAT *COULD* HAVE BEEN, AND WHICH *MAY YET* BE...
...WE CAN DEDUCE THAT IT IS HUMAN CONSCIOUSNESS MOVING THROUGH THIS CONSTRUCT THAT CREATES OUR PERCEPTION OF TIME... OF CHOICE...
...AND THEREFORE, WE CAN CONCLUSIVELY PROVE THAT FREE WILL CAN EXIST HARMONIOUSLY IN AN EINSTEINIAN UNIVERSE!
UH... AND JUNK LIKE THAT.
ARE THERE UH...
...ANY QUESTIONS?
JUST ONE.
CAN YOU **FIX** THE CLUBHOUSE OR **NOT**?
YES.
BUT IT'LL COST ABOUT FIFTY BUCKS.

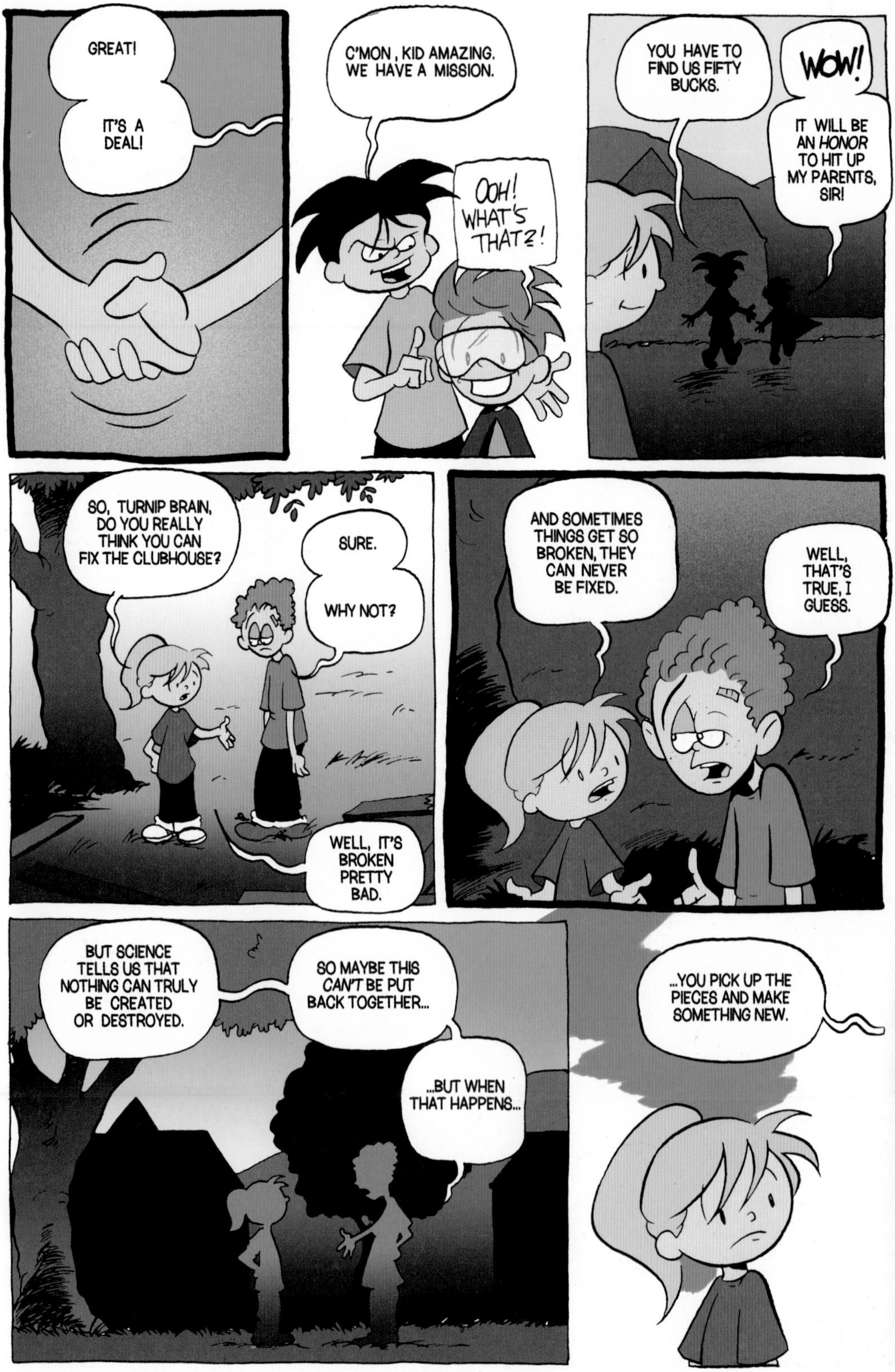
GREAT!
IT'S A DEAL!
C'MON, KID AMAZING. WE HAVE A MISSION.
OOH! WHAT'S THAT?!
YOU HAVE TO FIND US FIFTY BUCKS.
WOW!
IT WILL BE AN *HONOR* TO HIT UP MY PARENTS, SIR!
SO, TURNIP BRAIN, DO YOU REALLY THINK YOU CAN FIX THE CLUBHOUSE?
SURE.
WHY NOT?
WELL, IT'S BROKEN PRETTY BAD.
AND SOMETIMES THINGS GET SO BROKEN, THEY CAN NEVER BE FIXED.
WELL, THAT'S TRUE, I GUESS.
BUT SCIENCE TELLS US THAT NOTHING CAN TRULY BE CREATED OR DESTROYED.
SO MAYBE THIS *CAN'T* BE PUT BACK TOGETHER...
...BUT WHEN THAT HAPPENS...
...YOU PICK UP THE PIECES AND MAKE SOMETHING NEW.

OKAY...

...BEFORE MOM AND I LEFT NEW YORK, I SAW A DOCTOR ABOUT THE PROBLEM I WAS HAVING.

THIS IS WHAT HE TOLD ME:

SOMETIMES, A THING IS BROKEN SO BADLY, THERE'S NO WAY TO PUT IT BACK TOGETHER.

BUT NOW HERE'S TURNIP BRAIN SAYING:

IF YOU CAN'T PUT SOMETHING BACK TOGETHER, PICK UP THE PIECES AND MAKE SOMETHING NEW.

Y'KNOW, I THINK MR. HENDERSON IS RIGHT. THERE *IS* SOMETHING HOLDING ME BACK.

AND IT'S NOT THAT PRINCIPAL WRIGHT THINKS THAT I'M BAD.

IT'S THAT DEEP DOWN INSIDE...

I *AGREE* WITH HIM.

THAT WEEKEND, MY DAD WAS GOING TO NEW YORK TO COLLECT THE LAST OF HIS THINGS AND OFFICIALLY PUT OUR OLD PLACE UP FOR SALE.

HE ASKED IF I WANTED TO GO, AND AT FIRST I SAID NO. I DIDN'T WANT TO SEE OUR APARTMENT ALL EMPTY AND SAD.

BUT THEN I DECIDED TO CHANGE MY MIND.

I HAD A SCIENTIFIC THEORY TO TEST.

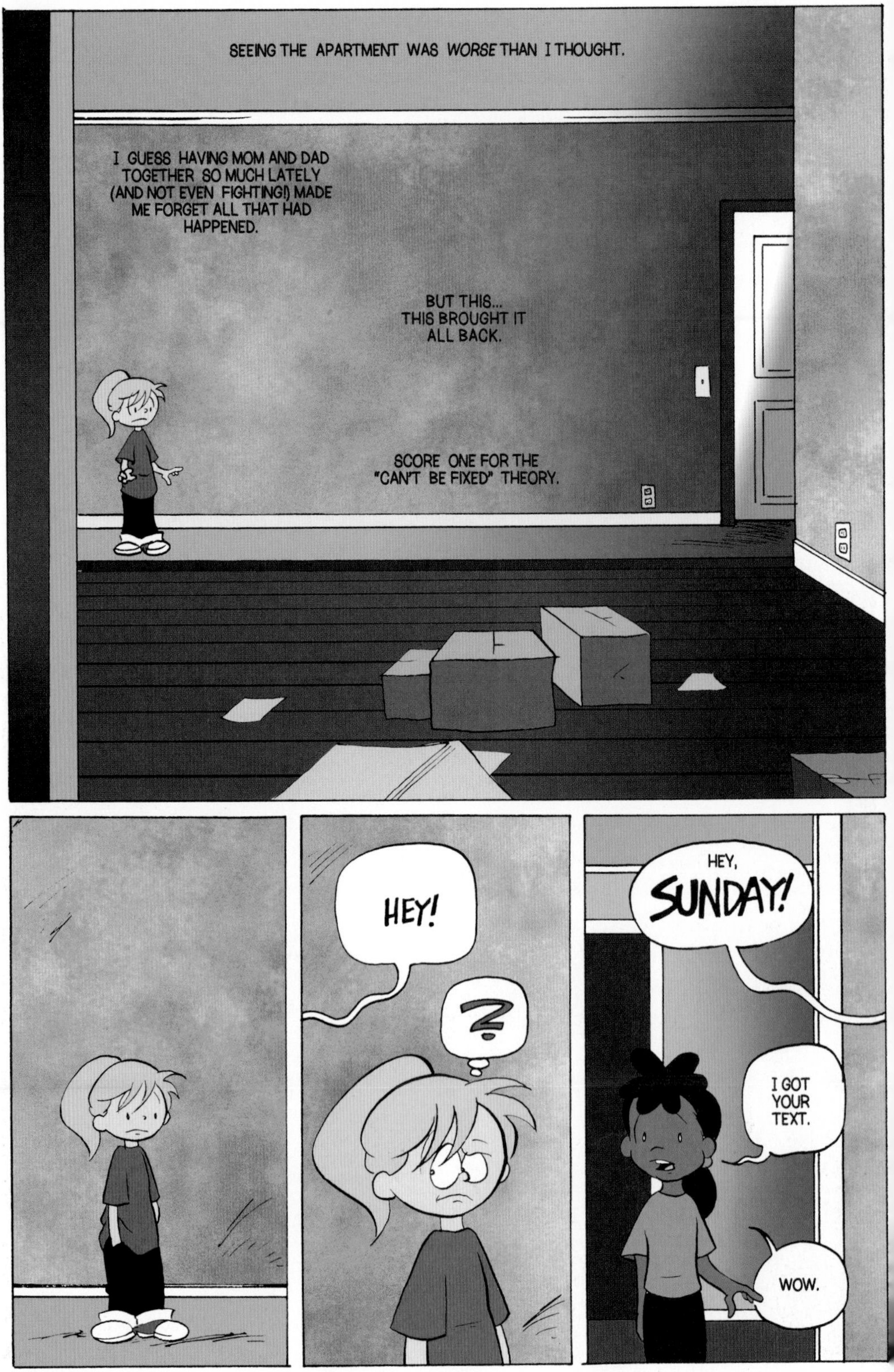
SEEING THE APARTMENT WAS *WORSE* THAN I THOUGHT.
I GUESS HAVING MOM AND DAD TOGETHER SO MUCH LATELY (AND NOT EVEN FIGHTING!) MADE ME FORGET ALL THAT HAD HAPPENED.
BUT THIS... THIS BROUGHT IT ALL BACK.
SCORE ONE FOR THE "CAN'T BE FIXED" THEORY.
HEY!
?
HEY, SUNDAY!
I GOT YOUR TEXT.
WOW.

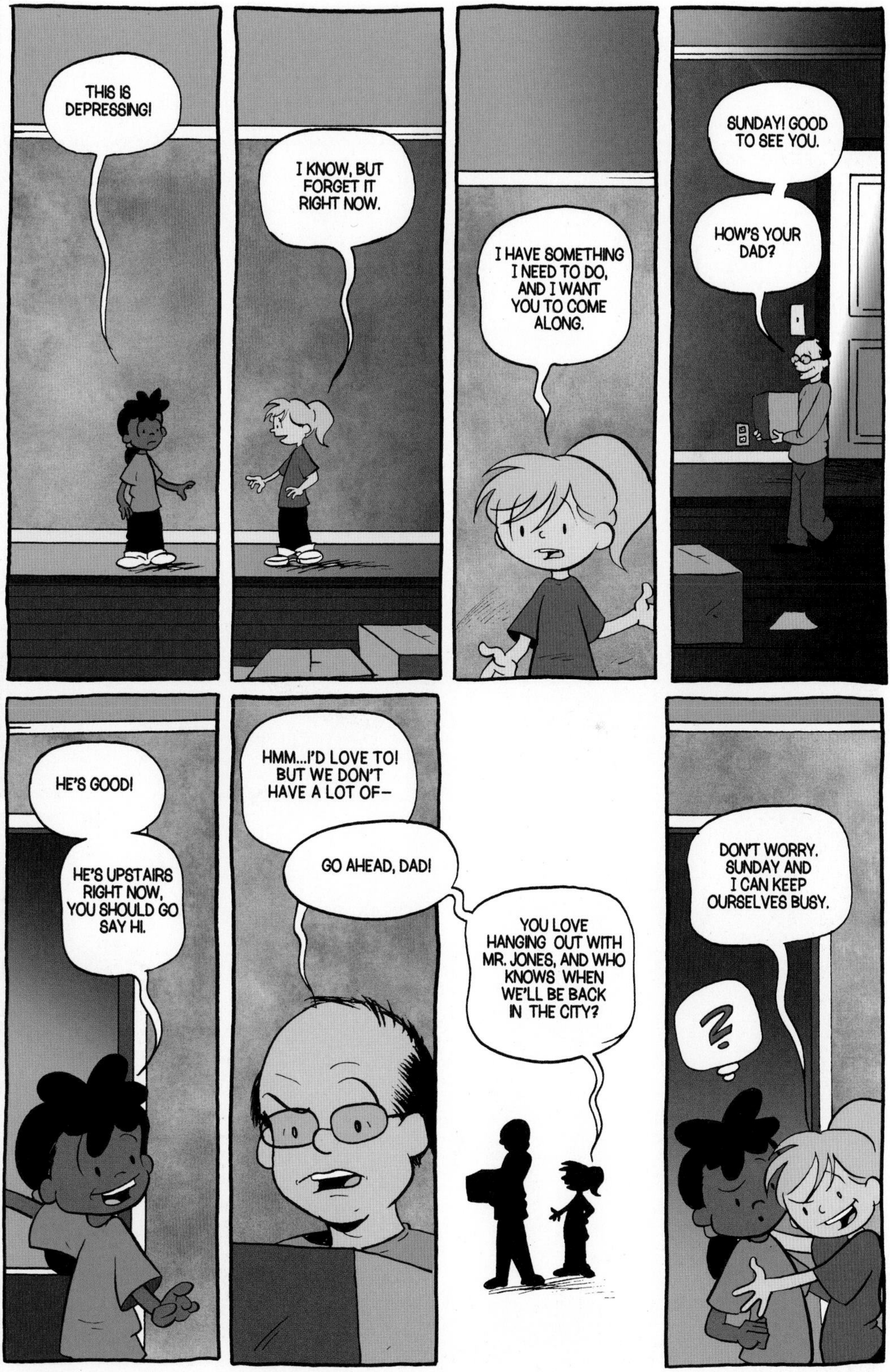
THIS IS DEPRESSING!
I KNOW, BUT FORGET IT RIGHT NOW.
I HAVE SOMETHING I NEED TO DO, AND I WANT YOU TO COME ALONG.
SUNDAY! GOOD TO SEE YOU.
HOW'S YOUR DAD?
HE'S GOOD!
HE'S UPSTAIRS RIGHT NOW, YOU SHOULD GO SAY HI.
HMM...I'D LOVE TO! BUT WE DON'T HAVE A LOT OF—
GO AHEAD, DAD!
YOU LOVE HANGING OUT WITH MR. JONES, AND WHO KNOWS WHEN WE'LL BE BACK IN THE CITY?
DON'T WORRY. SUNDAY AND I CAN KEEP OURSELVES BUSY.
?

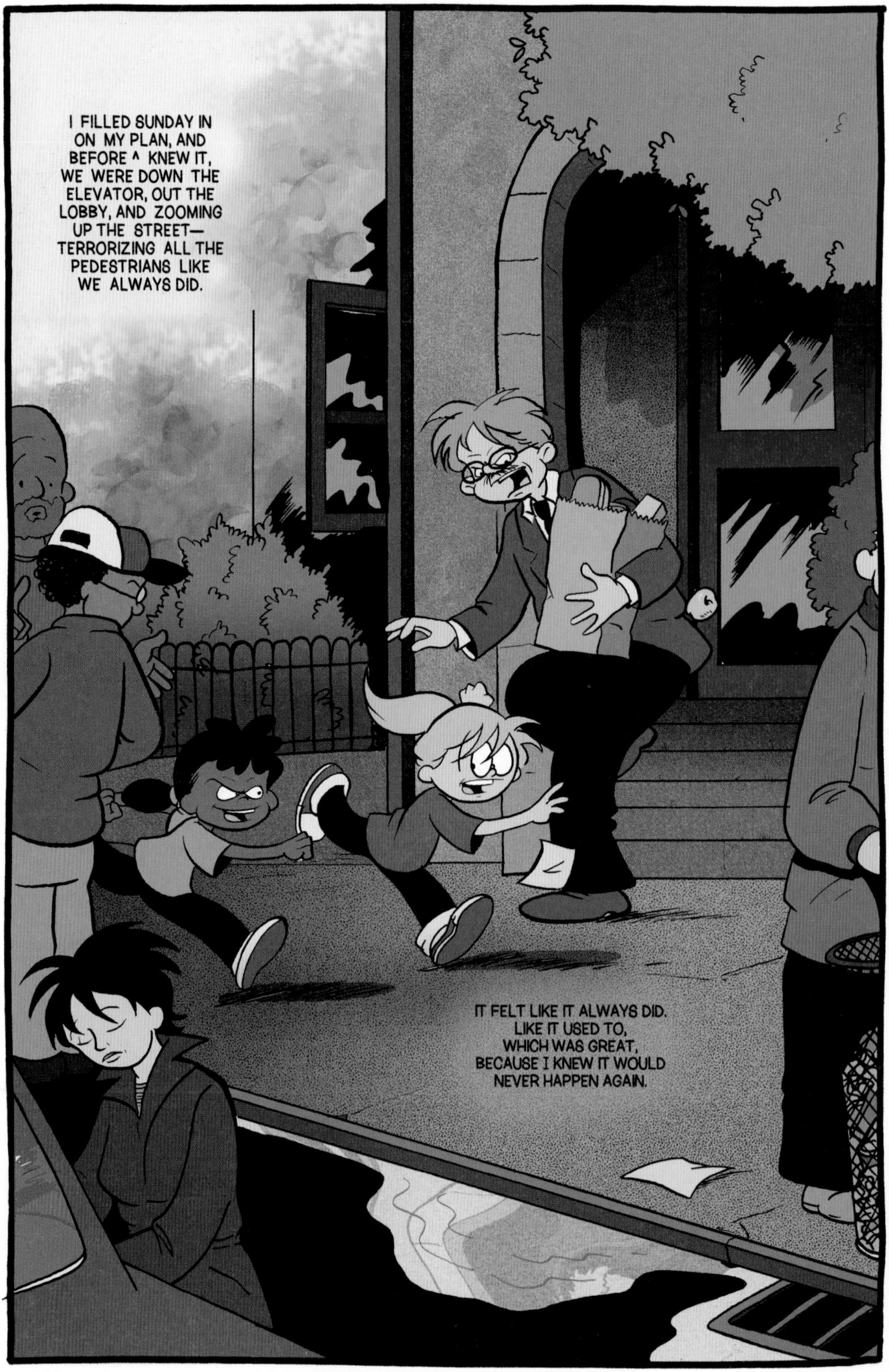
I FILLED SUNDAY IN ON MY PLAN, AND BEFORE ^ KNEW IT, WE WERE DOWN THE ELEVATOR, OUT THE LOBBY, AND ZOOMING UP THE STREET— TERRORIZING ALL THE PEDESTRIANS LIKE WE ALWAYS DID.
IT FELT LIKE IT ALWAYS DID. LIKE IT USED TO, WHICH WAS GREAT, BECAUSE I KNEW IT WOULD NEVER HAPPEN AGAIN.

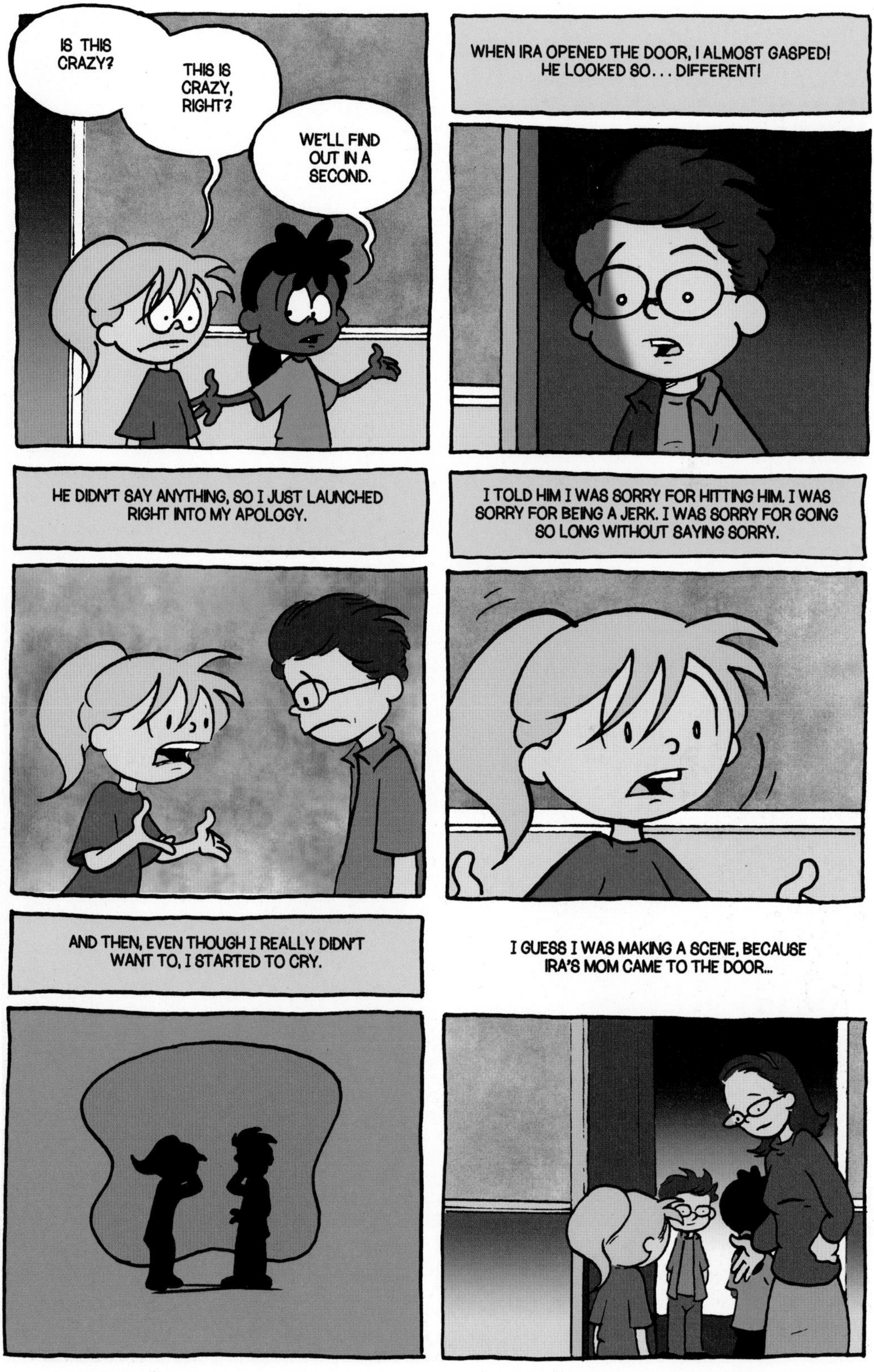

IS THIS CRAZY?
THIS IS CRAZY, RIGHT?
WE'LL FIND OUT IN A SECOND.
WHEN IRA OPENED THE DOOR, I ALMOST GASPED! HE LOOKED SO. . . DIFFERENT!
HE DIDN'T SAY ANYTHING, SO I JUST LAUNCHED RIGHT INTO MY APOLOGY.
I TOLD HIM I WAS SORRY FOR HITTING HIM. I WAS SORRY FOR BEING A JERK. I WAS SORRY FOR GOING SO LONG WITHOUT SAYING SORRY.
AND THEN, EVEN THOUGH I REALLY DIDN'T WANT TO, I STARTED TO CRY.
I GUESS I WAS MAKING A SCENE, BECAUSE IRA'S MOM CAME TO THE DOOR...

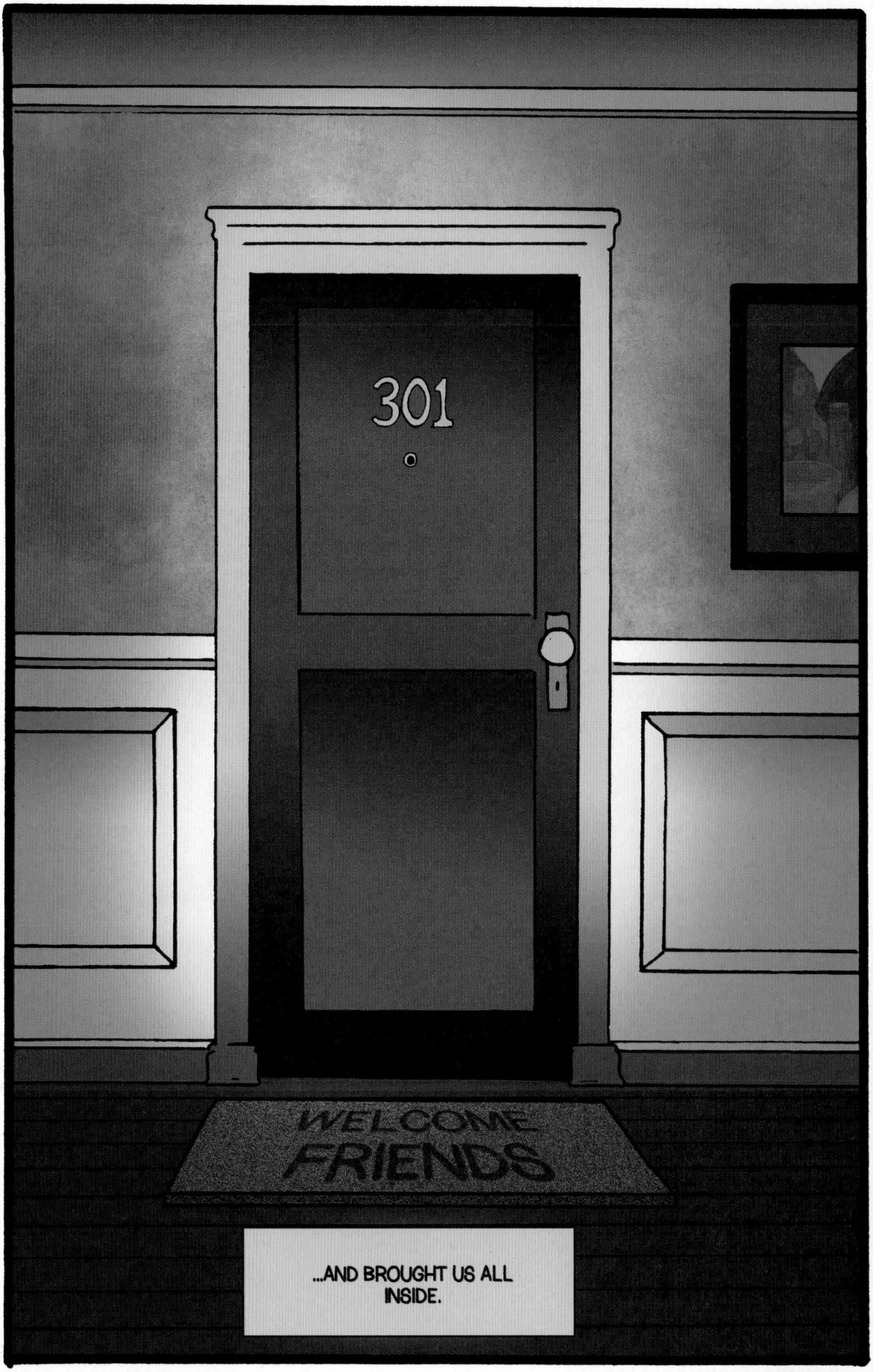
301
WELCOME
FRIENDS
...AND BROUGHT US ALL INSIDE.

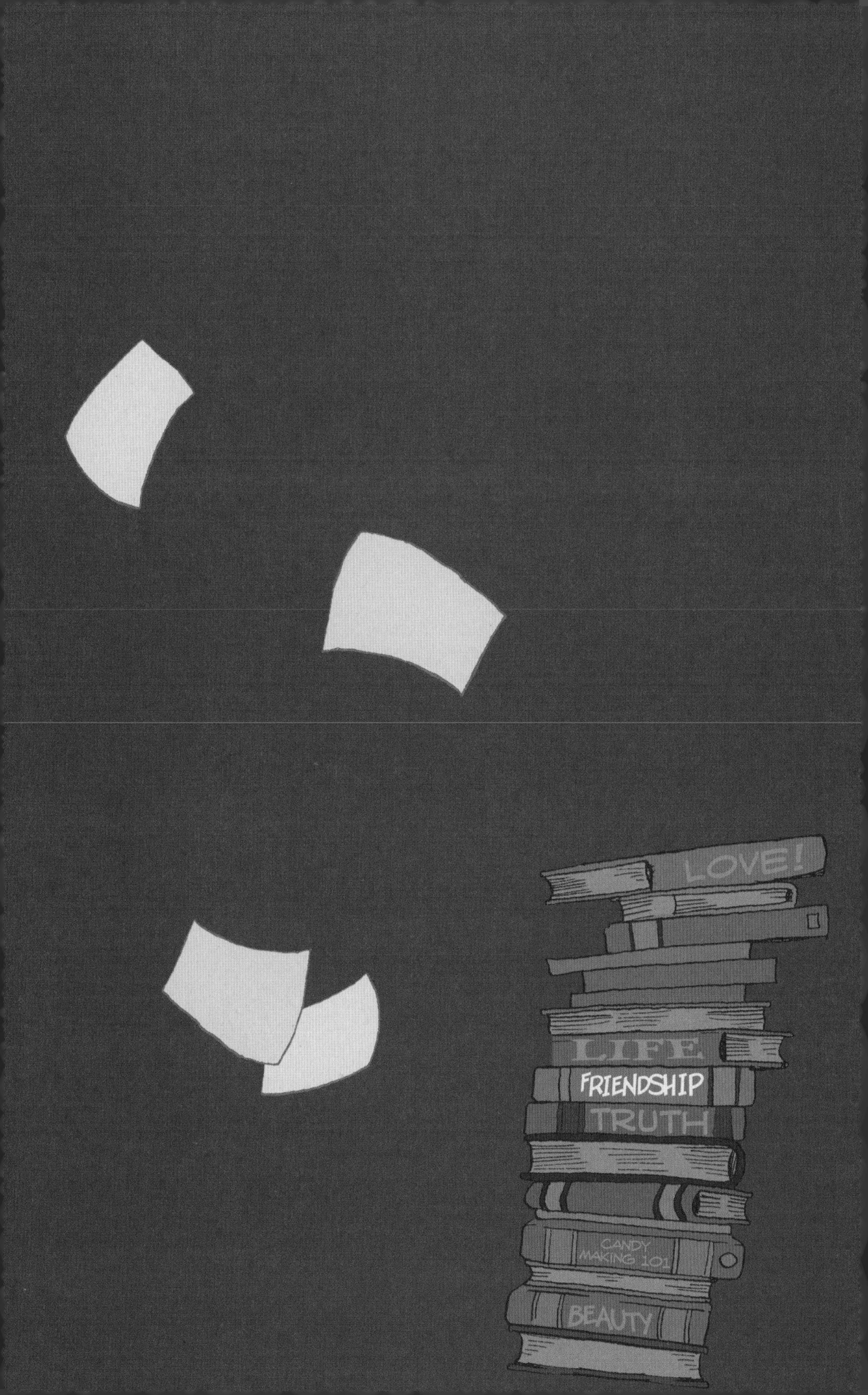
LOVE!
LIFE
FRIENDSHIP
TRUTH
CANDY MAKING 101
BEAUTY

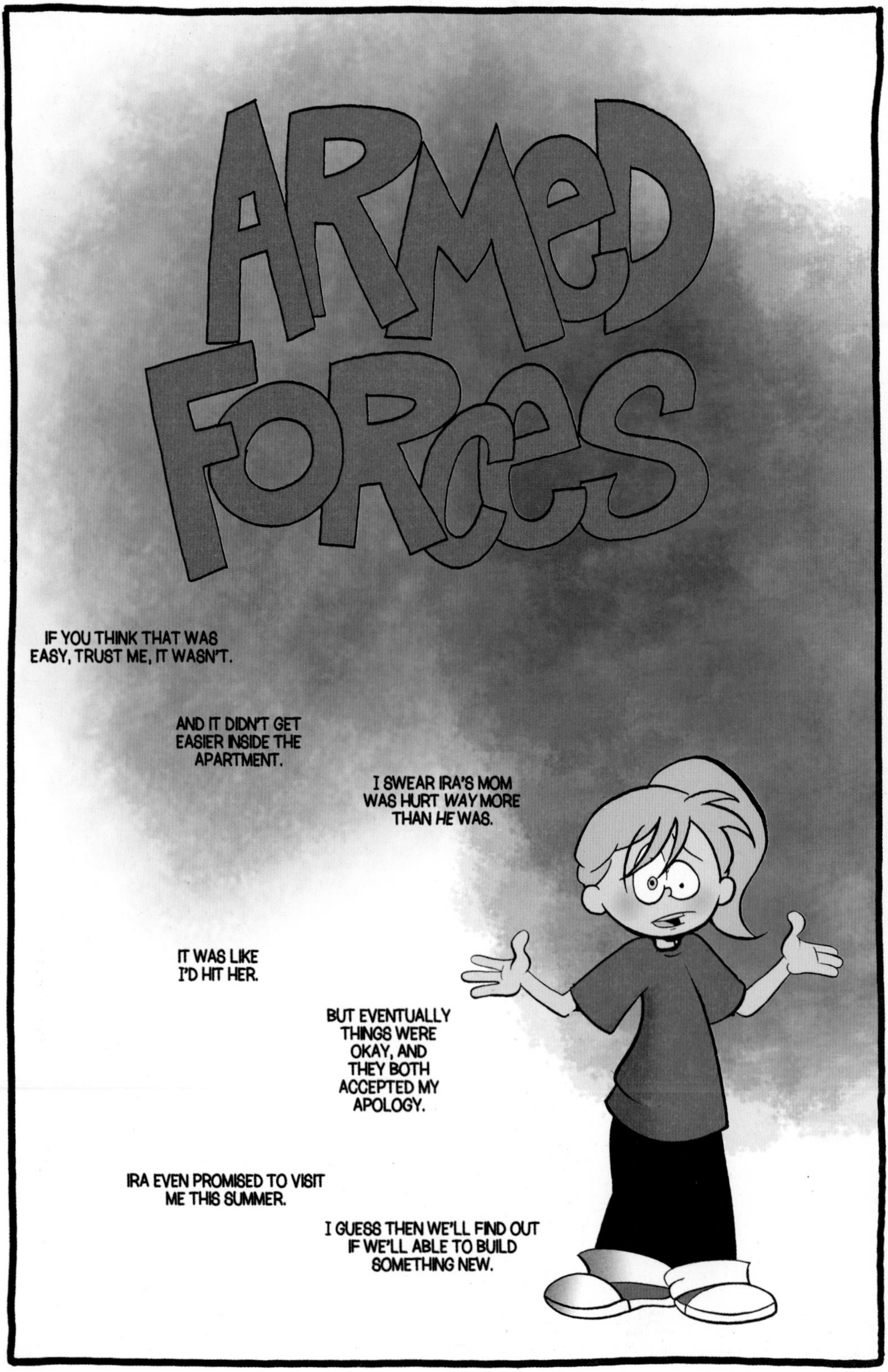
ARMED FORCES
IF YOU THINK THAT WAS EASY, TRUST ME, IT WASN'T.
AND IT DIDN'T GET EASIER INSIDE THE APARTMENT.
I SWEAR IRA'S MOM WAS HURT WAY MORE THAN HE WAS.
IT WAS LIKE I'D HIT HER.
BUT EVENTUALLY THINGS WERE OKAY, AND THEY BOTH ACCEPTED MY APOLOGY.
IRA EVEN PROMISED TO VISIT ME THIS SUMMER.
I GUESS THEN WE'LL FIND OUT IF WE'LL ABLE TO BUILD SOMETHING NEW.

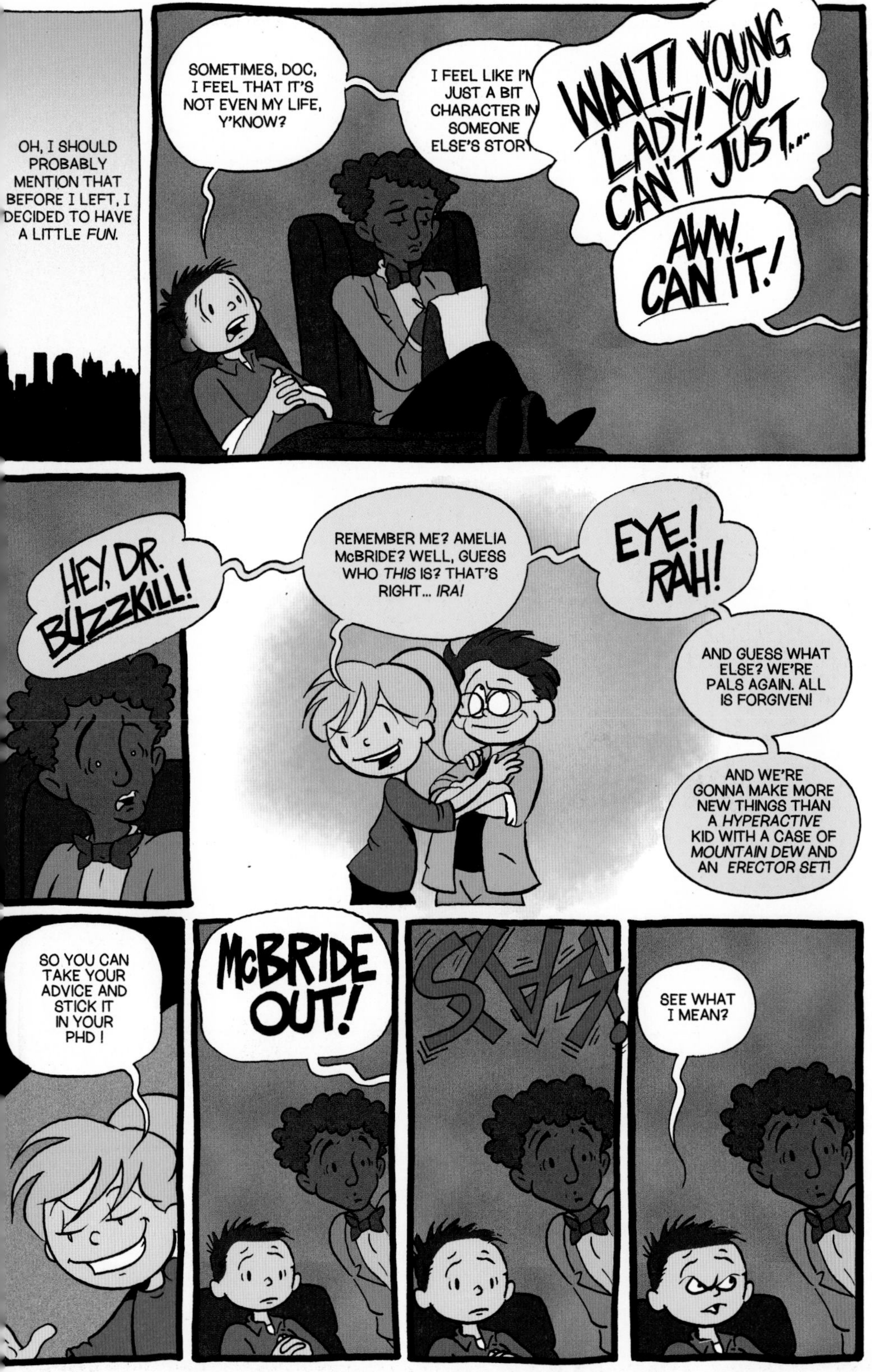

OH, I SHOULD PROBABLY MENTION THAT BEFORE I LEFT, I DECIDED TO HAVE A LITTLE *FUN*.
SOMETIMES, DOC, I FEEL THAT IT'S NOT EVEN MY LIFE, Y'KNOW?
I FEEL LIKE I'M JUST A BIT CHARACTER IN SOMEONE ELSE'S STORY
WAIT! YOUNG LADY! YOU CAN'T JUST....
AWW, CAN IT!
HEY, DR. BUZZKILL!
REMEMBER ME? AMELIA McBRIDE? WELL, GUESS WHO *THIS* IS? THAT'S RIGHT... *IRA!*
EYE! RAH!
AND GUESS WHAT ELSE? WE'RE PALS AGAIN. ALL IS FORGIVEN!
AND WE'RE GONNA MAKE MORE NEW THINGS THAN A *HYPERACTIVE* KID WITH A CASE OF *MOUNTAIN DEW* AND AN *ERECTOR SET*!
SO YOU CAN TAKE YOUR ADVICE AND STICK IT IN YOUR PHD !
McBRIDE OUT!
SLAM
SEE WHAT I MEAN?

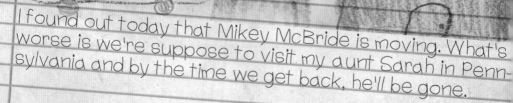

AFTER I GOT HOME, I WAS BACK TO
READING TANNER'S OLD DIARIES.
YOU CAN IMAGINE MY SURPRISE
WHEN I FOUND OUT THE LITTLE BOY
TANNER USED TO MOON OVER...

I found out today that Mikey McBride is moving. What's worse is we're suppose to visit my aunt Sarah in Pennsylvania and by the time we get back, he'll be gone.

I don't even want to go see Aunt Sarah. She's so dumb. She writes these kids' books and they're cool and all, bu she doesn't even sign her own name. So she's not even famous. PLUS, instead of living some place cool, like New York or Paris, she lives in some dumb town in Pennsylvania. I swear, if that ever happens to me, I hope somebody puts me out of my misery. AAGH!

I'm gonna miss Mikey. He was always nice and never called me a weirdo like everyone else. Mary's so dumb. Mikey totally liked her and she was never ever nice to him.

UPDATE: Get this: I told Mary that Mikey was moving and she cried! Are you kidding me?? She does nothing but tease him and call him names and the minute she finds out he won't be around, she loses it. I WILL NEVER UNDERSTAND PEOPLE! EVER!

...WAS MY *DAD!*

Tanner

BUT CAN YOU JUST IMAGINE?!

HEY, I'M GONNA GO HELP MY MOM MAKE MORE BON BOMBS. WANNA HELP?

UGH! No!

LAST TIME I HELPED, I ATE LIKE FORTY!

ME TOO!

AND THEN I HAD A DREAM I WAS DROWING IN THE CREAMY COOKIE FILLING, AND I HAD TO EAT MY WAY TO SAFETY.

IT WAS THE BEST DREAM I EVER HAD.

>SIIIIIIIIIIIIIGH<

HEY, RHONDA, AFTER MY MEETING, WE SHOULD GO OVER TO REGGIE'S.

SORRY, MY CAPE IS IN THE WASH.

DOES HE MISS ME?

OF COURSE!

C'MON, YOU NEVER HANG OUT WITH HIM ANYMORE.

GOOD.

113

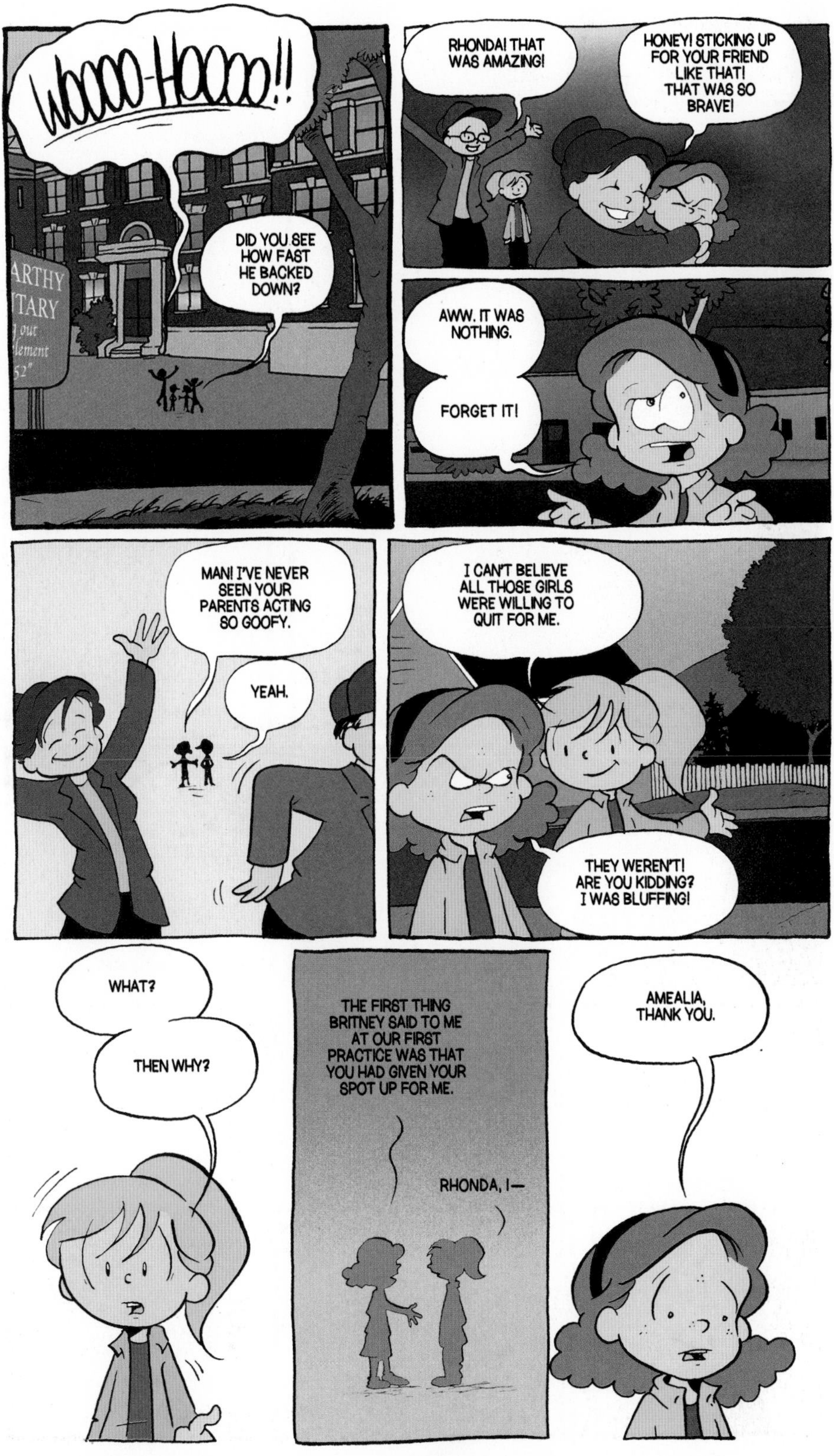
WOOOO-HOOOO!!
DID YOU SEE HOW FAST HE BACKED DOWN?
ARTHY
ITARY
RHONDA! THAT WAS AMAZING!
HONEY! STICKING UP FOR YOUR FRIEND LIKE THAT! THAT WAS SO BRAVE!
AWW. IT WAS NOTHING.
FORGET IT!
MAN! I'VE NEVER SEEN YOUR PARENTS ACTING SO GOOFY.
YEAH.
I CAN'T BELIEVE ALL THOSE GIRLS WERE WILLING TO QUIT FOR ME.
THEY WEREN'T! ARE YOU KIDDING? I WAS BLUFFING!
WHAT?
THEN WHY?
THE FIRST THING BRITNEY SAID TO ME AT OUR FIRST PRACTICE WAS THAT YOU HAD GIVEN YOUR SPOT UP FOR ME.
RHONDA, I—
AMEALIA, THANK YOU.

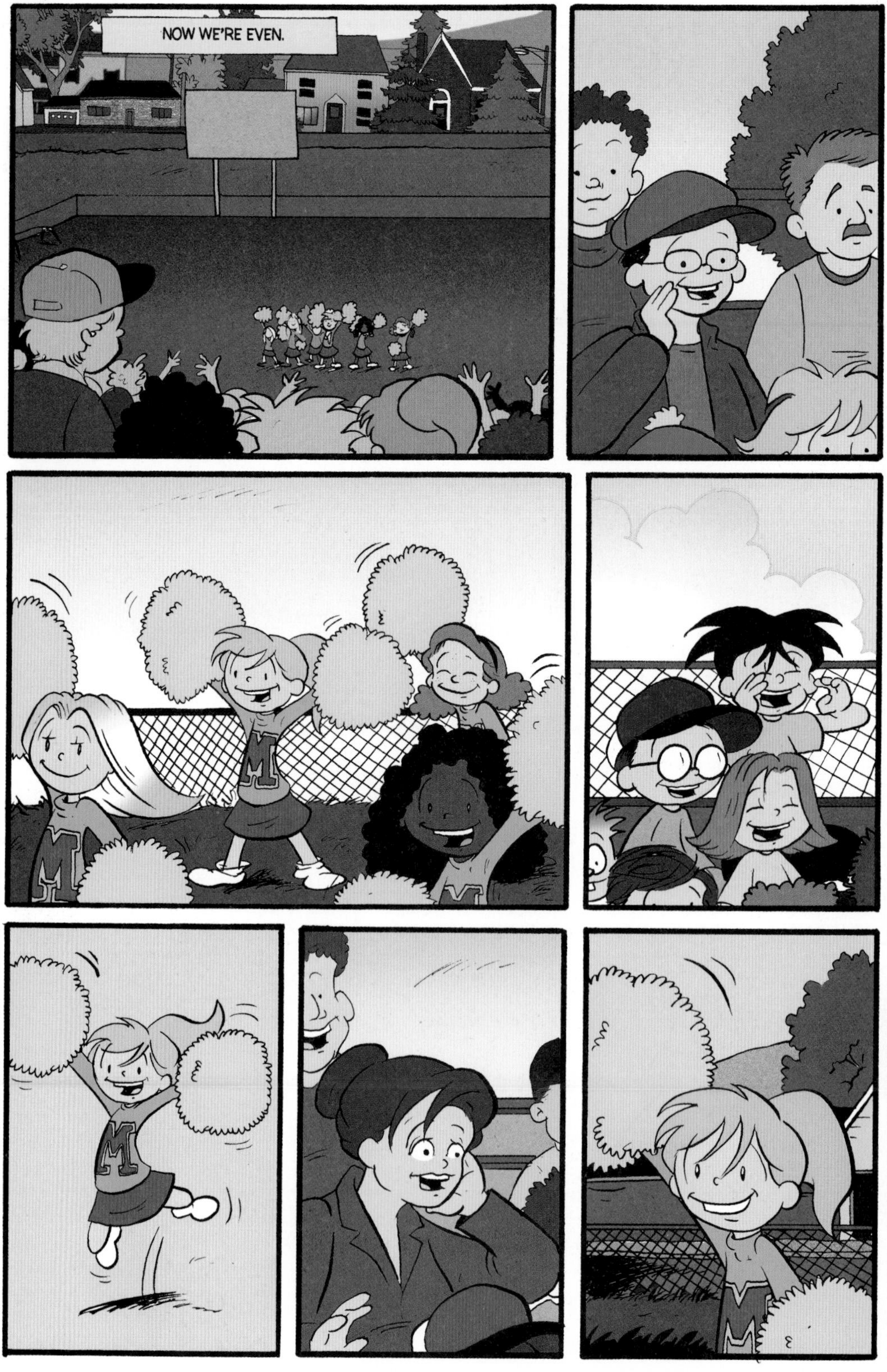
NOW WE'RE EVEN.

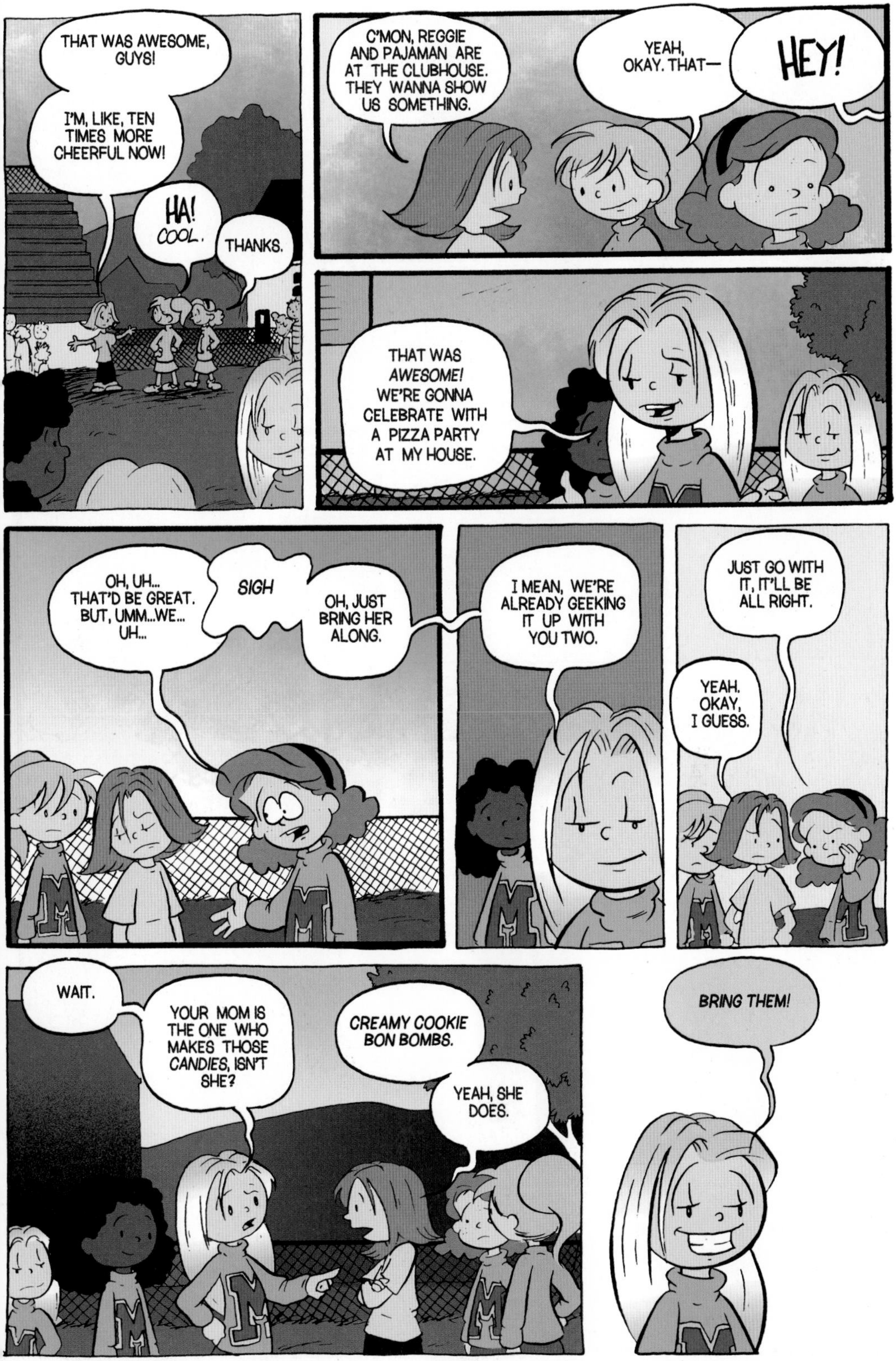
THAT WAS AWESOME, GUYS!
I'M, LIKE, TEN TIMES MORE CHEERFUL NOW!
HA! COOL.
THANKS.
C'MON, REGGIE AND PAJAMAN ARE AT THE CLUBHOUSE. THEY WANNA SHOW US SOMETHING.
YEAH, OKAY. THAT—
HEY!
THAT WAS AWESOME! WE'RE GONNA CELEBRATE WITH A PIZZA PARTY AT MY HOUSE.
OH, UH... THAT'D BE GREAT. BUT, UMM...WE... UH...
SIGH
OH, JUST BRING HER ALONG.
I MEAN, WE'RE ALREADY GEEKING IT UP WITH YOU TWO.
JUST GO WITH IT, IT'LL BE ALL RIGHT.
YEAH. OKAY, I GUESS.
WAIT.
YOUR MOM IS THE ONE WHO MAKES THOSE CANDIES, ISN'T SHE?
CREAMY COOKIE BON BOMBS.
YEAH, SHE DOES.
BRING THEM!

BRING LOTS OF THEM.

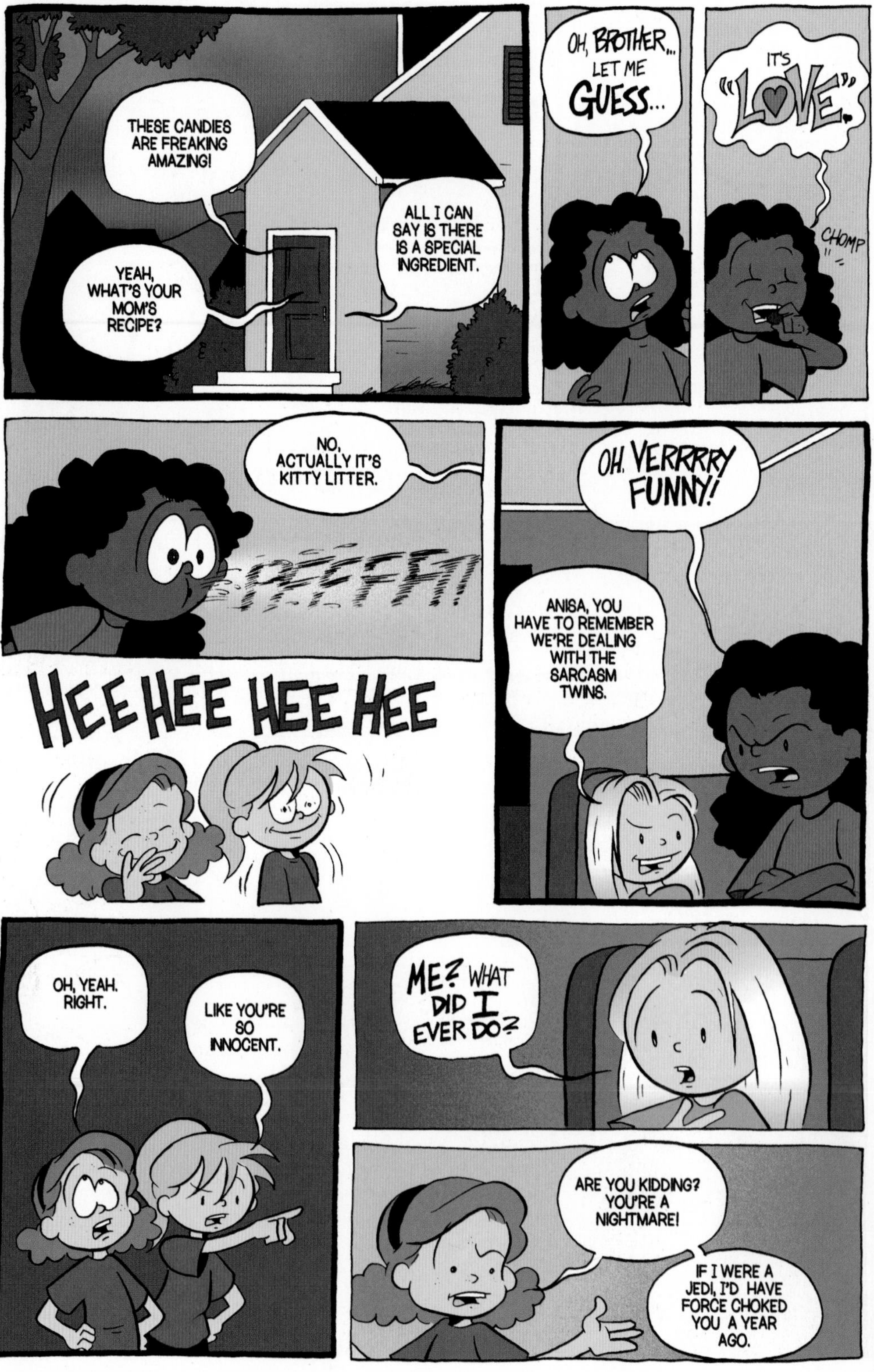
THESE CANDIES ARE FREAKING AMAZING!
YEAH, WHAT'S YOUR MOM'S RECIPE?
ALL I CAN SAY IS THERE IS A SPECIAL INGREDIENT.
OH, BROTHER... LET ME GUESS...
IT'S "LOVE".
CHOMP
NO, ACTUALLY IT'S KITTY LITTER.
PFFFFT!
HEE HEE HEE HEE
OH, VERRRRY FUNNY!
ANISA, YOU HAVE TO REMEMBER WE'RE DEALING WITH THE SARCASM TWINS.
OH, YEAH. RIGHT.
LIKE YOU'RE SO INNOCENT.
ME? WHAT DID I EVER DO?
ARE YOU KIDDING? YOU'RE A NIGHTMARE!
IF I WERE A JEDI, I'D HAVE FORCE CHOKED YOU A YEAR AGO.

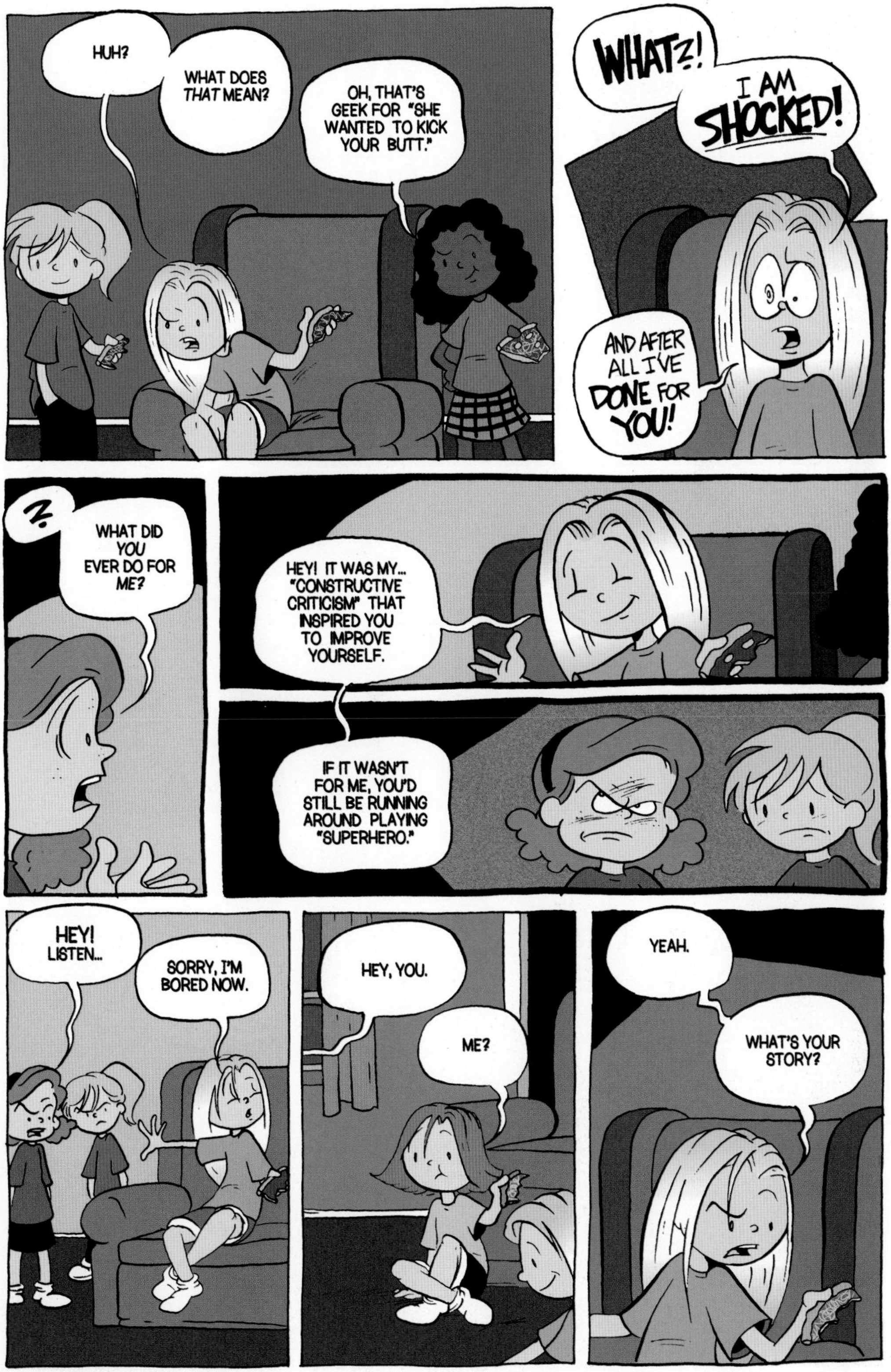
HUH?
WHAT DOES *THAT* MEAN?
OH, THAT'S GEEK FOR "SHE WANTED TO KICK YOUR BUTT."
WHAT?!
I AM SHOCKED!
AND AFTER ALL I'VE DONE FOR YOU!
?
WHAT DID *YOU* EVER DO FOR *ME*?
HEY! IT WAS MY... "CONSTRUCTIVE CRITICISM" THAT INSPIRED YOU TO IMPROVE YOURSELF.
IF IT WASN'T FOR ME, YOU'D STILL BE RUNNING AROUND PLAYING "SUPERHERO."
HEY! LISTEN...
SORRY, I'M BORED NOW.
HEY, YOU.
ME?
YEAH.
WHAT'S YOUR STORY?

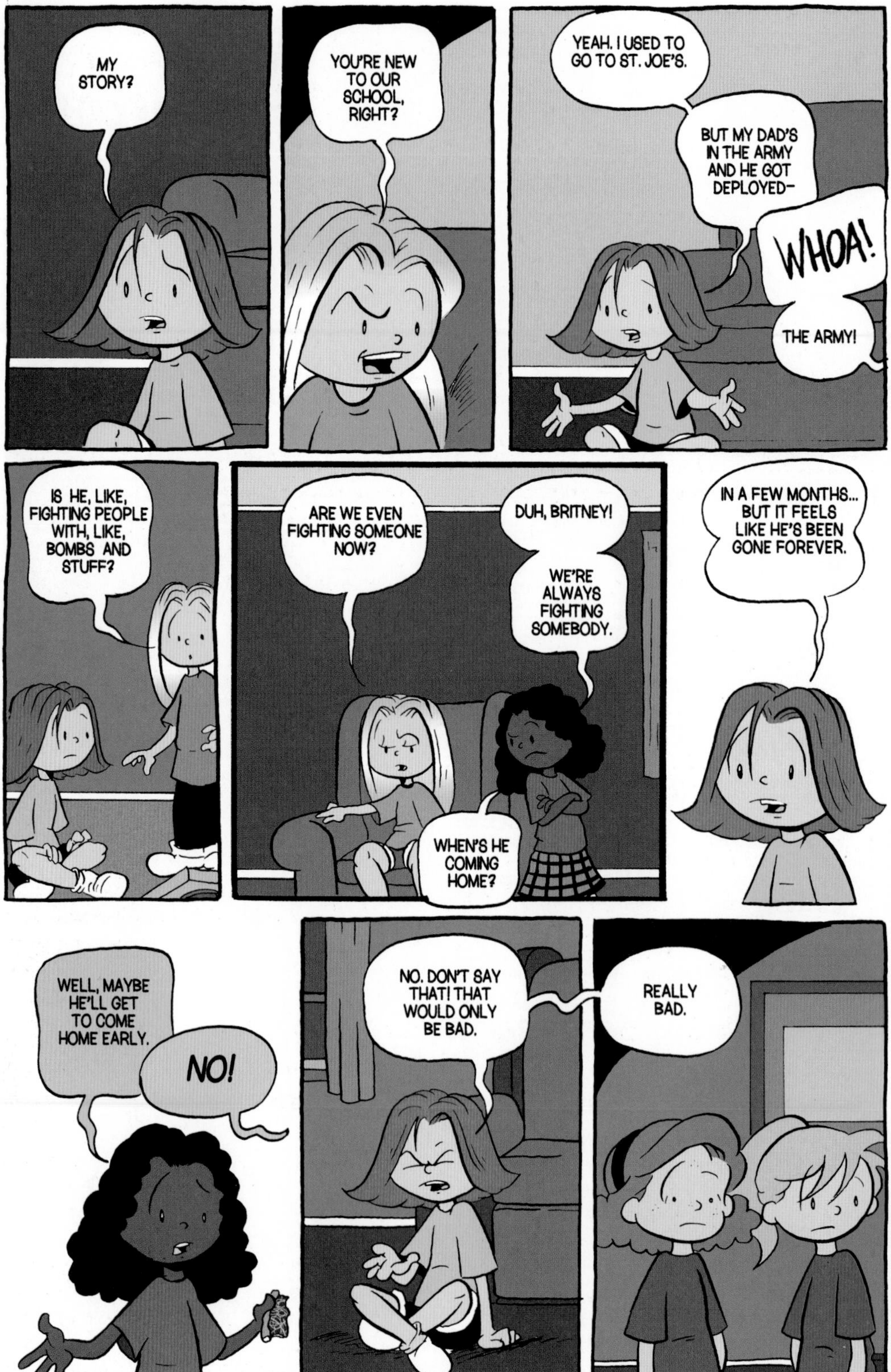

MY STORY?
YOU'RE NEW TO OUR SCHOOL, RIGHT?
YEAH. I USED TO GO TO ST. JOE'S.
BUT MY DAD'S IN THE ARMY AND HE GOT DEPLOYED–
WHOA!
THE ARMY!
IS HE, LIKE, FIGHTING PEOPLE WITH, LIKE, BOMBS AND STUFF?
ARE WE EVEN FIGHTING SOMEONE NOW?
DUH, BRITNEY!
WE'RE ALWAYS FIGHTING SOMEBODY.
WHEN'S HE COMING HOME?
IN A FEW MONTHS... BUT IT FEELS LIKE HE'S BEEN GONE FOREVER.
WELL, MAYBE HE'LL GET TO COME HOME EARLY.
NO!
NO. DON'T SAY THAT! THAT WOULD ONLY BE BAD.
REALLY BAD.

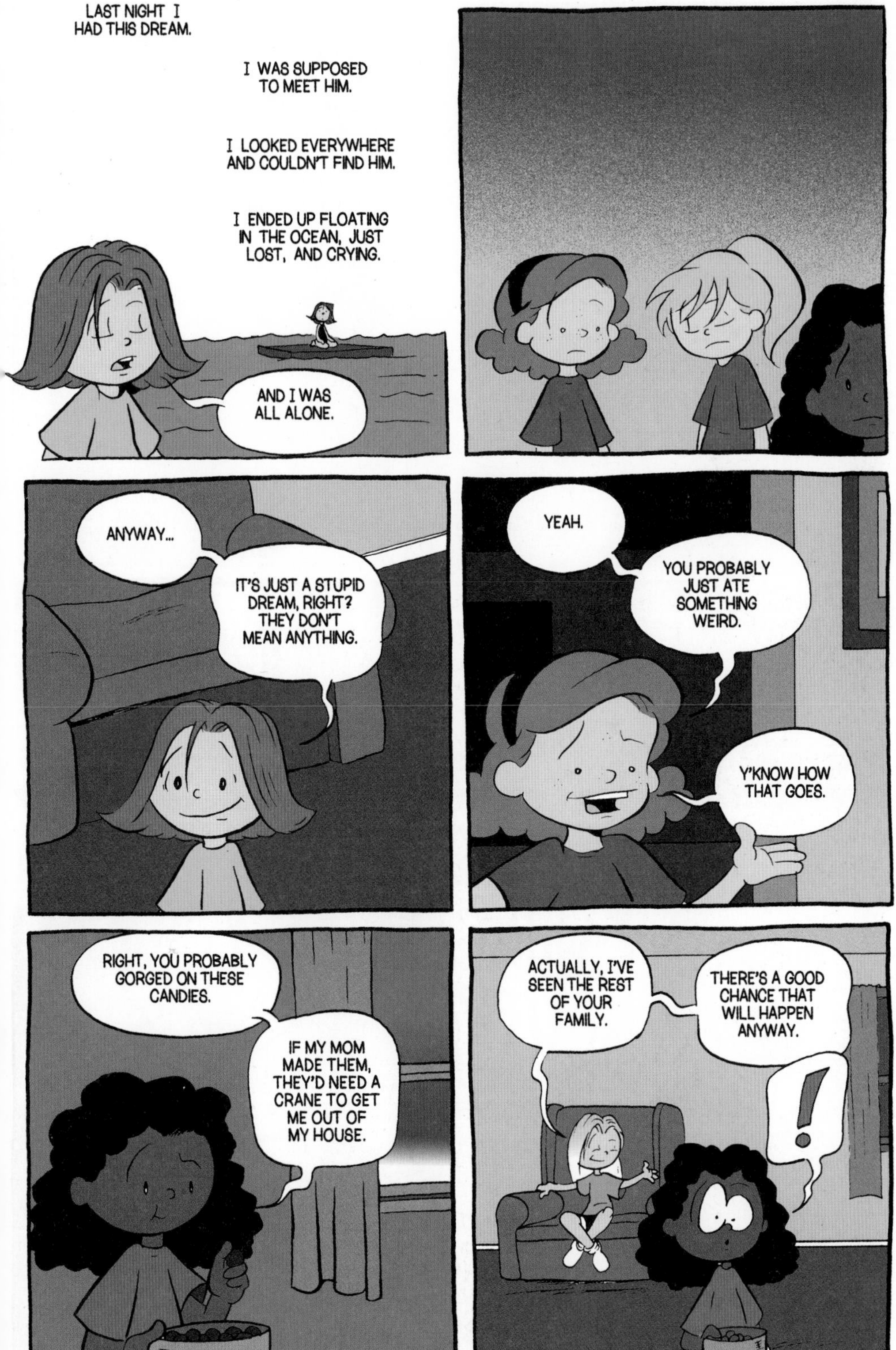
LAST NIGHT I HAD THIS DREAM.
I WAS SUPPOSED TO MEET HIM.
I LOOKED EVERYWHERE AND COULDN'T FIND HIM.
I ENDED UP FLOATING IN THE OCEAN, JUST LOST, AND CRYING.
AND I WAS ALL ALONE.
ANYWAY...
IT'S JUST A STUPID DREAM, RIGHT? THEY DON'T MEAN ANYTHING.
YEAH.
YOU PROBABLY JUST ATE SOMETHING WEIRD.
Y'KNOW HOW THAT GOES.
RIGHT, YOU PROBABLY GORGED ON THESE CANDIES.
IF MY MOM MADE THEM, THEY'D NEED A CRANE TO GET ME OUT OF MY HOUSE.
ACTUALLY, I'VE SEEN THE REST OF YOUR FAMILY.
THERE'S A GOOD CHANCE THAT WILL HAPPEN ANYWAY.
!

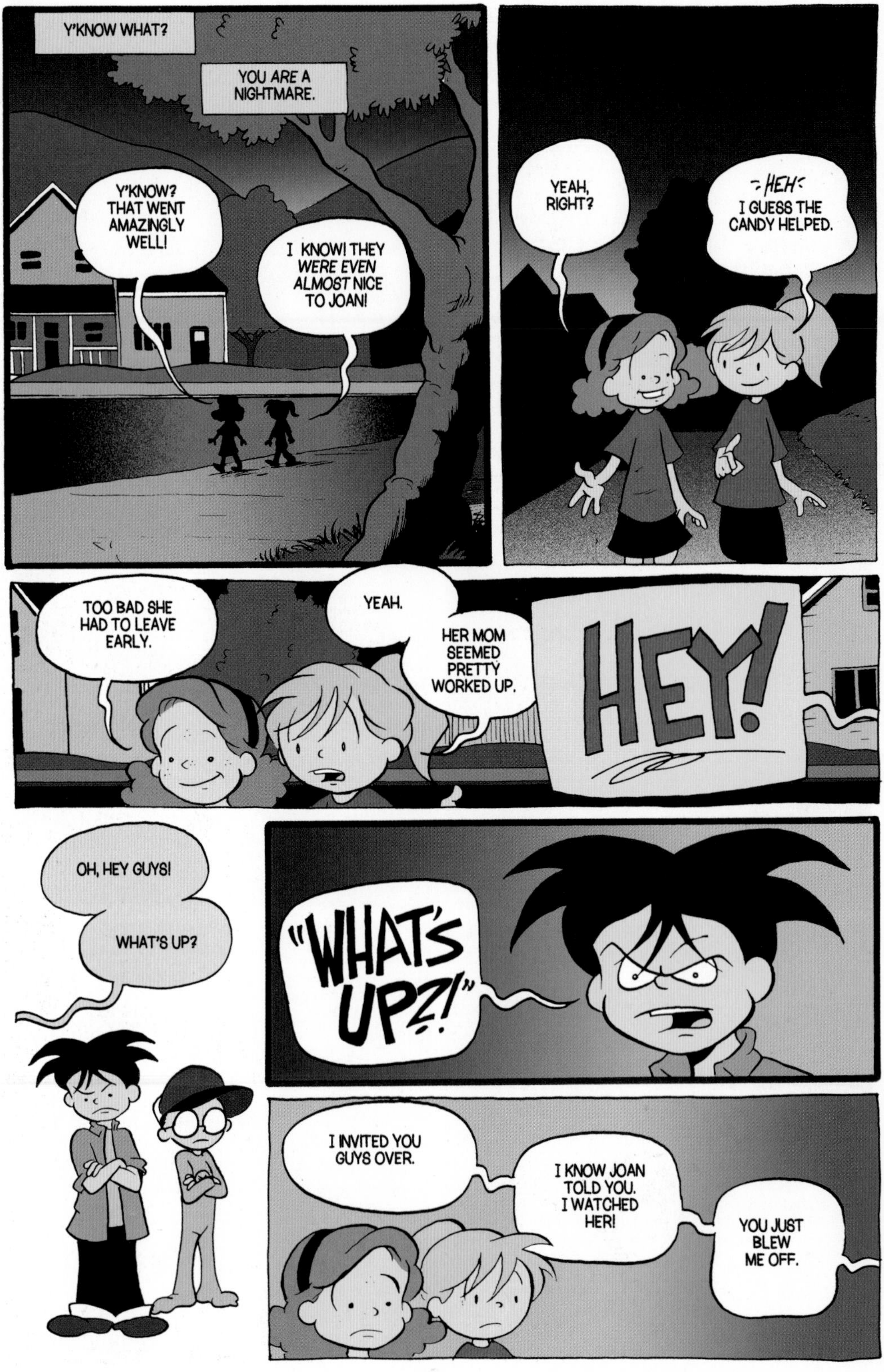
Y'KNOW WHAT?
YOU *ARE* A NIGHTMARE.
Y'KNOW? THAT WENT AMAZINGLY WELL!
I KNOW! THEY *WERE EVEN ALMOST* NICE TO JOAN!
YEAH, RIGHT?
HEH
I GUESS THE CANDY HELPED.
TOO BAD SHE HAD TO LEAVE EARLY.
YEAH.
HER MOM SEEMED PRETTY WORKED UP.
HEY!
OH, HEY GUYS!
WHAT'S UP?
"WHAT'S UP?!"
I INVITED YOU GUYS OVER.
I KNOW JOAN TOLD YOU. I WATCHED HER!
YOU JUST BLEW ME OFF.

124

WHEN WE GOT TO MY HOUSE, MY MOM WAS WAITING FOR US. AT FIRST I THOUGHT SHE WAS JUST OUT ENJOYING THE BEAUTIFUL WEATHER. BUT WHEN WE GOT CLOSER, I COULD SEE SHE LOOKED AWFUL, LIKE SHE WAS SICK — LIKE SHE'D SEEN A GHOST.

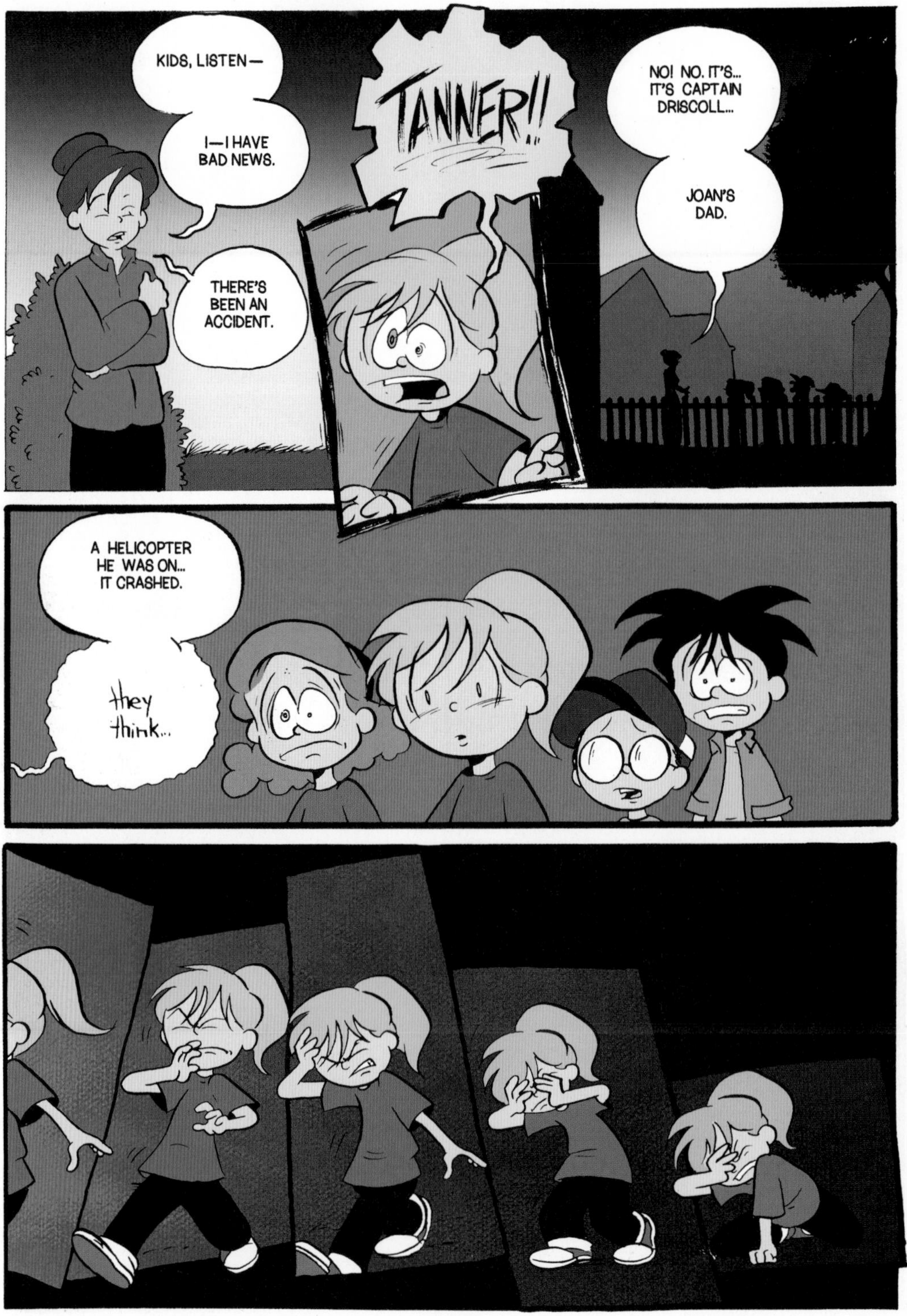
KIDS, LISTEN—
I—I HAVE BAD NEWS.
THERE'S BEEN AN ACCIDENT.
TANNER!!
NO! NO. IT'S... IT'S CAPTAIN DRISCOLL...
JOAN'S DAD.
A HELICOPTER HE WAS ON... IT CRASHED.
they think...

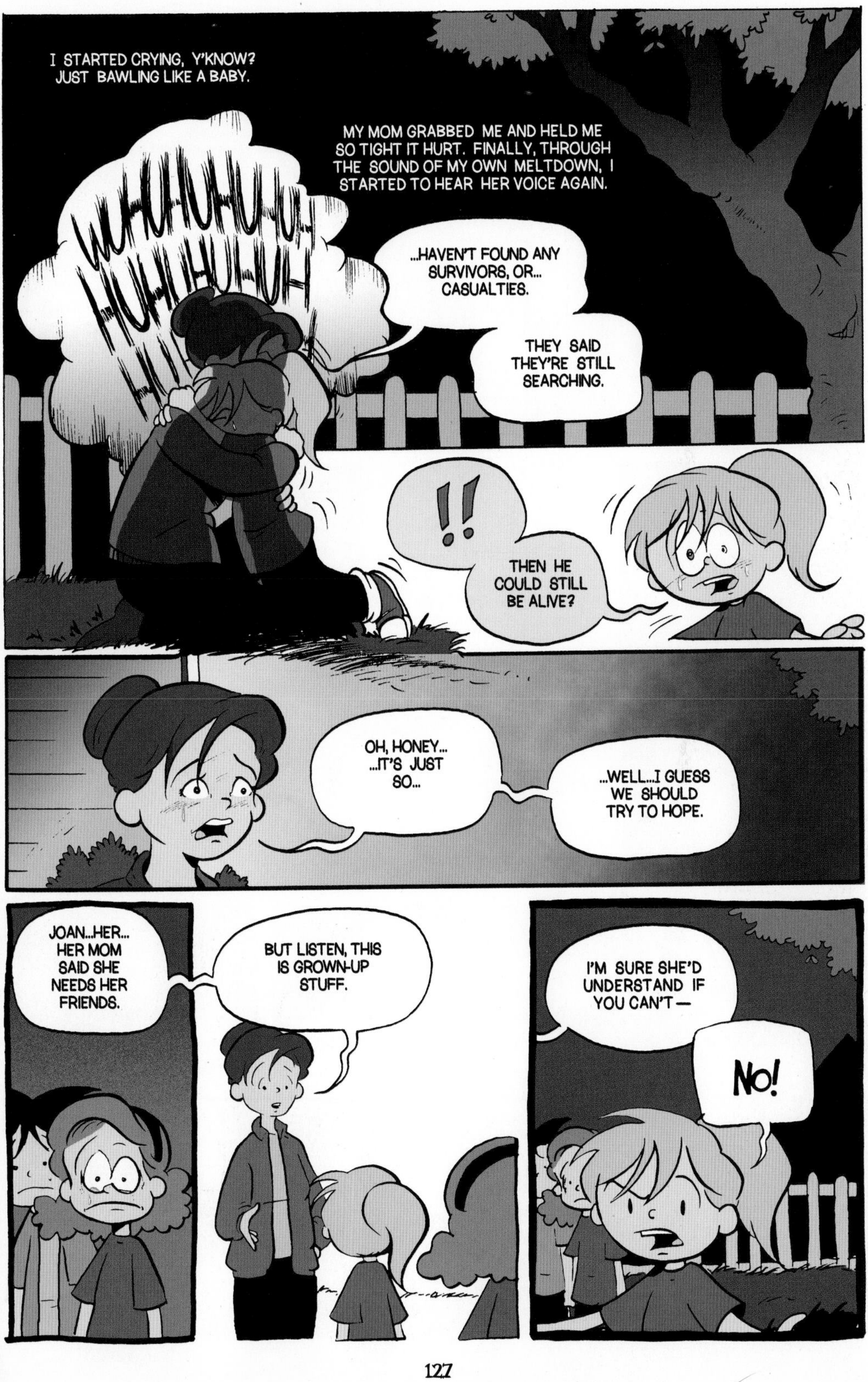
I STARTED CRYING, Y'KNOW? JUST BAWLING LIKE A BABY.
WHUHUHU-U-HUHUHUUH-HU
MY MOM GRABBED ME AND HELD ME SO TIGHT IT HURT. FINALLY, THROUGH THE SOUND OF MY OWN MELTDOWN, I STARTED TO HEAR HER VOICE AGAIN.
...HAVEN'T FOUND ANY SURVIVORS, OR... CASUALTIES.
THEY SAID THEY'RE STILL SEARCHING.
!!
THEN HE COULD STILL BE ALIVE?
OH, HONEY... ...IT'S JUST SO...
...WELL...I GUESS WE SHOULD TRY TO HOPE.
JOAN...HER... HER MOM SAID SHE NEEDS HER FRIENDS.
BUT LISTEN, THIS IS GROWN-UP STUFF.
I'M SURE SHE'D UNDERSTAND IF YOU CAN'T—
NO!

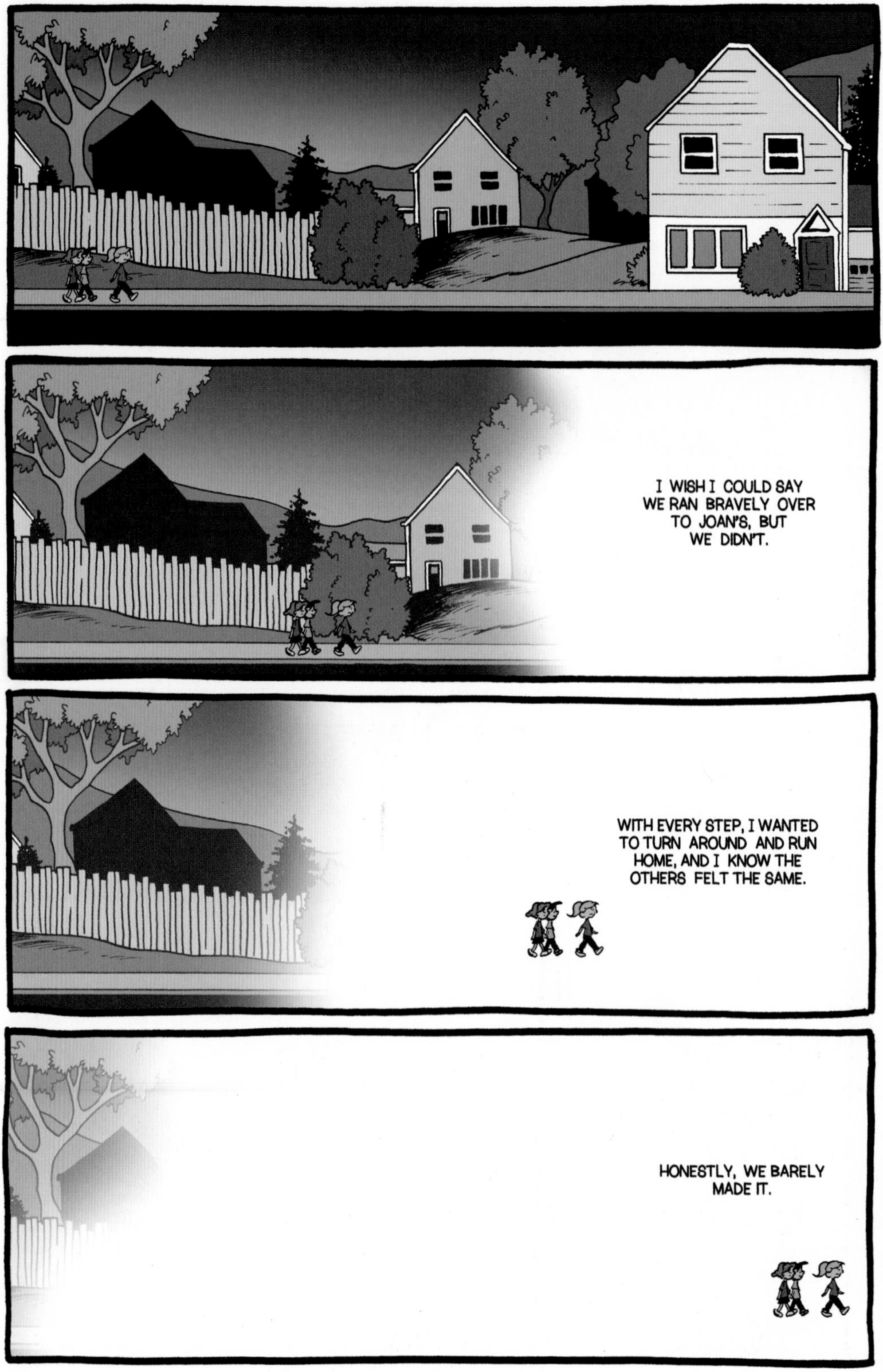
I WISH I COULD SAY WE RAN BRAVELY OVER TO JOAN'S, BUT WE DIDN'T.
WITH EVERY STEP, I WANTED TO TURN AROUND AND RUN HOME, AND I KNOW THE OTHERS FELT THE SAME.
HONESTLY, WE BARELY MADE IT.

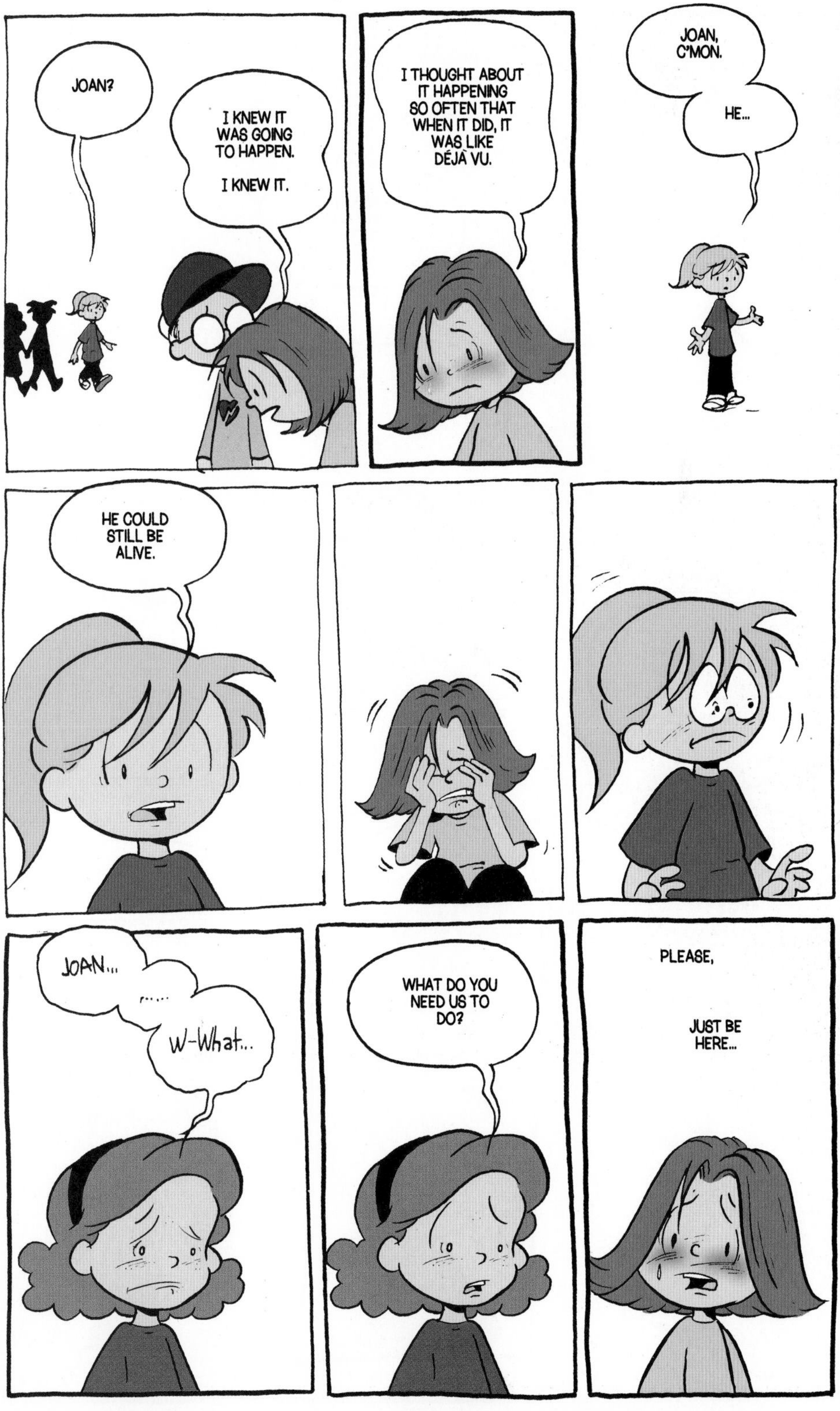
JOAN?
I KNEW IT WAS GOING TO HAPPEN.
I KNEW IT.
I THOUGHT ABOUT IT HAPPENING SO OFTEN THAT WHEN IT DID, IT WAS LIKE DÉJÀ VU.
JOAN, C'MON.
HE...
HE COULD STILL BE ALIVE.
JOAN...
...
W-What..
WHAT DO YOU NEED US TO DO?
PLEASE,
JUST BE HERE...

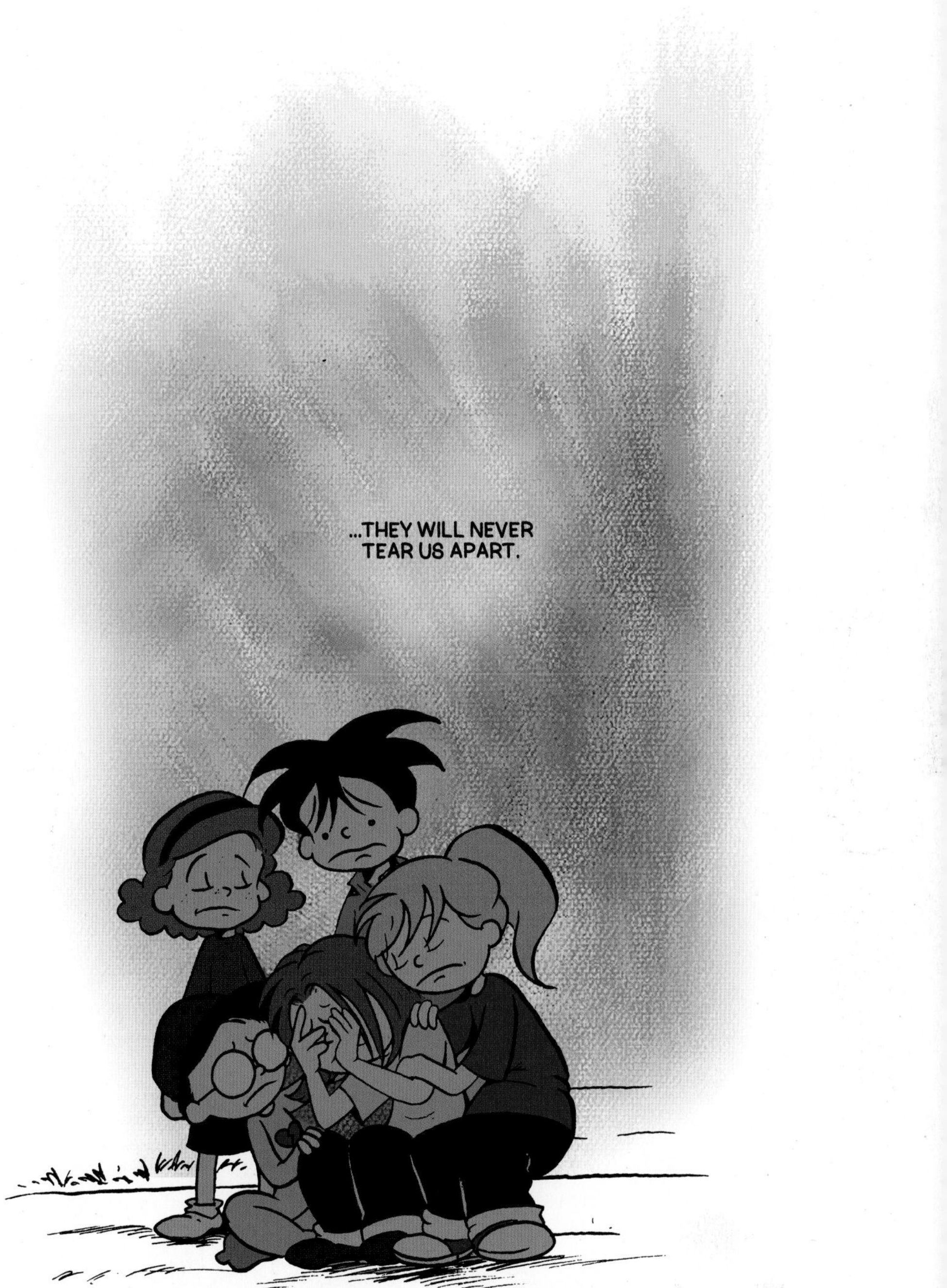
...THEY WILL NEVER
TEAR US APART.

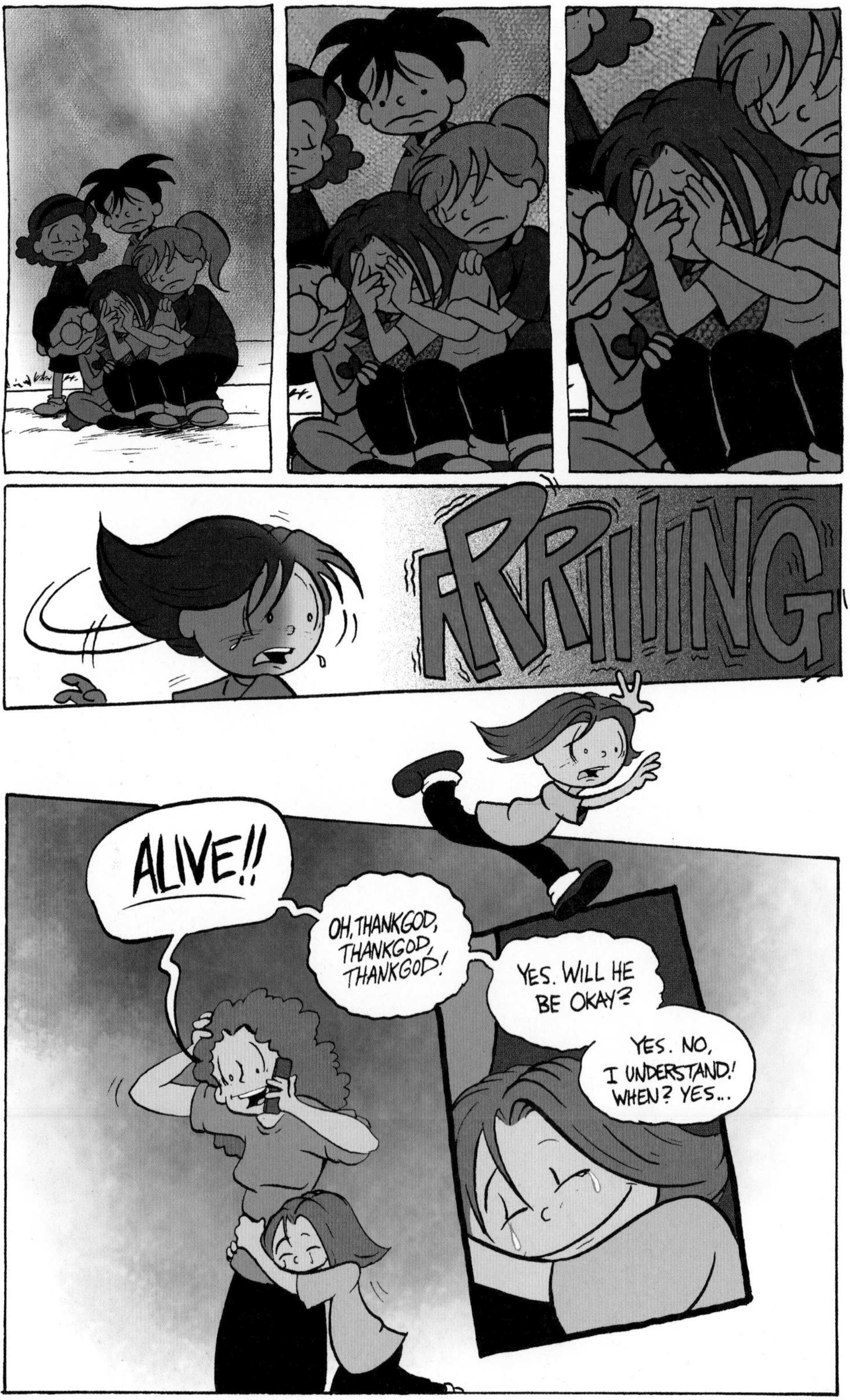
RRRIIIING
ALIVE!!
OH, THANKGOD, THANKGOD, THANKGOD!
YES. WILL HE BE OKAY?
YES. NO, I UNDERSTAND! WHEN? YES...

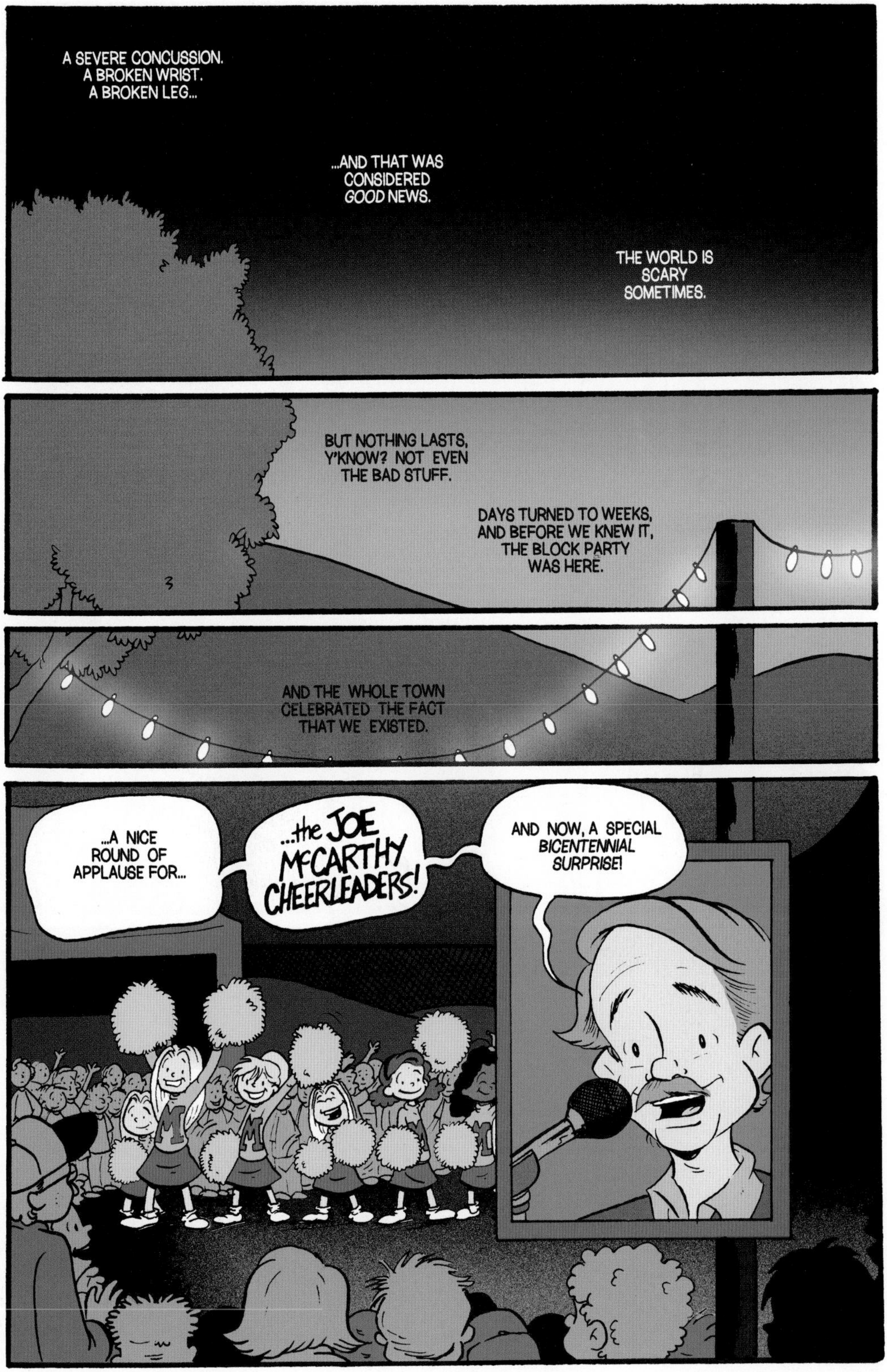

A SEVERE CONCUSSION.
A BROKEN WRIST.
A BROKEN LEG...
...AND THAT WAS CONSIDERED *GOOD* NEWS.
THE WORLD IS SCARY SOMETIMES.
BUT NOTHING LASTS, Y'KNOW? NOT EVEN THE BAD STUFF.
DAYS TURNED TO WEEKS, AND BEFORE WE KNEW IT, THE BLOCK PARTY WAS HERE.
AND THE WHOLE TOWN CELEBRATED THE FACT THAT WE EXISTED.
...A NICE ROUND OF APPLAUSE FOR...
...the JOE McCARTHY CHEERLEADERS!
AND NOW, A SPECIAL *BICENTENNIAL SURPRISE*!

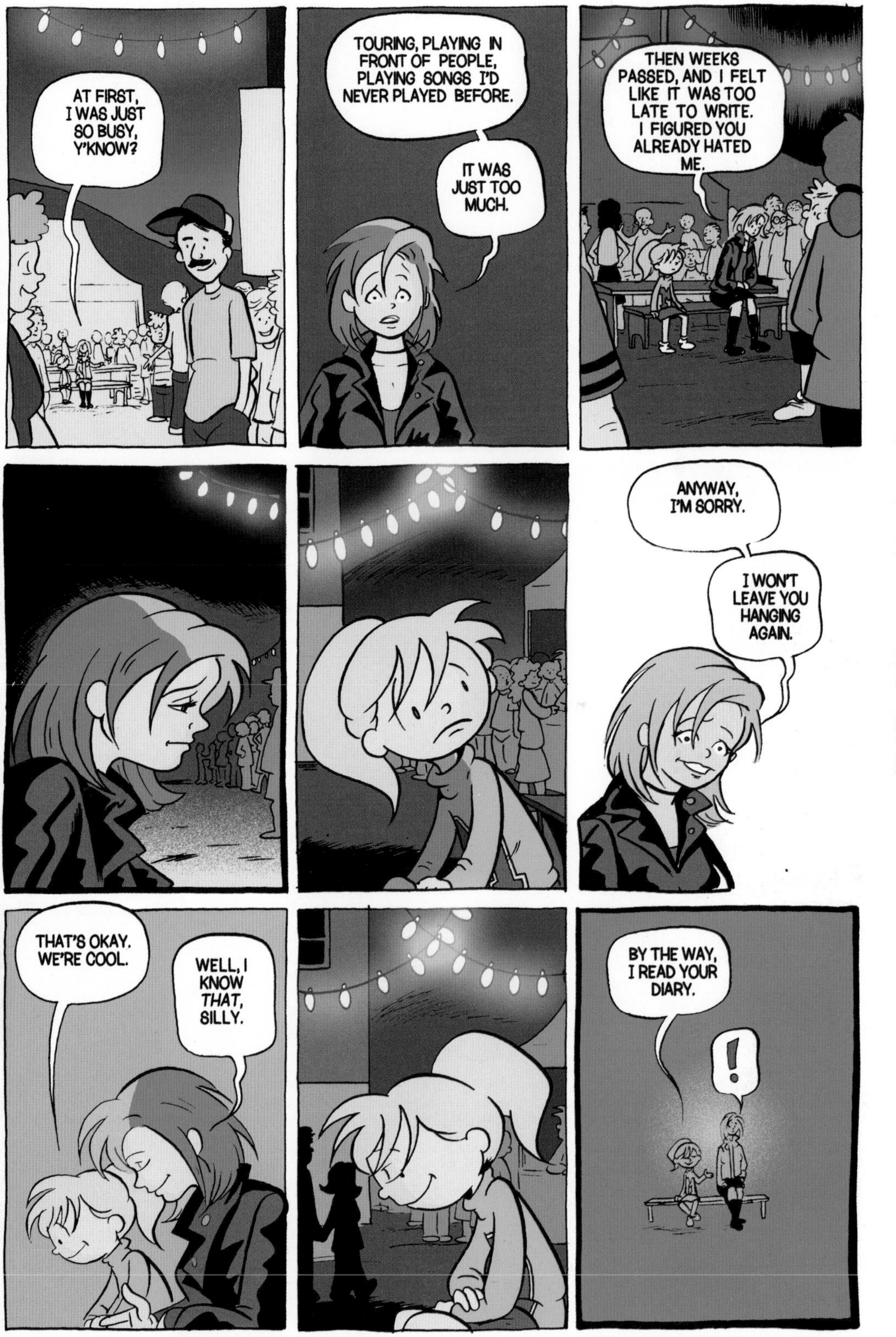
AT FIRST, I WAS JUST SO BUSY, Y'KNOW?
TOURING, PLAYING IN FRONT OF PEOPLE, PLAYING SONGS I'D NEVER PLAYED BEFORE.
IT WAS JUST TOO MUCH.
THEN WEEKS PASSED, AND I FELT LIKE IT WAS TOO LATE TO WRITE. I FIGURED YOU ALREADY HATED ME.
ANYWAY, I'M SORRY.
I WON'T LEAVE YOU HANGING AGAIN.
THAT'S OKAY. WE'RE COOL.
WELL, I KNOW *THAT*, SILLY.
BY THE WAY, I READ YOUR DIARY.
!

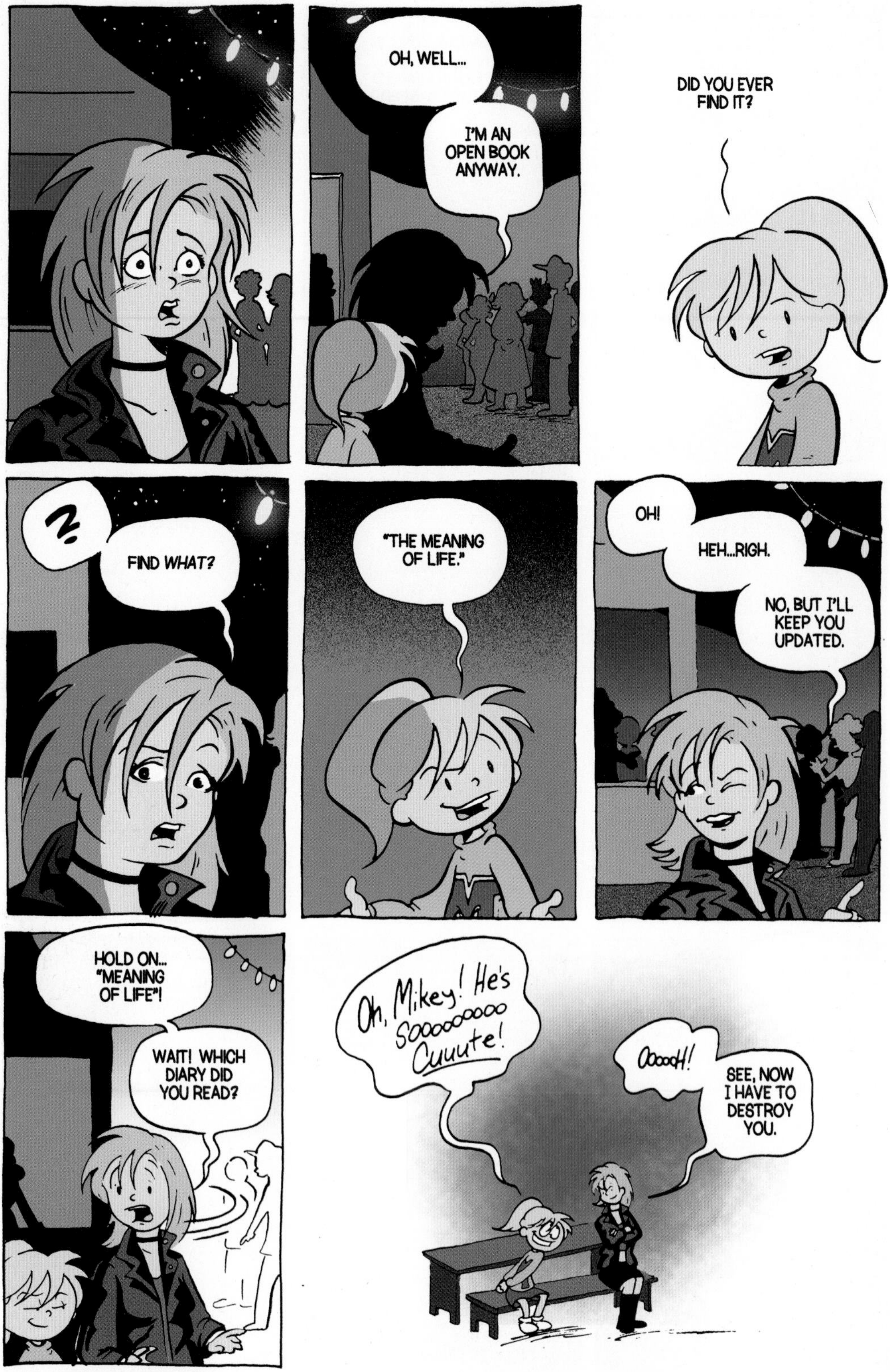
OH, WELL...
I'M AN OPEN BOOK ANYWAY.
DID YOU EVER FIND IT?
?
FIND WHAT?
"THE MEANING OF LIFE."
OH!
HEH...RIGH.
NO, BUT I'LL KEEP YOU UPDATED.
HOLD ON... "MEANING OF LIFE"!
WAIT! WHICH DIARY DID YOU READ?
Oh, Mikey! He's Sooooooooo Cuuute!
OooooH!
SEE, NOW I HAVE TO DESTROY YOU.

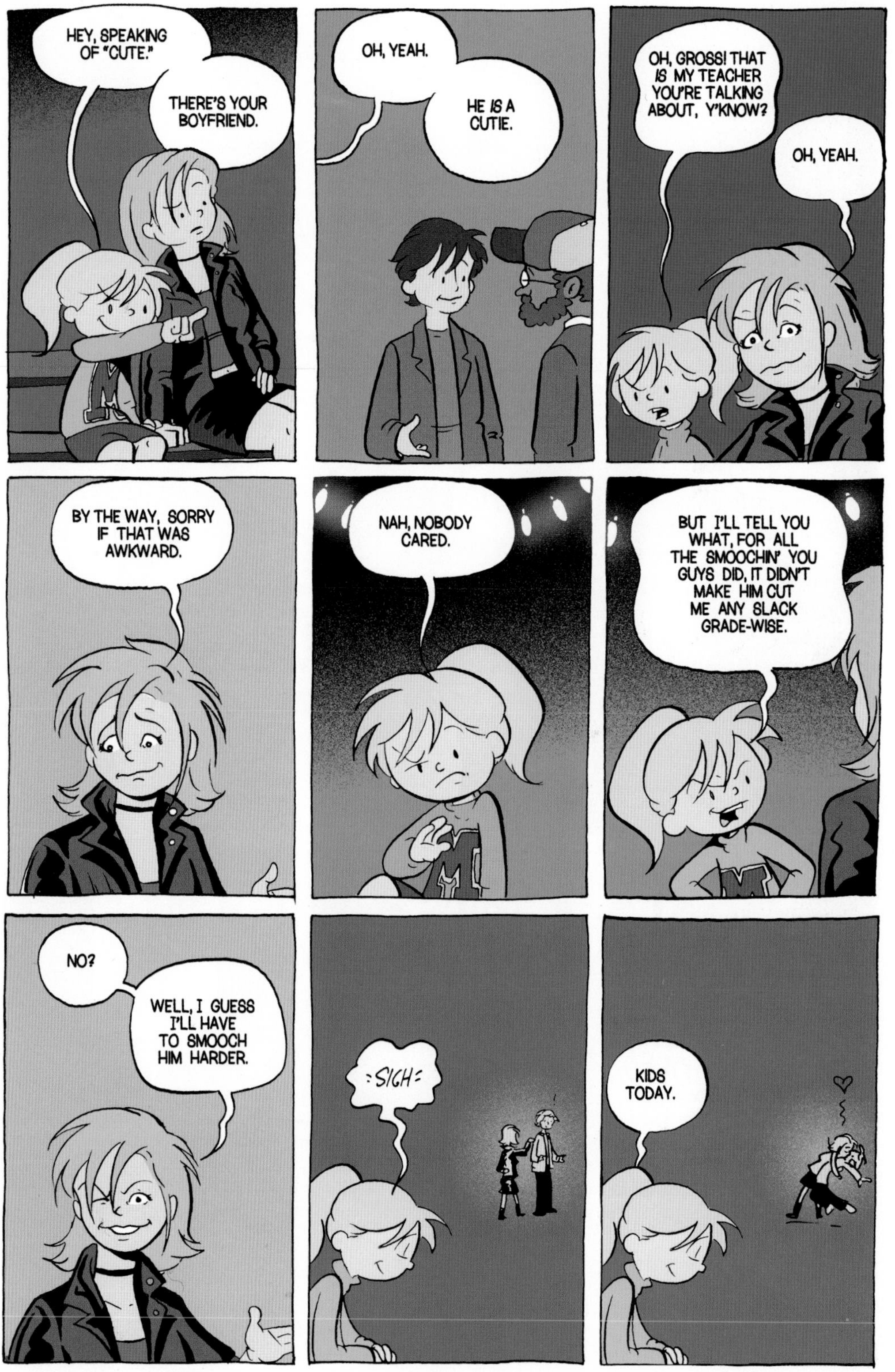
HEY, SPEAKING OF "CUTE."
THERE'S YOUR BOYFRIEND.
OH, YEAH.
HE IS A CUTIE.
OH, GROSS! THAT IS MY TEACHER YOU'RE TALKING ABOUT, Y'KNOW?
OH, YEAH.
BY THE WAY, SORRY IF THAT WAS AWKWARD.
NAH, NOBODY CARED.
BUT I'LL TELL YOU WHAT, FOR ALL THE SMOOCHIN' YOU GUYS DID, IT DIDN'T MAKE HIM CUT ME ANY SLACK GRADE-WISE.
NO?
WELL, I GUESS I'LL HAVE TO SMOOCH HIM HARDER.
SIGH
KIDS TODAY.

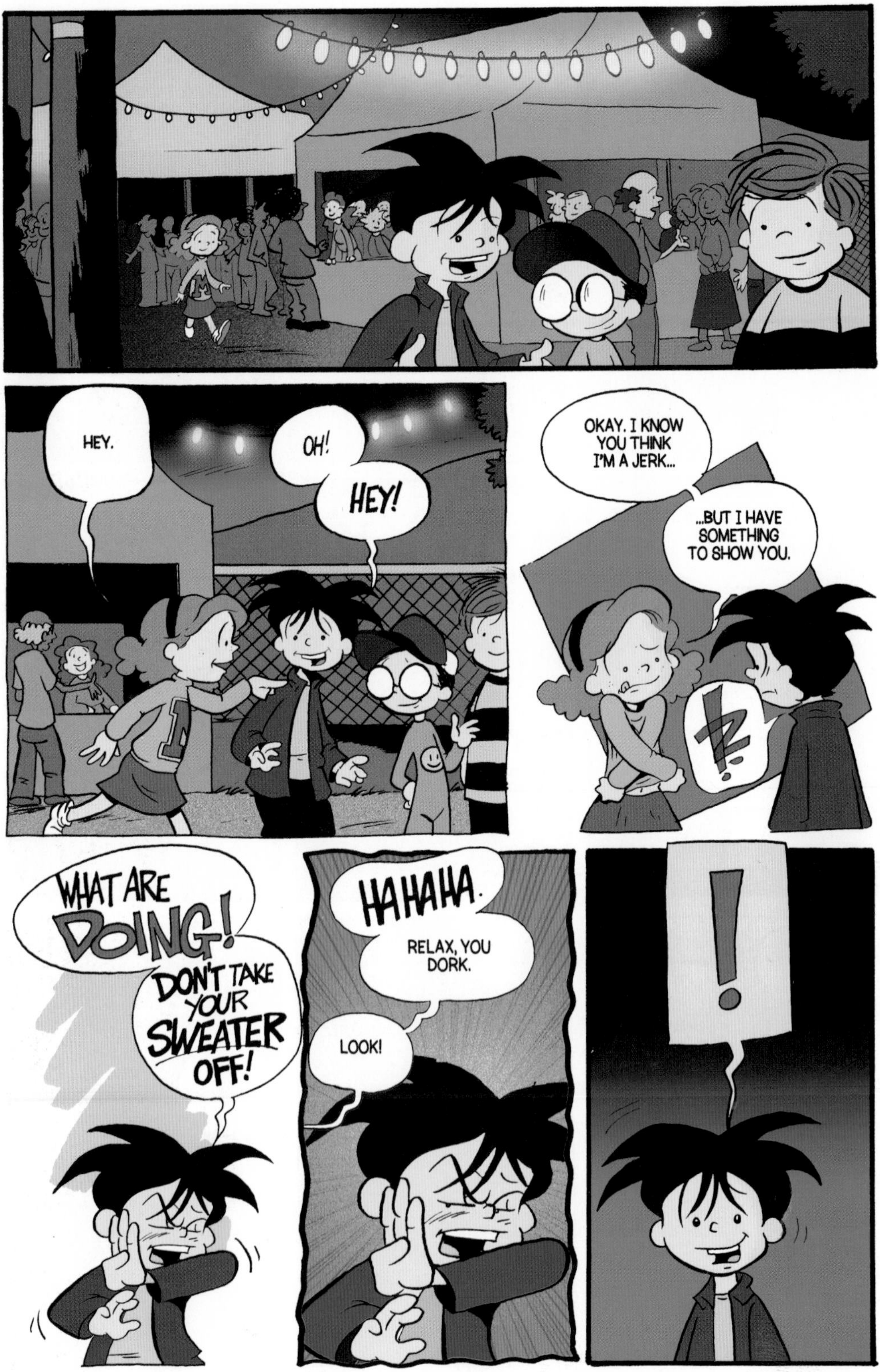
HEY.
OH!
HEY!
OKAY. I KNOW YOU THINK I'M A JERK...
...BUT I HAVE SOMETHING TO SHOW YOU.
?!
WHAT ARE DOING!
DON'T TAKE YOUR SWEATER OFF!
HAHAHA.
RELAX, YOU DORK.
LOOK!
!

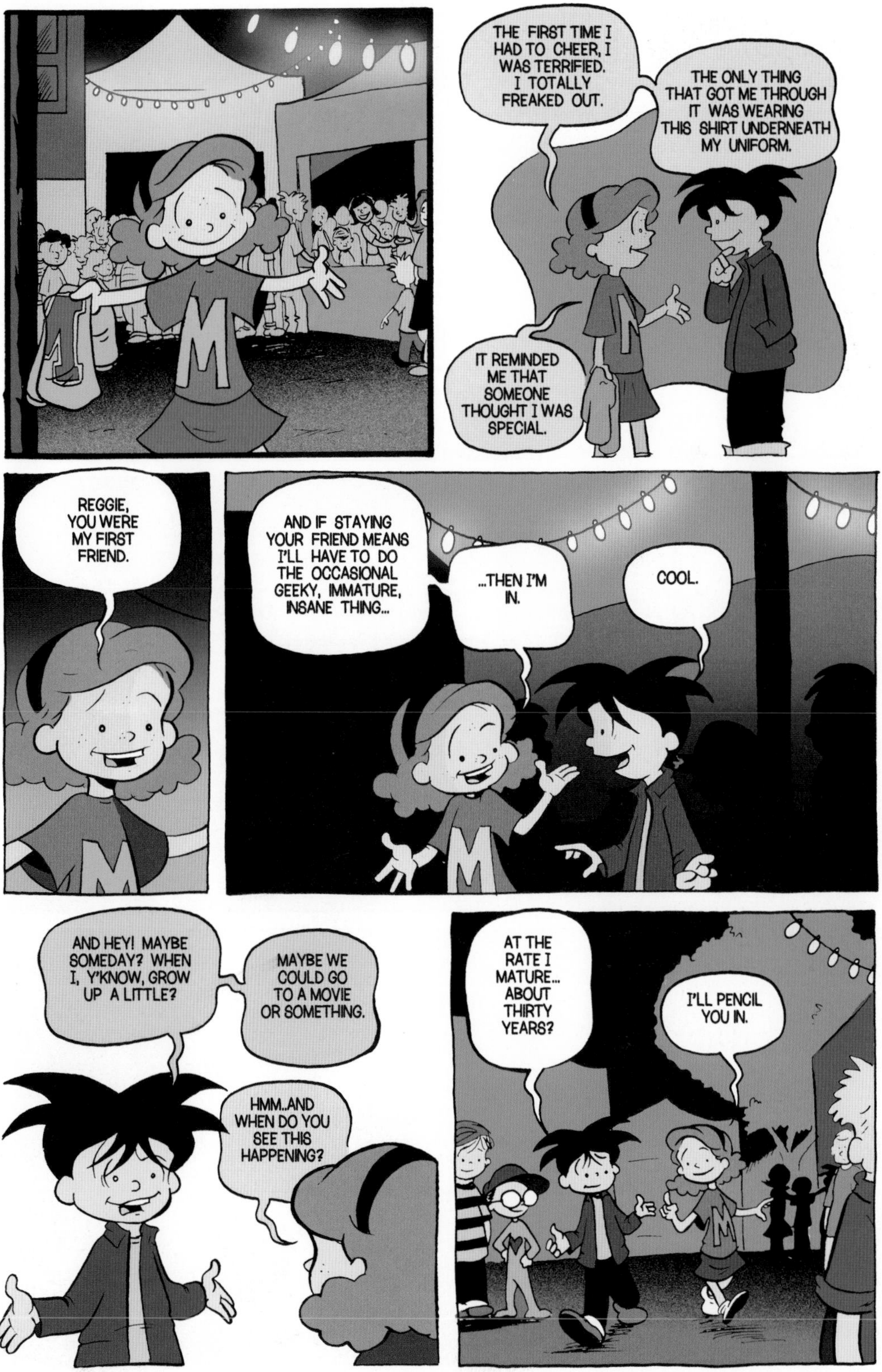
THE FIRST TIME I HAD TO CHEER, I WAS TERRIFIED. I TOTALLY FREAKED OUT.
THE ONLY THING THAT GOT ME THROUGH IT WAS WEARING THIS SHIRT UNDERNEATH MY UNIFORM.
IT REMINDED ME THAT SOMEONE THOUGHT I WAS SPECIAL.
REGGIE, YOU WERE MY FIRST FRIEND.
AND IF STAYING YOUR FRIEND MEANS I'LL HAVE TO DO THE OCCASIONAL GEEKY, IMMATURE, INSANE THING...
...THEN I'M IN.
COOL.
AND HEY! MAYBE SOMEDAY? WHEN I, Y'KNOW, GROW UP A LITTLE?
MAYBE WE COULD GO TO A MOVIE OR SOMETHING.
HMM..AND WHEN DO YOU SEE THIS HAPPENING?
AT THE RATE I MATURE... ABOUT THIRTY YEARS?
I'LL PENCIL YOU IN.

Sometimes the best way to get someone through the pain of their past or their present is just to be there with them

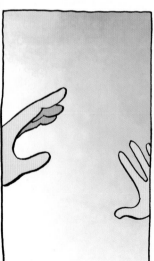

and to hold their hand

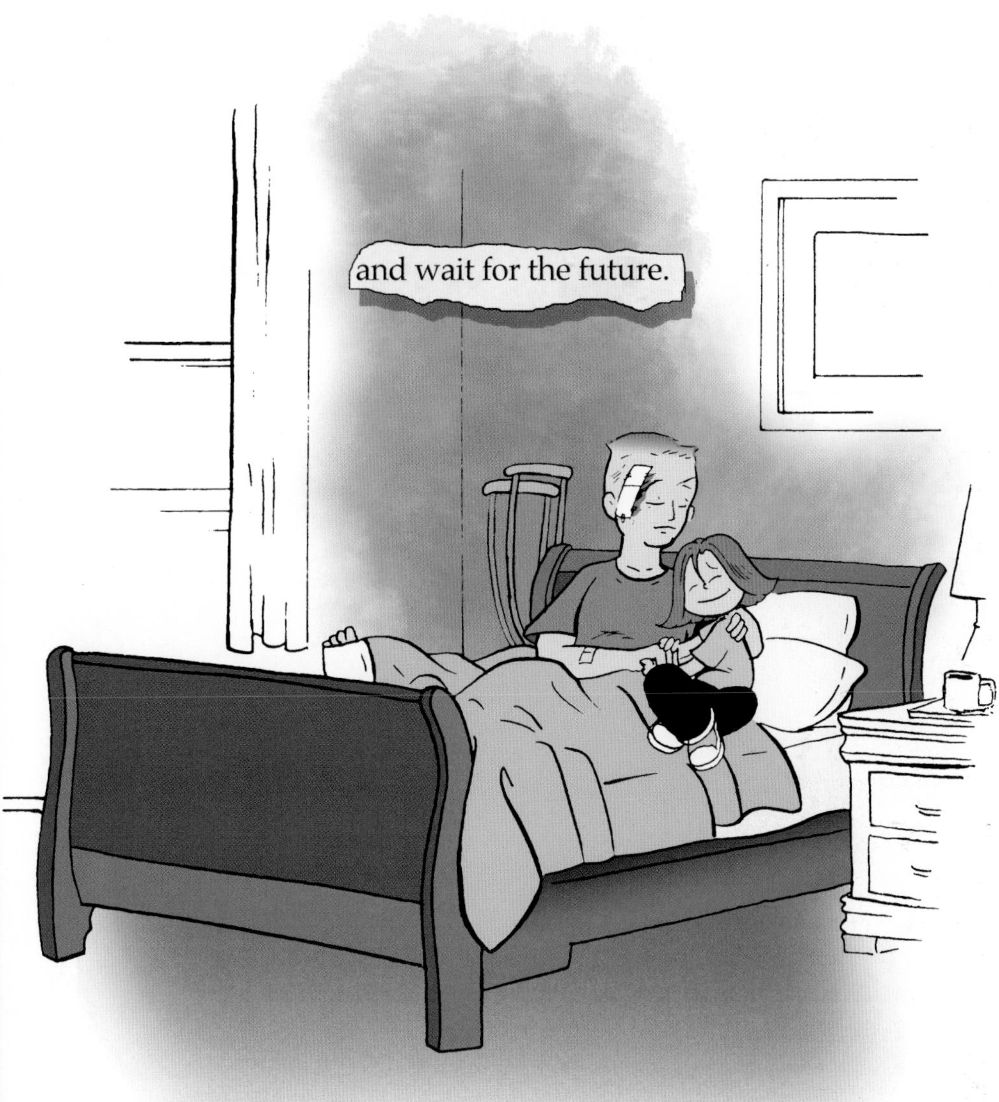
and wait for the future.

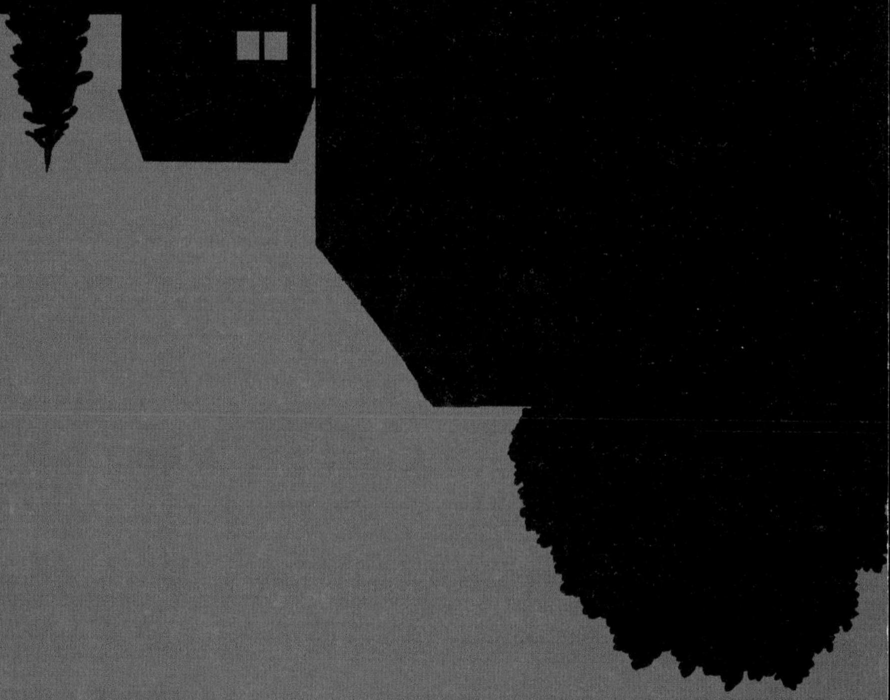